It's not just another ... *anothe*...!

FOR FRANK MALLORY, it's his life. He runs a major TV network, gets 300 G's a year, expense accounts, swank hotels, sensational women, and, of course, a limo—a silver Rolls-Royce, complete with four TV's, two phones, a bar, and a stereo. But it's a tough act to keep together when:

- Mallory's boss, THE BIG GUY, comes up with some bright ideas.

- his wife, MARCIA, turns out to be Pelham Manor's very own Mary Hartman.

- CINDY, his teen-aged daughter, disappears with a California surfer.

- his girl friend, SALLY HAWKES, decides to get him . . . or his career!

It's a hilarious, romantic romp, from Manhattan to Hollywood, for a shrewd, ambitious man in a power-crazy business.

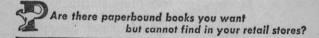

Dan Jenkins
and Edwin Shrake

LIMO

A KANGAROO BOOK
PUBLISHED BY POCKET BOOKS NEW YORK

LIMO

Atheneum edition published 1976

POCKET BOOK edition published November, 1977

This POCKET BOOK edition includes every word contained in
the original, higher-priced edition. It is printed from brand-
new plates made from completely reset, clear, easy-to-read type.
POCKET BOOK editions are published by
POCKET BOOKS,
a Simon & Schuster Division of
GULF & WESTERN CORPORATION
1230 Avenue of the Americas,
New York, N.Y. 10020.
Trademarks registered in the United States
and other countries.

ISBN: 0-671-81239-4.
Library of Congress Catalog Card Number: 76-11576.
This POCKET BOOK edition is published by arrangement
with Atheneum Publishers. Copyright, ©, 1976, by Dan
Jenkins and Edwin Shrake. All rights reserved. This book,
or portions thereof, may not be reproduced by any means
without permission of the original publisher: Atheneum
Publishers, 122 East 42nd Street, New York, New York 10017.

Printed in the U.S.A.

For our girls at home.
And all the boys in khaki.

Sometimes I take it as far as I can. . . .
Sometimes I don't even go.

WILLIE NELSON

PART
ONE

Chapter One

~~~~~~

It was a hot sticky night in Barcelona and all the good whores had the summer flu.

That's how I always thought the memoirs would begin. And after a lot of splendid things had happened to me over the years, mostly in wars and journalism and fucking, the book would end with Claudine or Inga walking back into this bar on the rainy side of some desolate Pacific island and apologizing for the Bolivian smuggler she had lent her soul to, and saying, "It's you, after all, Frank. It's you, Cairo, Tangier, that little sidewalk cafe in Crans-sur-Sierre, and your crazy jeep careening down a dirt slope in another African border skirmish. Vodka tonic, darling. And just hold me for a moment."

I could start that way now, of course, although I have managed to get involved in such things as television and families and analysts and love instead of real life. But maybe the only way I can begin to tell you about it—about all of those piercing, lurid months that changed prime-time TV into something a little bit wonderful, and changed the irritable but Christ-like

3

Frank Mallory into a more worthy human being—is to say that it all probably started when my wife gave me a lawyer for my birthday.

Most men find leaving home difficult, I think. Even though you may have discovered that your wife can throw a down-and-in from the bedroom to the fireplace with a jar of Elizabeth Arden's moisturizer, you stay trapped in the slush of good memories.

When you visualize leaving it always comes out the same. The wife and kids will stand there crying in the entrance hall while you try to cram the loafers and cashmeres into the golf bag with three or four suede jackets draped around your shoulders at once.

Maybe you've got some of your favorite stereo albums under your arm, and you're juggling the basketball autographed by the 1970 Knicks. Some guys give it up right there because of the tears. Or because they make the mistake of taking one last glance at the old leather chair in the den.

Others might get as far as the front lawn. And then they think about something vastly more sentimental: what the savings books will look like after the lawyers have folded them into party hats.

I did not, incidentally, unwrap a package on the morning of my forty-first birthday and find an actual person with a briefcase and a court order standing inside of it. What I found was a card from my wife Marcie. I found it on the butcher-block table in the kitchen of our warm and comforting home in Pelham Manor, New York.

I was alone that morning in October. The kids had done their poached eggs and gone off to their private schools to avoid the heroin addiction which Marcie felt was sweeping Westchester County.

Marcie was at the analyst's again, trying to find out why I was ambitious.

I was stumbling around recovering from another

Scotch-and-argument hangover, hoping to hit the coffee mug with a spoonful of instant Taster's Choice, when I saw the envelope.

The card was yellow and pink with a picture of a bowl of flowers on it. The sentiment was printed in rhyming script. It was the kind of card you would mail to an aunt who had never been altogether civil to you. Marcie had rewritten the last two lines, so that it now read:

> What a joy to know someone
> Who's always been the kind
> To offer me a helping hand
> Or hear what's on my mind
> For all of this, a birthday gift
> It's more than just a whim
> I'll pay for your half of our divorce
> To Phillips Nizer Benjamin & Krim.

A total collapse of meter, I thought, sitting there at the table.

The fact is, I probably would not have left home that day if it hadn't been for my friend D. Wayne Cooper.

Cooper had driven up from the city to Pelham Manor in the limousine the company provided for me. That wasn't unusual; it was Cooper's job. To look after me—the network biggie—and also to look after our silver Rolls limo.

D. Wayne Cooper was an old pal from Texas. He had done a bit of everything in his day, and a good deal of it in truck stops and honky-tonks, I'd say. I hired Cooper during the summer, right after I accepted the new job, which made it possible for me to afford him. Cooper was my driver, my personal appointments secretary, and you could say my bodyguard, seeing as how

5

I was in television. Mainly, he was my walk-around guy.

When Cooper came into the kitchen he didn't ask for coffee or even a beer. He just looked at me for a second, turned, and went out. He started going through the rest of the house, gathering up things from the closets and drawers. My casual ensembles. My serious suits for the lunches at "21." My handmade boots from Austin. And my wood-framed Wilson tennis racquet which put sting and mystery in my ground strokes.

Also, he sang.

"My front tracks are lookin' for a cold-water well . . . my back tracks are covered with snow. . . . Sometimes it's Heaven . . . Sometimes it's hell . . . Sometimes I don't even know."

A country song could speak for D. Wayne Cooper almost anytime. Occasionally for me as well. Those Willie Nelson lyrics were Cooper's idea of humor, given the circumstance.

Coming back to the kitchen, he said, "Gettin' your ass out of the house is my birthday present."

I said something like I didn't see how I could leave a cozy place like this, no matter how often I had threatened, or how worn out I was from hollering about the clouds that continually hovered over Pelham Manor.

"A poor man can," Cooper said. "A man with a lot to lose stays on too long. Look at you, Frank. Did you wash your face with ketchup? You never been one to crave agony. I just saw Marcie down the road crying and looking terrible."

Cooper picked up some pieces of bacon off a paper towel on a counter and wrapped them in a slice of white bread.

"You and Marcie don't do nothing these days but try to destroy each other," he said. "Who'd be the winner

6

if that happened? You got one of them three-hundred-thousand-dollar-a-year jobs. At least you've got it until some sissy tricks you out of it. You can afford a divorce just like you don't have nothing to lose but half interest in a refrigerator."

I showed him the card but he didn't laugh.

He said, "You got that Silver Goblet parked outside. It ain't like you got nowhere to go. Like you've said yourself, you got too good of an apartment stashed in the city to let it sit there for nothing better than one or two nights a week of sneak-lovin'."

D. Wayne Cooper had a way of getting it all down to where it belonged.

"Anyhow," he said, "you ain't been married to nobody but your work for twenty years. Shit. Give old Marcie a break."

I left Marcie a note taped to her Panasonic blender, where she would be sure to see it. The note said:

Dear Marcie:
I'm moving into the city for a while so we can both try to think clearly about our lives. Explain it to Cindy and Frankie in whatever way you think is best. I'll tell them my side of it later. I'm sure they not only will understand, but they might not even miss the sound of broken glass coming from our bedroom. Thanks for the lawyer. All I plan to tell him is that once you were a radiant light as you stood there on the dock, shining through the darkness that, in those days, was Lisbon. I love Jesus.

Frank.

About the job Cooper mentioned. I had the official title of Vice President, Entertainment, CBC–TV. I was in charge of prime-time programming for the Chambers Broadcasting Company, one of the four major networks.

Prime time is what they call those three hours of television entertainment—dramas, comedies, movies, specials—that come between the early evening local news, which tells you who's winning what wars, and the late evening local news, which tells you how many firemen and cops were killed during the day.

Prime time is the hours of the evening—eight to eleven, to be general—during which the commercials cost the most money because the audiences are the biggest. Which is why prime time has so often been referred to as the "showcase" of a network.

It's been said that the head of prime-time programming for a network doesn't have any more power than the king of a medium-sized country. I, on the other hand, had always worked in TV news. So it was my opinion that most programmers in the quarter century of television's existence had done little more than approve a pilot about a crippled orphan girl and her pet donkey.

The new job had brought with it a style of living that I thought was better and Marcie thought was gaudy. That I said was fun and she said was embarrassing. That I said was important and she said was irrelevant.

Not that Marcie ever refused to let the silver Rolls take her to Bendel's and Bloomingdale's. And not that she fought very hard to keep from taking advantage of the apartment in the city, which was big enough to put *Richard III* and the Coliseum Boat Show in at the same time. And not that she disapproved of what the salary boost did for her stature around the antique auctions.

It was just that I had stopped doing anything right a long time ago.

D. Wayne Cooper made sense as usual. It was time to move it on down the road, as he would say.

When the limo pulled away that day in the fall, I said to Cooper, "I know you're right, D. Wayne, but it still hurts."

"Yeah, I know," he said. "Life's a funny old dog, ain't she?"

When a married man suddenly finds himself out on the street for one reason or another, he is obliged to fuck himself into a coma.

It is some kind of law they passed a while back.

My first few months full-time in the apartment on Park Avenue I obeyed the law. I don't recall that it was all that much fun, especially with the fashion models. Cooper described my actions as purely human.

We did some remodeling in the apartment and created a suite for Cooper downstairs, but I don't know that he did a very good job of bodyguarding, or why would I remember that some of the most joyous occasions were those days when I could wake up and not find a wine glass or a wig or a Wellesley graduate in the bed?

I have been leading up to a day in April, about six months after I left Pelham. I like to think back on it as the day God struck. I say God because I checked. Nobody else confessed.

It was a day when the career of Frank Mallory was going to get tossed up in the air so everybody at the network could run around with Hefty trash bags trying to catch pieces of it when it fluttered back into the music and laughter of Manhattan.

I speak of a fine spring morning, one of those days when the air quality would be acceptable to WCBC–TV, our local station.

The sun rays were shimmering white instead of filtered New Jersey green as they came through the sliding glass doors of my bedroom.

Without a headache, I would have wanted to go out on the terrace and look at the sights. At Central Park and the reservoir across to the west. To the city's skyline posing for another Instamatic on my left. Or north and upstate past Harlem and Yankee Stadium toward the Marcies and station wagons of the world.

I was just crumpled up on the bed, trying to remember what last night was like, and maybe wondering if there might be another East Side contessa beside me, when I heard Cooper's voice.

"Frank, you got to get with it. You got to meet the Big Guy up in Greenwich before noon," Cooper said.

The Big Guy was Harley O. Chambers. Harley O. Chambers was the founder, chairman, monarch and bat boy of the Chambers Corporation, which of course owned CBC–TV. The Big Guy owned most everything else you could think of on the financial pages.

I patted around on the sheets.

"You slept by yourself," Cooper said. "Our last stop was Clarke's. You went for a swim in the J&B. Sat with the usuals. And the mayor for a while."

I opened one eye.

"After you solved all the problems of pollution and football, you did Cary Grant, Cagney, John Wayne. The mayor hadn't heard you do 'em in months. Julia got pissed and split."

I asked Cooper if there was any plausible reason why he hadn't brought me straight home after dinner at Elaine's, which was a restaurant where I went to watch heiresses eat fettucini.

He said, "You fell in love with Julia, who you met at dinner."

I said, "That girl I had a date with . . . Eloise? She didn't want to go to Clarke's?"

"Not with you and Julia," Cooper said.

10

When he hit you with a sensible reply like that, Cooper had a way of grinning that barely parted his lips but caused dimples to appear on either side of his mouth like suck-holes in the sand. Cooper reached up with hands that had three silver-and-turquoise Navajo rings on them, and pushed back his hair to clear it away from his ears. His hair hung down a couple of inches past the collar of his Levi jacket.

The silver-and-turquoise rings were chipped and spotted with tooth marks, but not because Cooper chewed on them.

"As a matter of fact, Eloise compared you to some kind of turd that can only be found in Texas or Egypt," Cooper said.

Cooper kept grinning and walked toward the bathroom in his pool hall slouch, with a hishi necklace bumping against his thin chest and bracelets sliding down his wrists. If you knew what to look for, you could see his right calf was thicker than his left. That was because he had what he called his Binniss, a .32 snubnose Smith & Wesson, stuffed into his right boot under the Levis. He carried his cash in the left boot.

"Eloise said something else," Cooper said. "She said she's been out with a lot of big shots in her time and you don't give good enough head to get away with flirting with a dirtyleg while in the company of a lady."

I said I didn't remember Eloise saying that.

"You were already out of the limo by then and heading into Clarke's with Julia," Cooper said.

Two fuzzy little Yorkshires rushed into the room yapping like a herd of nuns. They jumped onto the bed. I had given the dogs to Marcie for Christmas. The kids named them Dump and Ling. Marcie gave Dump and Ling back to me right after I moved out of the house. Brought them to Gotham herself and straight up to the penthouse and shut them in the bathroom where they ate the five-hundred-dollar hairbrush that was

11

presented to me by the West Coast news department when I left CBS.

Marcie said since I was going to be spending the night with a lot of dogs from now on anyhow, I might as well have this pair that would lie down and roll over without me having to shove hundred-dollar bills at them.

I could swear my prize hairbrush smelled like liverwurst when I finally trapped Dump and Ling out on the terrace and stopped them from pulling it in different directions. Rotten, low-minded, scum-level paranoia is what Marcie called the notion.

She said she had shut Dump and Ling in the bathroom so they wouldn't piss a map of Indonesia on my carpet like they had on hers.

While I was trying to remember what had made Eloise act like a bad sport, Dump and Ling scrambled under the covers, and the big orange tabby cat who had been sleeping under there spoke straight animal talk which made them flee onto the terrace. André, the cat, was my all-time favorite animal. That cat understood everything I said, could leap eight feet off the ground, and loved to watch television and movies with me on the eight-screen lashup in the den of the penthouse.

If André stayed with your show all the way to the end, you had a quality piece. But maybe not a hit. André was not a Nielsen cat.

I heard the shower. I got out of bed and started putting on my warmup suit and my red Pumas. Cooper looked at me from the bathroom door.

"You ain't got time to run no laps," he said.

"What do all those Tanzanian fuckers do the mile in?" I asked.

In the mornings I ran two miles around the reservoir in Central Park. Unless I was some place like Beverly Hills or London, of course. I had tracks

12

laid out everywhere, and I always tried to do two miles a day. Some days I would get to staggering and taste the chili coming up and have to quit and lie down. But usually if I kept on running I would break through the sour part, even on the really bad days, and just run right on through it and out the other side.

It was your normal lap around the reservoir. I passed a wino asleep in a hedge, then a teenage couple sprawled in a flower bed, then four black dudes who tried to trip me with a tire chain, then a group of twelve-year-olds who offered me a joint. That was in the first half-mile.

The scenery always made me think of tour guides. Welcome to our garden island. Have you been to the fern grotto? Have you visited the lookout over the canyon? Have you driven through the river valley?

I overtook two young girls riding English saddle. Their expressions told me their fathers paid an apartment maintenance on Fifth Avenue that would feed an emerging nation for a month.

On the reservoir path, even though I zigzagged around two chows on a leash, an old lady's purse caught me with a solid blow—and my elbow rang for the next one hundred yards.

Near the end, I was gaining on a younger guy who looked like a trackman. He was either a serious NYU strider or a backgammon ace who had just left the Regency Club and was running off the $6,000 he had dropped.

I put on a hard burst, which wasn't entirely easy, and passed him. I kept going and his gray sweatsuit fell back in the distance. He couldn't have been a trackman. His shoes were too new and I thought I got a whiff of Old Spice Lime.

I still felt good about passing him until I came onto a group of guys with film cameras behind some trees.

They said I'd ruined a good take of the commercial they were shooting.

The silver Rolls was waiting in front of the building when I came down from showering and slipping into my Saturday outfit: suede jacket, pigskin pants and boots. Cooper was wiping the hood of the limo with a soft cloth. Chester, one of the doormen, was watching Cooper and admiring the car.

"I've been meaning to ask what you've got to do to get one of these," Chester said.

Cooper said, "There ain't but one auto-mobile like the Silver Goblet. To get it, you got to be Frank Mallory."

Chester opened a rear door of the limo for me as Cooper slid in behind the wheel. Chester then imitated a golf swing and held the pose on the followthrough, watching the flight of an imaginary ball.

"Fine morning to knock out some whaps, Mr. Mallory," he said.

"Can I tell you something about that swing, Chester," I said. "Don't take it out of town."

I sat back in the limo and opened up the *New York Times,* then, to see if I had been fired or promoted.

Chapter
Two

~~~~~~

You could hear it said among almost any group of coal miners that a man did not need a silver Rolls limo to be happy. You could probably hear that a man did not need one with four television sets arranged in a wood panel in the back seat. A coal miner would say that a man did not need to be able to watch CBC, NBC, ABC and CBS—all four networks—at once. Riding in a car.

A man might not need a bar and liquor cabinet in his limo. Or a built-in oven and hot plate. Or two phones. Or the leather seats and carpeting that mine had.

Or the round clock set in the middle of the TV sets to tell whether everybody's shows were getting on and off the air on schedule.

He might not need to have the limo stocked every morning with the *Times, Daily News, Women's Wear, Billboard, Variety* and a few other publications so he could keep up with mankind and Hollywood.

I happened to have all this because I asked for it. And just like the penthouse, the salary, the stock, and the paid-up life insurance policy, the Chambers Corporation came up with all of it. The lures were dangled in a lot of directions to jolt me away from CBS.

I was more than satisfied at CBS and I had all the challenges I could handle, having worked my way up near the top of network news. And if I might just sneak this in, the old network was a place where I had seen my share of Emmys and Peabodys, which are awards they give to executives instead of the technicians who deserve them.

In some ways, television is a game to see which network executive can get the best toys. I negotiated for as many toys as I could get before I left CBS to go to Chambers. I wasn't going to leave a winner and move to a network basically noted for its decline in everything but sports and soaps without all the stripes I could stitch on my sleeve.

Anyhow, that's why I had the Rolls.

While Cooper and I often giggled about the absurdity of having a limo like the Silver Goblet, we also enjoyed the hell out of it. And as much as anything, I enjoyed the fact that it made somebody like Herb Grant want to drive nails into my hands.

Herb Grant had somehow slithered up as close to the Big Guy as anyone could get. Grant was Group President of Chambers Communications. In other words, he presided over TV, radio, film, books, records, cassettes—all communications divisions. And Grant reported only to the Big Guy, a fact he seldom allowed you to forget.

He was a man of whom it was said around the merry corridors of Madison Avenue, where Grant came from, that if the Big Guy ever got constipated, Herb Grant's head would shrink up to the size of a pinto bean.

As for the meeting in Greenwich on Saturday, I knew only that I was supposed to be there with Herb

16

Grant and Stanley Coffman. Stanley Coffman was president of the television network. He was my direct boss and the man most responsible for hiring me at CBC.

After a procession of programmers who had risen out of the sales division, CBC had slowly dug itself into a deep hole as the fourth network in prime time. The Big Guy ordered Stanley Coffman to do something about it, even if it was drastic.

I was drastic. A news man.

In the office on Friday I had asked Stanley if he knew what the Greenwich meeting was about.

"He probably wants to discuss our oversupply of paper clips and rubber bands," Stanley said of the Big Guy. "Or maybe he wants to ask why we changed the fucking logo—which was two years ago."

Stanley and I had been friends before I joined CBC. I had known him from around bars, which is where most TV people are introduced to each other. I first met him in the Polo Lounge in Beverly Hills. Stanley was sitting in a booth with his arm around a starlet talking long distance to his wife in New Canaan.

"Bernice," Stanley said into the phone that night. "Don't pay the ransom. I just escaped."

The day Stanley made the big pitch to hire me, he said, "Look around the business today and what do you see? Broads are running daytime. Punks out of college are doing late-night humor. Entertainment guys are in charge of sports. Why can't a news guy bring something to prime time?"

No reason, I said.

"Besides," Stanley said. "You're more fucking expensive than Israel."

So there I was. Drastic. Expensive. And on my way to a mystery luncheon with the Big Guy.

If the meeting was going to involve a problem with

17

programming, I didn't need it. I already had several, and one of them rang on the phone in the limo as we were sailing up the Merritt Parkway and I was buttering my English muffin.

It was Melvin, a director of specials, calling from the Coast. Melvin Gottlieb. Always a nervous man, he now sounded exhausted. Hearing Melvin's voice, I could envision him sitting on his bed, fully clothed, since he'd been up all night. He would have a compatible girl-child in freaky denim on the floor at his knees in the hotel suite, and they would be taking snorts of coke, using a coffee spoon for a scoop.

"Frank, listen," Melvin's voice said. "I got something I want you to hear." I didn't hear anything.

"Hear that, Frank?" Melvin said. "That's my heart, Frank. Know who made it sound like that? Peggy did it. I'm sorry, Frank. Peggy has to die."

I looked at my watch and checked it against the limo clock. New York time was 9:31, which meant Melvin had just survived another apricot sunrise in California.

"She can't sing or dance, so what use is she to us alive?" Melvin said. "You get the drift?"

There was a noise over the phone like a hog wading into dinner.

"I overdid it that time!" Melvin said. "Knew I'd do it sooner or later. Want to hear a heart explode, Frank? Go off like a goddam sky rocket. Got any curiosity about that?"

I told Melvin to take it easy. In his condition I might as well have told him to swim to Catalina.

I expected from directors, actors and writers a certain amount of what Marcie described as self-destructive behavior. But I didn't think they were self-destructive so much as they were vulnerable to attacks of fear. They were terrified that people would decide

18

they really didn't know what they were doing, and probably never had.

The old bravado would crack, and out would come a frightened baby monster that would try to arrange it so we could all fall in the same pile. Whether a director, for example, ordinarily knew what he was doing or not didn't matter while the fear was showing. That was especially true in Hollywood, where nobody was sure of anything until after it had happened.

If you brought in all the nuts from the county farm, dressed them up in Guccis and things from the men's department in Giorgio, and put them to running Woolworth's, you would get a pretty good picture of how Hollywood works.

I told Melvin to swallow a couple of Valiums and go to sleep.

"Just as soon as the black bitch is dead," he said.

Melvin got me about halfway nervous. The Peggy Hanley special was my first big personal production in the new job. I had already handled, or tried to fix, a number of shows I had been stuck with when I took the job. And I had some pilots shooting for the fall which Herb Grant hated.

But the Peggy Hanley thing would be the first show of my own I'd had time to get on the air. I saw Peggy do some songs and a comedy skit one night at the Improv, caught her in a dramatic role at a theater in the Village, and when she turned up as the singing and dancing surprise of a Broadway musical, where she was on stage for a total of seven minutes and made the first paragraph of every critic, I signed her for a special.

Then I signed Melvin Gottlieb to direct it.

Marcie had often suggested that I was capable of error.

I told Melvin it was in his contract that he was forbidden to bruise the star.

19

"I'll stick a hot wire in her ear. Won't leave a mark on her," he said. He cackled and coughed and sounded as if he might be involved in a scuffle of some sort. You may wonder why I did not fire Melvin at that moment. The reason was that Melvin was an excellent director when he was sane, and occasionally brilliant when he was crazy. And the taping, which would be in front of a live audience, was less than a week off. And Herb Grant would inquire why I ever hired Melvin in the first place, and I did not want to say that I was capable of error at that point.

Melvin was assured I would take care of the situation.

"Peggy has a beautiful ass," he said, calmly and slowly. "I would like to drag her through the grass on it."

I had already picked up the other phone and called my secretary, Arleene. When I hung up on Melvin, Arleene was waiting. Arleene was wonderful, kind, patient and intelligent. She should have been a psychiatric nurse.

"Call L.A. and tell them to send someone who is physically very powerful over to the Beverly Wilshire and make Melvin swallow a fistful of Valiums, even if the fist has to be stuck down Melvin's throat," I said. "This same person is to keep an eye on Melvin day and night until after the taping."

"Right. One baby-sitter for Melvin," Arleene said.

I turned on the hot plate, glanced out of the window at the trees rushing past, and asked what was happening around the network that morning. Arleene said I was due for a call from News.

"They want to pre-empt tonight for an hour on the earthquake in Peru. Grant was in earlier and he said nobody wants to see dead babies in prime time on Saturday night," Arleene said.

I said the News guys must have some great footage to ask for an hour.

"Your basic fire and rubble and a better-than-average tidal wave," Arleene said. "Also the writers on *Satan Sucks* want a conference with you."

"What about?"

"You know how writers are. Either they won't tell you anything, or they tell you too much. This was their day for secrets."

"Put them down for Monday afternoon," I said.

"Satan Sucks," as Arleene named it, was a movie of the week that I had been unable to cancel. The real title was "Satan Takes a Bride." My predecessor as head of prime-time programming had signed contracts for it that could only be broken at terrific expense. Instead of squandering a fortune on lawyers, I had spent a few thousand on new writers who were supposed to transform "Satan Takes a Bride" into something we could enter at Cannes.

"A woman named Eloise called. She said she had decided to do the lead in some new play in London, last night was goodbye, and she hoped you dehydrated in your sauna. The rest of the messages are nothing you need to think about while you are on your way to have lunch with the Big Guy. Your horoscope for today says you should strive for internal peace and be close to your loved ones."

When Arleene was off the phone, I looked through the magazines and papers, glanced at the cartoon shows on the four TVs in the back of the limo and drank some coffee.

"Do people live in these things? I don't ever see nobody," Cooper said. We were passing through an area of big homes and wide, green lawns.

"I guess everybody died trying to pay the bills," Cooper said.

I said some of the corpses kept going back and forth

on the New Haven. Made me think of the Flying Dutchman, I said. Cooper said he never heard a tune by the Flying Dutchman. I said it was a ghost ship.

"Goddamn, I think I saw it one time when I was in the Marine Corps. If it was a big deal with sails on it, I saw it go in a fog bank and not come out. Did seem kind of peculiar," he said.

When Cooper was in the Marine Corps in Korea— fighting, he said, for my right to go to what he called Texas University—he got a commendation from the General.

Cooper drove the General in a jeep from Pusan Harbor up to the Yalu River, which took a while, and then walked out with the General in the snow after the Chinese came in. I read the commendation.

The General said he was amazed at how Cooper never got tired. The General said Cooper was ever vigilant and had such incredible eyesight he could spot enemy targets where nobody else in the entire Marine Corps could see them. The General said Cooper could spot enemy targets that even the radar couldn't see. The General gave Cooper a Silver Star for that. Of course the General had never heard of amphetamines.

Cooper got his Purple Heart from being sprayed by a white phosphorous grenade while he was walking in the snow with the General. That's how Cooper got the scars on his back. He said he saw the enemy up there heaving the grenade, all right, but he was too cold to do anything about it.

"I found me a place," Cooper said as he steered the limo into the country club driveway. "Down at Park Avenue South and Fifteenth Street. Small dance floor. Bar up front. Got a bunch of labor coming in there Monday to start fixing it up."

"You sure Gotham needs another shitkicker night-club?" I said.

22

"Hell, Gotham could use a good one," Cooper said. "There's nine radio stations around here that don't play nothing but shitkicker music. You might not be hip to that, because a radio don't have a picture in it."

I said Cooper could count me in for five-thousand-dollars' worth of his nightclub. Cooper had wanted to have his own bar with good live Country & Western music ever since I'd known him, and that was approaching thirty years ago, when I was in the fourth grade and Cooper came in the fifth grade to boss the school.

"I done got you in for twice that much," Cooper said.

I got out of the limo at the clubhouse entrance and noted a member, a caddy, a groundskeeper and what might have been a barber, all of them staring not at me or the Silver Goblet, but at Cooper. He had on his brown beaver cowboy hat, the gold earring in his left ear, and his hair touched the bottom of the car window. His blue eyes looked up at me, and he grinned a couple of leathery dimples.

"I'm a personal friend of Dolly Parton," he said.

Chapter
Three

~~~~~~

When I walked into the men's grill at the country club I found the Big Guy, Herb Grant and Stanley Coffman at a table, and no one else in the room except some black waiters alert to anyone's requests. The members of the club understood that the Big Guy didn't use the facilities too often, and when he did he liked his privacy. I imagined how the tweed coats all got up and discreetly shuffled away when he arrived. Otherwise, they had to fear the Big Guy would put out a hit on their croquet mallets.

As far as I knew, the Big Guy had always been called the Big Guy. Even to his little pink face and wispy white hair people addressed him as Big Guy. Well, sometimes Chief. But mostly Big Guy.

He liked it. He enjoyed being called Big Guy.

I suppose if I had ever owned a television network, paper mills, steel plants, computer firms, ships, electronics industries, plastics companies, magazines, oil fields and banks—on four different continents—I would have been able to comprehend it.

But I was not Harley O. Chambers, the Big Guy,

so I did not know what it was like to be able to order my country into war just to get the economy on the upswing.

I called him Chief. I established that right away. I just never would have been capable of saying, at some future time when I might hope to get away with it, "Excuse me, *Big Guy,* but you've got piss stains on your lap." Chief I could say.

The Big Guy was sipping a glass of buttermilk. As I entered I realized he was telling the same old story about throwing double sixes when he had to, and how there are moments when the will can overcome pure luck. He was wearing his bow tie, dark suit, railroad shoes and white socks. He was somewhere in his seventies and he spoke in a soft and serious voice.

He merely smiled at me when I sat down at the table. He was busy. A waiter had brought him his blade putter and put a golf ball on the carpet and Herb Grant had leaped up to place a water glass on the floor, about eight feet away from the ball.

While a waiter was tying a napkin around the Big Guy's eyes and leading him with the putter to a stance over the ball, Herb Grant turned to me and said:

"I hear you left Clarke's this morning to a beautiful sunrise."

I said something witty like, yeah, well, the Shah had to get home for the prayer.

The Big Guy said, "Observe that my eyes are now blind-folded. But I have my memory, my sense of place, and my determination."

"A hundred he makes it," Grant said to Stanley.

"Jesus, I never bet against the Big Guy," Stanley said, all too cheerfully.

The Big Guy stroked the putt lightly and it did of course wobble along the carpet and go directly into the water glass. Whereupon he whipped off the napkin from around his eyes and gave us all the look of a man who had been certain it would happen.

"Would you call that one chance in thirty-six, Big Guy?" Stanley asked.

"If so, it's a metaphor for our industry," Grant said.

"Gentlemen," the Big Guy said. "As Jesus said in the Bible . . . and I agree . . . facing the truth is like facing a mountain of scabs. But I say . . . not to face the mountain would be to eat the coconut without hearing the ukulele. I think I've proved something here with my little trick. I want to get further into it after paddle tennis."

I whispered to Stanley, "Paddle tennis? You told me golf."

"Grant's idea," Stanley said. "It's his best game."

My own personal theory is, people who are good at paddle tennis, like expert skiers, aren't exceptional at any other sport. It's a game played with a paddle and a ball inside of a chicken coop on a platform. You can't run much because there's no room, unless you want to throw a side body-block on your partner. You can play the rubber ball off the wall screens before it hits the floor, but only if you don't get your other hand or your feet caught in the wire when you're scrambling after it.

One thing you can do. If you get beat as badly as Herb Grant and the Big Guy beat Stanley and Me— not that the Big Guy did much except squeal—you can sling your paddle across the court and up against the screen.

In the shower before lunch Herb Grant and I got into an exchange which had been overdue since the day I arrived at CBC.

First of all, Herb Grant was the kind of guy you only had to look at to know everything about. Tall, well-dressed, well-preserved. A man in his fifties with an out-of-season tan, a safe haircut, short and neat, and a killer handshake. Authoritative voice. Very big in the bar at "21." Big hello to the right people, small hello to the possibles.

Grant thought he knew all about the production, sales and p.r. side of television because he came from the ad agency business, which used to run TV, and in some ways still does.

The only thing Herb Grant really knew anything about was how to make the right marriage to get a mansion in Locust Valley and another in Southampton.

In Locust Valley and Southampton they would probably tell you that Herb Grant knew about three other things: wine, country club committees and the yellow peril.

In Locust Valley and Southampton, that would almost qualify Grant as a serious intellectual.

The riddle of how the Herb Grants of this planet reach the positions they attain in business stopped bewildering me a long time ago. A Herb Grant may think he has charmed and slicked his way into the Big Guy's favor, but the Big Guy knows the value of a Herb Grant. Every Big Guy needs a cutthroat asshole to watch the money. To a Big Guy, a cutthroat asshole is more trustworthy than someone with creative talent. Someone with creative talent is smarter than a Big Guy and understands the accidents by which fools get rich in the first place, and therefore the creatively talented person does not care so much about money. Creative talent has to be watched closely and kept in the pit, or creative talent will spend all the money on fun and something imaginative. We will never know whether that would generate more money because it never gets that far. The cutthroat asshole steps in. The Big Guy and the cutthroat asshole are afraid that if you let creative talent run loose, the only thing it will do is multiply and take up all the good parking places.

In the shower, Herb Grant said, "You play a pretty good game of paddle, old man, for a fellow who causes me some grief."

I said, "If I spent most of my time at country clubs, I'd have beat me worse than you did."

Grant said, "I'm sure it's no secret to you that I didn't have a damn thing to do with bringing you over to our store. Stanley sold you to the Big Guy when I wasn't looking. But that's okay. I think the way the Big Guy does. You run with your network president and your programmer until they go over the cliff."

I said I was shocked to learn that Herb hadn't personally hired me.

"Hard for me to understand what the hell a news guy's expertise could be in prime-time entertainment," Grant said.

I said the same thing could be said for someone who came out of the agency business.

"Oh, I don't know," Grant said. "I think the industry's done a pretty fair job of keeping the country entertained. All the ad boys have ever done is make sure of what they were buying. Wasn't too long ago, back there in the sixties, when the ad boys were the main program source."

That was right, I said. Who could ever forget that great writing team of Procter and Gamble?

"Personally, I think you're going to get slapped in the face with some of your new projects," Grant said. "In prime time, my friend, you're reaching for thirty-five to fifty million people, not that feeble fifteen to twenty million your old chum Cronkite gets. I'm talking about people who can *select* what they want to watch. Not a Senate hearing you've shoved down their throats."

28

I said I didn't have any comedy pilots working about a Senate hearing.

Grant said, "Not all that crap they did at that place where you came from worked. I'll give CBS credit for breaking down a few barriers, sure. But they're paying the rent with the same old cops and doctors."

Maybe we ought to just give up, I said, and play paddle tennis most of the year.

"Well, that's my nickel's worth," he said. "I'll go along with whatever you do that makes financial sense and shows good taste, but . . ."

I'd certainly come to him on questions of taste, I said.

". . . but I'm not interested in scaling any artistic mountains when I can build the same pile staying on my own level ground."

I asked what he would do if he found out he could build as big a pile and enlighten people at the same time.

"I'd say I've been in the industry long enough to know it can't happen," Grant said. "I'd also say I'm talking to a sophomore who's going to be riding around enlightened in a used Pontiac instead of a silver limo."

We were toweling off when Grant said:

"By the way. Our News Department get hold of you about that earthquake they want to cut in with tonight at seven thirty?"

I said Stanley had told News to go ahead. News didn't usually ask to pre-empt unless they had something worthwhile.

"For what it'll cost, we better see a lot of dead spicks in Peru," he said.

"You know something, Herb?" I said. "Even though you're a prince on Earth, all your Guccis are gonna have holes some day."

Herb Grant was at least good to have around for

office jokes. I once received a memo from Stanley Coffman which read:

TO: Frank Mallory
FROM: Stanley Coffman
SUBJECT: Proposed Sports Show.

I have the answer to our summer problem in competing on Sunday afternoons with Celebrity Mountain Climbing and Demolition Ice Dancing. We should call it Super Assholes. The 10 events (compete in your best of seven) would be:

1. Wine-Discussing.
2. Maitre d'-Handling.
3. Name-Dropping.
4. Subject-Evading.
5. Credit Card-Calling.
6. Spinnaker-Flying.
7. Entrée-Ordering.
8. Blazer-Wearing.
9. Chairman of the Board-Sucking.
10. Paddle Tennis.

My money's on Herb Grant. He's an outsider, but I like his chances.

At the end of lunch in Greenwich the Big Guy had another glass of buttermilk while the rest of us settled back with our coffee to listen.

We heard again how he had been a boy of only twelve when he ran away from home in Chicago. He would like to have been a pirate, he said, because he was quick on his feet, he was a good sword-fighter, and he could climb things.

He wanted to invent the airplane, but at the time he didn't know what an airplane was.

He said he hitchhiked and rode the rails, and found

work where he could. He remembered working on his first oil derrick. He didn't think much about oil then, but a shrewd old farmer told him cars and trucks were going to need it.

It was a fast-talking man in a checkered suit and a straw hat, he said, who told him about riverboats and a place called Mississippi. He said the man probably mistook him for Huckleberry Twist. He was likable, he said, and people told him things.

In Mississippi, he said, he learned to play card games in hotel rooms with older men. Sometimes he had to accept leases from them instead of money. He said he didn't know what a lease was at first but he kept them. Never throw anything away, he said.

One day, he said, he went out to look at a pasture on one of his leases. He stepped in a puddle of black glue. Oh, my, he said. And he remembered what a banjo player on a freight train had told him.

If you ever fall in a puddle like that, a banjo man said, never tell anyone where it is who has a tattoo.

He said he wanted to find an honest man for a partner who would build him an oil derrick. He looked around in a church. He found such a man. Wonderful Mr. Rankin, the banker.

Mr. Rankin said they would become partners. Mr. Rankin would build the oil derrick and if they found oil Mr. Rankin said the Big Guy could keep an eighth of the royalty.

It was a tragedy, he said, that a heavy tool fell from high on the derrick one night and killed Mr. Rankin only a week before the gusher hit. Accidents are dreadful, he said.

Oil was good because it provided jobs for people, he said. Jobs kept people from robbing grocery stores. Without oil, there wouldn't be a Chambers Corporation, either. People should not forget that.

But to be truthful, he said, radio was more fun than

31

oil. Oh, what happy days those were when he moved back to Chicago and started what came to be known as the first American suburb. And surely all of us knew that Harley O. Chambers also had started the first radio station west of the Hudson? Think of it. The first of the CBC network.

He did it because he liked gadgets, he said. Ah, the old crystal set. The first transmitter on his hill that some Italian—what's his name—invented for him.

There was only one reason why people went running around buying radios, he said. To hear "Harley O. Chambers Tonight." His show was just a hobby, but people liked the songs he sang for them, the poems he made up, and the little tales he told about the local merchants.

Surely all of us knew that Harley O. Chambers thought up the first radio commercial. That was more than his fellow pioneers, Bill Paley and General Sarnoff, could say. He felt that the merchants ought to pay for his little tales about them. Most of them were Jewish, after all, he said.

Oh, it was too bad we had all missed the great days of broadcasting, he said. Some of those old radio jingles were still among his favorite tunes.

But news broadcasts thrilled him as much as anything, he said.

"Caboom," the Big Guy said, lifting his eyebrows and smiling. "Vroom . . . burrrooom."

Stanley and I tended to exchange glances on this part.

"The city is an inferno and we can only guess how many sniveling Germans are hunkering in their shelters beneath the scorched and trembling earth," he said.

He talked into his empty buttermilk glass for sound quality.

"The lights are going out all over Paris," he said.

"She is like a beautiful lady with the blood slowly oozing from her veins— Tromp, tromp, tromp . . . I can hear the vile bootsteps of the menacing gray suits and armbands. . . . *Eeekter deeter bine nect der swine kemmel!* . . . But wait! . . . I can hear something else. . . . It comes from overhead. . . . The roar of a thousand Allied planes. The sky is snowflaked with Freedom's parachutes. Grinning little corporals from Iowa are floating into that turbulent hell beyond the Rhine. . . . And how, Mr. Hitler, do you like *those* apples?"

The Big Guy looked off. He put his glass down. Two whole minutes of silence.

Stanley and I hid in our coffee cups.

"Gentlemen," he said, returning to us. "A simple plumber came into my home the other day. He's the same plumber who has been there before, and he had the same look of contempt on his face."

This was new.

"Gentlemen, a smile can drive contempt through the snow like a bear chased by Eskimos," he said. "But I had no smile for that plumber's contempt. Does anyone know why?"

I didn't. Stanley didn't. I don't think Herb Grant did, although he sat up straight and cleared his throat.

"I know why," the Big Guy said. "That plumber was showing me his contempt for the squalid policeman, the gangster fiends, the cattle-rustlers and the ignoramus football players we give him to look at on television. That is why we are No. 4."

No one said anything.

The Big Guy said, "An insurance policy is only fragrant if the hand that holds it has known the richness of good dirt."

Herb Grant said, "Big Guy, if what you're getting

at is that this nation of ours—and correct me if I'm wrong—has allowed itself . . ."

The Big Guy smiled Herb into quick submission. And he turned to me.

"People need to smile, Frank," he said. "I think you're aware of it. That plumber started me to thinking many months ago that little people need to see little people on television. Their petty pursuits need not be altogether humdrum."

"Talking about a game show for plumbers, Big Guy?" Stanley said. "Got a title. 'Name That Wrench.' "

Stanley whooped alone.

The Big Guy said, "All these several months, Frank, that plumber's contempt has preyed on my mind. It got me to thinking about this wonderful land and all the interesting things people do. They cook. They sew. They polish guns. They toil over their homework. They converse. They put plastic saucers on the linoleum for cats and puppies."

Stanley tried again.

"When you mentioned plumbers, Big Guy, I thought maybe something had gone wrong with the moat."

I was beginning to get a little worried.

"Frank," the Big Guy said, "one of the reasons I let Stanley bring you on board our vessel was because he told me of all the great things you had done. I can't recite them all. The deceitful Vietnamese, for example. The seedy Washington politicians. Exposing Italians and Miami Beach. He convinced me you could do anything, and I believe him. And I want to say, if I have failed to do so already, that I am proud to have you loading our prime-time cannons. Now, I feel that with a talent like yours in our midst to help the coachmen thrash the horses, we can begin to move our ditch from under the shadows."

Here it came.

"Gentlemen, I've made a decision," the Big Guy said. "We are going into the homes of real Americans *live*. The people beckon. We're going to do a live show showing real people at home. I would like to see it called 'Just Up the Street.' I thought that up myself. I want to see it on the air as soon as possible."

"A few human-interest interviews can't hurt anything," Herb Grant said. "Hell of an idea, Big Guy."

"No interviews," said the Big Guy. "Just wonderful American people, doing whatever they do. We don't want to interrupt them with interviews. We shall simply chronicle their adventures on a typical evening at home."

Stanley said, "We can throw an hour in there on Wednesday night. Fewer sets in use that night, I think."

"Gentlemen, let's be generous," the Big Guy said. "Let's don't short-change America. 'Just Up the Street' must be a three-hour show. An entire evening of prime time celebrating the American spirit!"

"Three hours?" Stanley said, trying not to scream.

I dwelled, just momentarily, on three consecutive hours of prime-time Silex cleansing.

The Big Guy said, "Wednesday sounds fine, Stanley. Fewer sets in use, you say? Excellent. This will get them out of their bowling alleys and back to their sets where they belong."

He said, "Think of it. Three happy hours in prime time. Our network bringing the true America to the true America. Unrehearsed, spontaneous . . . pure theater, like those incessant Stukas over London."

Stanley mumbled, "We can clear the slot. I mean, what do we lose but reruns? A dummy D.A. and his Puerto Rican assistant . . . the dolphin that flies his own glider. . . ."

The Big Guy stood up then, and we noticed that two military chiefs in full dress uniform, weighted down with campaign ribbons, had appeared in the doorway of the men's grill. The Big Guy went over to them and they interlocked arms.

In the doorway the Big Guy smiled at me and said: "This is your baby, Frank. You rock it."

I couldn't say exactly how long we all sat there before anyone spoke. My own thoughts were largely about a little man with a pink face and wispy white hair.

It was Stanley who finally said, "What'd he call it? 'Just Up the Street'? We ought to call it 'Just Out of Work.' "

Herb Grant had leaned back in his chair and lit up a Vantage blue. He was not so stupid that it hadn't already occurred to him I'd been given a ridiculous assignment and if it failed as miserably as it had a perfect right to do, I would be waist-deep in quicksand. And so would Stanley. A network president is only as good as his programming guy.

"Looks like you've got yourself one of those challenges you relish," Grant said to me. "We can sure as hell forget about selling it to anyone. We'll have to eat the time, but if that's how the Big Guy wants to spend his money, there's no skin off my butt. I think I'll just have some laughs watching you try to turn this bag of crap into something *intelligent* and *enlightening*. Lots of luck, genius."

Cooper was waiting beside the Rolls when we came out of the clubhouse. He slumped against the door in his Levis and cowboy hat and jewelry, looking lean and dangerous. Grant said there was no place in the network's table of organization for a man like Cooper, so Cooper didn't exist. Grant wouldn't look at him.

Usually when Stanley saw the Rolls limo he would whistle and say, "Didn't know the Greek was in town." Or, "How does it handle in a heavy sea?" That day he just got in his Chrysler and drove off. Grant was picked up by his wife in a Buick station wagon. She

36

was a pretty woman except for a Piping Rock grimace.

"What would your old daddy say if he'd ever seen you knockin' a ball around inside a chicken coop?" Cooper said as our limo rolled past the paddle tennis courts and the country club gate.

I said, "Remember back in Sunset when we lost that bi-district game because they claimed I caught that pass out of bounds?"

Cooper said, "Damned old stickup's all it was."

"That's about how I feel right now," I said.

We drove along in silence for a while. I didn't turn on the TVs or pick up the papers or magazines. I made myself a Bombay martini with four olives in it and looked at Cooper's hair curling over his collar.

Finally Cooper said, "Well, if you're that pissed, you sure have learned to act grownup about it. I remember when they stole that touchdown from us, you screamed and pulled up grass and like to have got throwed out of the stadium. My daddy prayed for you that night."

"I remember," I said.

Cooper's daddy was Brother Dwight Wright Cooper, the evangelist. Brother Cooper prayed for me out loud in front of the whole crowd in the tent in the vacant lot at the evangelical meeting the night after the game. He prayed that I would rededicate my life to Christ and quit cussing. My own daddy lost fifty dollars on the game. Fifty dollars was a load of money for a railroad brakeman to come up with in those days. When I had checked in as a freshman at Hill Hall, the University of Texas athletic dorm, I had eight dollars, two pairs of Levis, several T-shirts, a windbreaker and a pair of loafers. Riding in the Rolls, I thought about those days and tried to be philosophical about what the Big Guy had put on me.

I said, "I've got a puzzle for you, D. Wayne. Is all

this fun I'm having in this business worth where I'm going—and where's that? And when I get there can I keep it—and will they love me?"

Cooper said, "What the hell does that mean?"

I said, "I fell in a trap. I'm supposed to do something impossible."

Cooper said, "I reckon you'll do it then."

I said I didn't, quite frankly, at the moment, see how.

"Lordy, it ain't all bluebirds and lemonade in the big league," Cooper said.

Without asking, he aimed the Rolls toward Pelham Manor.

Chapter
Four

~~~~~~~~~~~~~~~~~~~~~~~~~~~~~~~~~~~~~~

Marcie was in front of the house in a flower bed snipping at the rose bushes, and Cindy was sitting on a bamboo mat on the lawn, holding up a reflector to bounce the sun onto her face. I saw them both look around at the Silver Goblet wheeling into the drive. Marcie gestured at Cindy, who reluctantly put down the reflector, walked over to the flower bed and gave her mother a cigarette.

My daughter was sixteen years old and did not smoke. She hated smoking. In fact, as far as I knew, she didn't even smoke dope. If during one of her periodic searches of the house Marcie had ever found so much as one joint hidden in Cindy's underwear drawer, the noise would have set dogs to howling as far off as southern Canada.

But Cindy had observed plenty of her mother's fits. That's not why Cindy didn't smoke. She said she didn't smoke because she wanted to keep her two lungs for her whole life. A vulgarian might remark that if you could develop lungs like Cindy had at sixteen by not smoking cigarettes, every woman smoker in America would reach for an ashtray for the last time. Of course, a little girl's own daddy would never make a remark like that.

After fifteen or twenty years of two to four packs a day, Marcie had been trying to quit. Her approach to the problem was typical of the way Marcie operated. She kept cigarettes close by at all times for the feeling of security that a nicotine panic could be stopped before her eyeballs started rolling. But Marcie refused to smoke a cigarette unless Cindy gave it to her and lit it for her. The look of reproof on Cindy's face made Marcie feel guilty about asking. That cut her smoking way down.

As the limo pulled into the circular driveway, Cindy was lighting her mother's cigarette. Seeing the two of them standing together, Marcie in white shorts with a blouse knotted below the breasts, and Cindy in a crocheted bikini, I had an immense rush of pride that I'd had something to do with those two being there. I was overwhelmed with warm, sentimental memories of the good times. Cindy turned to let me know she would run to hug her wonderful old daddy just as soon as she got that cigarette lit, and I was flooded with love for my family.

I said, "D. Wayne, I must have been a stupid bastard to have let you walk in here and move me out of my home."

I met Cindy about ten feet from the Rolls. We hugged and kissed. She smelled like coconut oil. Her forehead left a coconut oil smudge on my cotton shirt.

"Daddy!" Cindy said.

"Baby!" I said.

"I'll go tell Frankie you're here," she said. "He's starting analysis this afternoon."

I watched Cindy run up onto the porch, swing around a column with one arm and then disappear through the door. In the front seat of the limo, Cooper

40

had put on his mirror glasses so we couldn't tell exactly what he was looking at.

Cindy bounded out the door again.

"Hi, D.W.C.," she yelled.

D.W.C. was what the kids called D. Wayne Cooper. Dimples popped into Cooper's cheeks, and he waved a little two-finger salute that started at the right eyebrow, like Gary Cooper did in *Morocco*. Then Cindy went back inside.

Marcie had taken off her gloves and dropped them in the flower bed beside the shears. She puffed on the cigarette. Smoke came out of her nose.

"Who told Frankie he needs analysis?" I said.

"We are supposed to communicate through our attorneys," Marcie said.

"Every time our lawyers nod to each other on the sidewalk, it costs another thousand," I said.

Marcie bent over and picked up the gloves and the shears.

Exciting things happened with the short shorts and the knotted blouse when she bent over, as Marcie very well knew. I might confess right here that all during our marriage, Marcie could inspire me to gulping, passionate, sexual desire any time she wanted. Which she had not been so interested in doing since she had turned serious.

In the early years of our marriage, Marcie's conversation was mostly about movies, food, diets, opera, children, doctors and whether it was too hot or too cold. In those years we fucked like cuckoos. In the old Plymouth parked on Mt. Bonnell in Austin. On the grass in the chiggers behind the frame house we rented in Austin. In the tile whirlpool shower at her parents' home in Houston. On the linoleum drainboard of the kitchen in our student housing apartment in Dallas. Behind the couch at the ranch-style house we later bought in North Dallas. On the terrace of our apartment in Philadelphia. On airplanes, in taxicabs, etc. I should mention that we did it a lot in beds, too.

Those early days, Marcie loved to put on little shows when there was a risk we might be seen by strangers. Like while we were driving somewhere. Or under the table at a restaurant. Or in a hotel room with the curtains open. She called it "being naughty."

Marcie would never consider jumping out of her duds at a party, no matter how drunk she was, no matter how clever the game, no matter how great a body she had. She didn't go for groups. Once she suggested a naked swim at a farewell affair the night before we moved to Philadelphia. This was when I was offered a better job than the one I had in Dallas. WCAU–TV in Philadelphia was a step closer to New York and the Apple. Marcie had her dress only half unzipped by the time five or six of us were already in the water. Then she ran inside and stayed until it was time to leave. Her charms were for my eyes only, is what she said that night. But when I would come back from some thrilling hurricane or political convention, Marcie would tremble when she met me. Her eyes would go out of focus when I touched her. I was like some kind of hero out of the pages of *Young Lust* comics.

But that was a long time ago. Before she turned serious.

Now Marcie straightened up with the gloves and shears in her hands and the cigarette in her mouth. My giddy desire to ravish her in the flower bed passed into history.

"What is this about Frankie in analysis?" I said.

Marcie said, "You're hostile toward analysis because you have a compulsion to run everyone else's affairs. This is a hysterical device to prevent other people from realizing how truly and deeply screwed up you are when it comes to running your own affairs."

I said where I grew up you had to run your own affairs pretty damn well or you got your ass whipped.

"Predictably, you respond with another story about growing up poor in Dallas," she said.

All in all, I liked it better when Marcie talked about banana bread.

"A fourteen-year-old boy doesn't belong in analysis," I said.

"Your son does," Marcie said.

Cindy opened the door and yelled, "Frankie won't come out. He's listening to music."

I started toward the porch.

"I don't know why you should be allowed inside a house you walked out of," Marcie said.

I said, "Why can't we talk to each other like two people who used to be practically the same thing as in love?"

"You don't realize what a tremendous negative force you set up around you," Marcie said.

I followed her into the house.

The living room was as tidy as a compulsive cleaner and arranger could make it with the help of a maid five days a week. Marcie had attacks during which she would go all over the house and yard picking up the "messies" and "nasties." The oil portrait of Marcie in the pearls and strapless gown had been moved from the mantel to a lesser position. She said that was a step in her struggle with ego. In place of the portrait was an impressionist painting she bought at a Fifty-seventh Street gallery. I could have sent a camera crew to Moscow for what it cost. The white carpet, white velvet couches and chairs and onyx tables dared any ignorant human to touch them with a muddy shoe or a drop of wine.

Opening off the living room was another room that I called the den and Marcie called the library. At least a hundred record albums were thrown around on the floor in that room. One tennis shoe sat on what had formerly been my typewriter. The other shoe leaned against a vase. The vase had turned over and spilled water and flowers on the desk. There was an apple core on a bookshelf, a sweatshirt on a lamp, a guitar case in my leather swivel chair and a tennis racquet on top of the TV.

Frankie Junior lay on his back with stereo earphones on his head and a guitar on his chest. His eyes moved toward us. He lifted a hand. It was hard to tell if it was a greeting or a gesture for silence.

"Frankie doesn't need analysis. He needs his Honda donated to charity," I said.

Frankie must have read my lips. He took off the earphones and said, "Be with you in a minute, Dad." You could hear noise pouring out of the earphones before he put them on again.

"Look at this mess," Marcie said. "The boy has no sense of responsibility. He's failing half his courses in school. He can barely read or write. He won't take out the garbage. He doesn't listen to what I tell him. He forgets things. Last week he went to school with one shoe on. All he does is eat and sleep and play his guitar."

"He stays in the shower for an hour at a time," Cindy said.

I turned off the power switch for the stereo. Frankie sat up blinking and removed the earphones.

"What did you have to do that for?" he said.

"I want to talk to you," I said.

"Everybody wants to talk to me all of a sudden. What's the deal?" Frankie said. "Yesterday, Dr. Fornet took me out for a malt. A malt, you dig it? What's a thirty-year-old guy drinking a malt for? I mean what the hell for?"

Frankie was stirring around, gathering his limbs under himself like a frog.

"Who is Dr. Fornet?" I said.

"Dr. Regis Fornet is the leading existential psychiatrist in the area. One of the leaders in the field in the entire country," Marcie said.

Frankie got hold of my desk and pulled himself to his feet.

He was tall for a fourteen-year-old, and skinny. He yawned and the braces on his teeth sparkled with spit. I didn't have any real yearning to kiss him at that moment. But I kissed him on the cheek. It was awkward. My folks didn't believe in kissing when I was a kid, so I thought it would be nice for Cindy and Frankie to get a lot of kissing from their parents. Cindy loved any show of affection. Frankie seemed embarrassed by it.

Frankie said he thought he would go take a shower.

"How about a ride in the Silver Goblet?" I said.

Frankie said, "Puke."

"Dr. Fornet is here," Cindy said from the window.

Frankie said, "Puke and snot."

We heard a car door slam and went to the front door to see a Porsche convertible parked behind the Rolls. Dr. Fornet was looking at the limo and then at the house, back and forth. He had a red beard and wore white pants, sandals and the kind of white frilly shirt they sell in Acapulco or Calcutta.

I said, "This psychiatrist makes house calls? On Saturdays?"

"He was here five times this week," Frankie said.

"Dr. Fornet was counseling me about Frankie," Marcie said.

"One time he stayed until after midnight," Frankie said.

"At seventy-five dollars an hour?" I said.

"There was no charge for the exploratory sessions," Marcie said.

I didn't like the way she said it.

Dr. Fornet walked only about two paces from the

Porsche. He put his hands up to his mouth and called:

"Halloooooo, the house! Is Frankie in there?"

"He's scared to come in with you here, Dad," Frankie said.

"Don't be an idiot. Dr. Fornet is not afraid of anything," Marcie said. She walked to the door and yelled, "Come in, Dr. Fornet."

"Such a beautiful day. Smell the breeze. Send Frankie outside," Dr. Fornet called.

Marcie grabbed Frankie by the elbow and marched him outside. Marcie's butt moved like something you dream of squeezing two handfuls of. Her legs were as brown and firm as the first day I ever saw her. That was when she was runner-up for freshman sweetheart at the University of Texas. Marcie was a voice major. In the section of South Dallas where I grew up, we thought if you went to college it was to play sports or to learn something practical like tooth-pulling or how to sue people. Going to college to learn how to sing struck me as downright exotic.

I used to wait for Marcie outside the Music Building and walk with her to Littlefield dorm, where she lived. I could hear voices singing and pianos playing through open windows of the Music Building while I waited. That was a strange and wonderful sound. Then Marcie would come out, maybe in a sweater and skirt, and we would walk along on a soft, yellow afternoon, and she might sing for me. Right about then I began to suspect I had found something I had rather do on afternoons in the fall and spring than practice football. To be honest, Marcie wasn't the only reason I quit the team in my sophomore year. Another reason was I saw I was not going to be a starter after the NCAA changed college football rules to one-platoon just in time for my freshman season in '53.

Without a scholarship, I managed to last out my junior year at Texas by working nights at the Austin newspaper. In the late spring, when I was a junior and Marcie was a sophomore, we thought she was pregnant. We ran off to Lampasas and got married in a country church. To support our new family I applied for a job at the *Dallas Times Herald*. They hired me. We moved to Dallas in the summer. Then it turned out she wasn't pregnant after all. But Marcie and I were happy to be married, anyhow. She studied voice at SMU, and I learned news reporting at the *Times Herald*. We lived in an old asbestos-siding apartment building with an attic fan on Yale Boulevard near the campus. I made forty-five dollars a week. Marcie's daddy in Houston sent us two hundred a month so she could stay in school. We had a new Mercury and a Muntz TV which were wedding presents. We could drink beer and eat pizza at Gordo's, and every few months blow twenty-five dollars on wine and a good dinner. It seemed like a great life at the time, but being in our twenties, we thought we were stuck with it forever.

So how did it happen that a red-bearded psychiatrist would be halloooooing in front of a big house that I didn't live in but was paying for in Pelham Manor, New York?

"You want to meet him," Cindy said, looking at me.

"Yeah, I'd like to ask him a question," I said.

"Oh boy, I wouldn't miss this for anything," Cindy said.

She hugged me again.

Dr. Fornet watched me coming toward him. He seemed wary. No doubt from having listened to Marcie for five nights in the past week. Some of the stories Marcie told about me were not lies, exactly, but they did not present me in the best possible light, either.

"You must be Mallory," Fornet said.

I said, "What is analysis going to do for Frankie?"

Fornet stepped sideways toward the rose bushes with an expression on his face that said there could be a world trophy American Beauty hidden in there some place, if only he could find it.

"Dr. Fornet is going to teach me how to cope," Frankie said.

"All you'll learn from him is how to hustle," I said.

"That was a very good rap we had yesterday, Frankie. I probably got as much out of it as you did," Dr. Fornet said.

"Yeah. Maybe more," Frankie said.

Cooper watched from the front seat of the Rolls through the mirror glasses.

"I think you are trying to sell my kid a package of bullshit," I said to Fornet.

"Your infantile aggression never ceases to amaze me," Marcie said.

"One can hardly dismiss existential psychiatry as bullshit," Dr. Fornet said with a twisted little smile. "Even if one does view the world from the mind of a television person."

"I just did it," I said. "It was an existential act."

"I'm gonna go play my guitar," Frankie said.

Frankie walked slowly toward the house.

"The boy hates you, I'm afraid," Dr. Fornet said.

"He thinks I'm a hell of a guy," I said.

Frankie paused to listen.

"He's repressing his hatred," Fornet said. "Beneath the impassivity you have forced him to cultivate, there lies a vast pool of rage, fear, pain . . . and a sickening disappointment in his father."

"Frankie, you sure you want to be analyzed by a man who confuses jack-off fatigue with repressed hatred?" I said.

Frankie shrugged and said, "He's about the same as everybody else."

"I'll tell you what you might try," I said to Frankie. "Instead of existential psychiatry, you might try work-

48

ing hard to be good at something. It's worth the trouble, and it can be a pleasure."

"Your ambition has broken out of its cage again," Marcie said. "Tell Frankie how they call you Captain Success, and then do a quick exit with a couple of gags to cover it up."

"Dad, that's what I'm doing with my guitar," Frankie said. "I mean, getting good at it."

I felt pretty stupid for not having understood that a lot earlier. I know this does not excuse it, but at least I understood it now that Frankie had explained it to me, and that was more than could be said for Fornet.

"We are dealing with moment-to-moment reality," Fornet said. "Do you feel threatened by having your son learn to deal with his life as *he* lives it, rather than with the distorted picture of a life that is forced upon him in your quest for power?"

I said, "Listen, Fornet, I grew up poor in Dallas, and that is why I am going to knock you on your ass, in case you later on are digging for a reason."

"My god, Frank, what kind of example is that for a father to be?" Marcie said.

I motioned for the kids to come closer. I said this was going to be an example of how to cope with moment-to-moment reality.

Cooper got out of the limo.

"I should point out that I get off on karate," Fornet said.

Fornet arranged his body in a karate stance. He looked like a grasshopper. Cooper sidled in between us.

"Why don't we take it on home before the museums close?" Cooper said.

"That's a good idea, D. Wayne, but first I have to rearrange this bowl of fruit," I said.

"You wish I were a homosexual, but your jealous anger indicates you're afraid I'm not," Fornet said, moving his hands like a spastic.

49

I jumped at Fornet and clutched him by the throat. I intended to choke him and kick him and punch him and generally enjoy myself at his expense.

Instead, we fell over into the rose bushes.

Fornet landed on bottom. I fell on him and felt the stuffing shift like when you fall on a soccer ball.

Fornet screamed, "The thorns! The thorns!"

I got up. Fornet clawed at himself.

"My shirt is torn. My back is ripped. My god, I'm bleeding. Do you see the blood?" he said.

Marcie helped Fornet up. She was very tender with him. She led him toward the house.

"From now on, Frank, let's use the lawyers, huh?" Marcie said, looking back at me.

Cooper grinned two deep dimples. Cindy rubbed my hands where they were scratched. The braces shone as Frankie's mouth hung open. He was probably thinking about Segovia.

"Mama's going to get really tired of Dr. Fornet," Cindy said.

"I'm bound to run him off before long," Frankie said.

"Real good move you put on that sucker," Cooper said.

It was a joy to be with my family.

Chapter
Five

~~~~~~

I spent the rest of the weekend in the apartment watching television and staring into space. I was thinking about a show titled "Just Up the Street" and one of the things that came to my mind was that you could shoot the whole three hours at the Mallory home in Pelham Manor easily enough. Plenty of wonderful Americans there, doing happy things.

On Monday morning I was getting ready to go to the office and start quizzing production people for ideas for "Just Up the Street" when another crisis erupted, and I had to get Cooper to drive me to the Jersey shore, to a town called Bay Head. You can get there in a little over an hour, but who would go unless you favored swimming in a red tide? Or unless some deranged person had selected it as a location for scenes in "Satan Takes a Bride"? Norris, the director, had phoned. He said he had a problem with the star, Pete Stern.

Pete was infuriated at the crew and he had locked himself in the ladies' room of a service station. He refused to come out.

"He's supposed to be leaping from one houseboat to another, chasing the mysterious force, but he's locked in the john instead," Norris said. "He's mad because one of the guys in the crew said he jumps like a fag."

The Silver Goblet pulled up to the location before I realized it. I had been staring at one of those full-page ads in *Variety* an executive producer usually pays for himself. Somebody named Aaron Furness was being congratulated for another hit TV series on ABC about a lovable heart surgeon.

Norris opened the rear door of the limo before Cooper could get out. "He's been in there for over two goddam hours," Norris said. We walked toward the ladies' room. The crew sat around. Some played cards. Others enjoyed naps.

I didn't want this to take long.

"Pete," I said, rapping on the door of the toilet. "This is Frank Mallory. Have you got amoebic dysentery or something? There are thirty people out here about to go on overtime."

A bitter laugh came from behind the door.

I looked at Norris.

"It wasn't too bad when he chased the head witch down the alley," Norris said. "He runs okay. It was the jumping. You know how little kids look when they crouch down and put their feet together and swing their arms back and forth?"

"What's left of the shooting?"

"Two days if he gets out of the can in the next five minutes," Norris said.

I said, "Pete, we need you out here."

"You damn well need me out there," Pete Stern said.

"Who said he jumps like a fag?" I asked Norris.

Norris said, "Joe said it. Pete wants him fired. You know what a hassle that would be with the union?"

Joe was a light gaffer. I walked over to interrupt his card game.

"Want to give me a break, Joe?" I asked. "Take a couple of days in the Poconos on full pay and expenses?"

"I ain't leaving," Joe said. "He jumps like a fag."

I said Joe could take the wife and kids with him.

"To a hotel?"

Get a suite, I said. Do a lot of room service.

I went back to the ladies' room.

"Pete, I got rid of the guy who insulted you," I said. "Open the door."

A latch unbolted and Pete Stern stepped out. He was tall and blond and he could look rugged if he stood still and wasn't asked to deliver more than one line of dialogue at a time. He had been discovered by an aging actress when he went to her home in Beverly Hills to measure her dining room for new carpet. She got him in a number of beach party pictures. He became a star when he landed in a TV western series in which all he had to do was not drop his gun and say, now and then, "I don't rightly know, Ma'am."

"Hello, Frank," said Pete Stern. "I knew you'd take care of this."

"Let's go to work," I said.

"Not with this crew," Pete said. "I want a different crew. They all laughed."

He shouted at the crew.

"I want all of you off the set!"

"In other words," I said, "you want to be here on the Jersey shore, all by yourself, making your own movie."

"Frank, I want that crew deported!" Pete said. He stepped back into the ladies' room, slammed the door, and bolted it again.

"Did you ever see him in that remake of *The*

Maverick Queen?" Norris asked. "He slid off his horse like Fred Astaire coming down a staircase."

I said, "Shoot around him today. Double him. Long shots. Over the shoulder stuff. We'll come up with a new ending so you don't need him at all, and you can wrap it on time."

I headed toward the limo.

"Oh, and don't tell Pete," I said. "Let him spend the whole day in there looking at himself in the mirror."

Going past the card game, I said, "You're right, Joe. He jumps like a fag."

Joe said, "I could be wrong. I could think about it in the Poconos."

Chapter
Six

〰〰〰〰〰〰〰〰〰〰〰〰〰〰〰〰〰〰

It was after lunch when I got back from the Jersey shore, but Cooper had stocked the limo with a pizza featuring many of the architectural wonders of Florence, so I hadn't missed a meal.

My office was in a corner of the twentieth floor of the Chambers building, a floor where people worked for a living in behalf of CBC. Stanley Coffman's office was on the same floor, in another glassed-in corner with a similiar wide-angled view of Gotham.

To find the Big Guy or Herb Grant or the executive dining room, you had to take a special elevator up to the thirty-fourth floor and show your I.D. card to an armed guard.

Stanley had a theory about the security.

"Grant doesn't want anyone to catch him by surprise when he's playing with his Frisbee," Stanley said.

The Chambers building was on Sixth Avenue in the fifties, near CBS, ABC, Time-Life, McGraw-Hill, all of those relatively new skyscrapers that crept away from NBC and the skating rink but kept Rockefeller

Center for an address. You could say the Chambers building was part of Rockefeller Center's encroachment on cut-rate jewelers, porno shops and clothing stores for the man who fancied orange tuxedoes.

When I stepped off the elevator on twenty, Stanley was in the hall chatting with a tall, long-haired production girl.

As I walked by, Stanley took the girl's arm and held it out to me.

"Could that throw a knuckler?" he said.

I smiled at the girl.

"This is Melissa," Stanley said. "Melissa struck out twelve yesterday against Channel Seven in the park. Our guys kicked their ass."

More importantly, I said, had anybody seen any numbers on the earthquake?

"God, our footage was incredible. Half of Peru was under water," the girl said. "The rest was on fire."

Stanley said, "Fucking thing did a thirteen share. Right in the old flusher. The female private eye got it up against the ropes and hammered it. The bounty hunter put it down for the count. And the campus dean with the two retarded kids pulled down his pants and shit on the whole hour."

I said we did what we could in an effort to serve the public.

"Grant's marbles bounced all over the floor this morning," Stanley said. "Know what I want where I work next, Frank? A window that'll open. Then when the certifiable dunce comes around, I can do a bird thing for him."

Stanley was as capable as any network president could be, but he knew as well as anyone how quickly they come and go. The Big Guy had selected Stanley as network president because he did a good job of running the station in Los Angeles. Stanley was a West

Coast guy. He went to USC and he was one of the few people I liked who ever came up through sales.

Stanley did not have the best of marriages. His wife missed her swimming pool, and his kids missed wrecking their cars. On my way down the hall I could hear Stanley talking to Melissa.

"Might blow a few trains tonight," he said. "What's the story on the clap? Cleared up and everything?"

When I got to my own corner of the floor Arleene was at her desk in the outer office reading a copy of *Rolling Stone*. She was a handsome, gray-haired, tailored woman in her early fifties. She had the kind of alertness, efficient style, wit and curiosity that I had found only among New Yorkers.

Arleene had raised two daughters by herself and had never ceased to be astounded by the fact that both of them had chosen to marry Ivy League types with connections in brokerage firms. She attributed this flaw in their character to the genes of their father.

Even if he had survived the crash of his wounded torpedo plane on the flight deck of a carrier during World War II, he would have returned home and tried to start a mail-order business, she said.

"All I really knew about him was that his uniform fit and his wings looked swell," she had told me.

When I said to Arleene once that there was more than one kind of patriot in that war, she said, "I love my daughters, but I could have collected tinfoil or coat hangers, right?"

Arleene had been my secretary through all of my overachieving at CBS, and I insisted that she be another part of the package when I changed networks.

"Your writers on *Satan Sucks* have been in your office for thirty minutes," Arleene said.

"How stoned are they?"

"I don't know," she said, "but a while ago in there it sounded like six ducks playing basketball."

My office had two sides of floor-to-ceiling glass, one side filled by a programming chart that showed what every network put on the air in every minute of prime time throughout the season, and one wall of four TV monitors built in above a long shelf designed to hold the framed photographs, objects of humor, awards, and other trivia that a man can't resist keeping on display until he either dies or retires and his children store them in a damp basement.

It was a reasonably large office, with plenty of room to pace across the carpet, with a small bar in a corner, and the desk, chairs, sofa and tables had all succumbed to Arleene's recent infatuation with leather and stainless steel.

The writers were Thurlow Watts and Larry Travers. Watts was a partially bald and bearded man in his forties. Before he turned to TV and movie writing, he had done fourteen novels nobody remembered, and the libretto of a Broadway musical about sugar-cane growers that closed the second night. He tended to dress in the tank tops and denims of a younger man. He looked especially silly when he carried his shoulder bag and wore a cap like Lenin's.

His partner, Travers, was only twenty-two, wore dark glasses, had permed hair, a goatee, a mustache, baggy trousers that covered his sneakers, and a knee-length fatigue jacket over a faded football jersey. Travers considered the craft of writing only a brief stopover on his way to becoming a Hollywood mogul or perhaps Pope.

They had met and agreed to become collaborators, I believe, after sharing a mutual experience. In a studio screening room they had simultaneously laughed out loud and convulsively at the part of a highly praised dramatic film where the heroine got both her legs amputated.

Watts was sitting on my desk top with his legs

folded under him. Travers was doing pushups on the carpet.

"Okay," I said, entering. "What we need is a new ending with the same setups as the old one. But not a word from Pete in the last few pages. You have to know he's around without getting a real look at him."

Travers went from pushups to situps.

"What if he turns into a werewolf? Then we can put a funny face on him and change his voice," he said.

Watts growled, "Pete gobbles starlets."

I gestured for Watts to get off my desk and take a chair. I sat down and rather wearily rubbed my forehead.

"I was thinking more like Pete could get grabbed by a giant bat that's hovering around," I said.

Travers began sidestraddle hops. I asked him to stop. He plopped down quickly on the sofa, crossed his legs, and began swinging one foot rapidly and tapping the other.

"What if he's chasing the boss witch down the alley, and he gets mugged by one thousand rats. We can't see him under the rats," Travers said.

"And by the time the rats are off, his face looks like dog food," said Watts.

"What if we dub a speech for the boss witch while she's running down the alley," Travers said, "and she says, 'Satan, come suck this parasite off of me.' And then the giant bat . . ."

"Or a flying rhinoceros, who gives a shit . . ." Watts said.

". . . bangs down with a boom of lightning," Travers said, "and Satan's voice is like thunder in the background, and Pete is gone. Which is sudden and tragic, but the girl takes over and knocks the witches off."

Watts said, "What if the girl escapes from the motel just in time to see Pete jerked away by this giant bat, and she realizes what she's got with her is the boss witch's magic catfish bone. . . ."

"And then since Pete's out of range in the maw of the giant bat, she raids the coven by herself and whacks out all the witches with a perfectly formed catfish bone," Travers said.

"Maybe it's shaped like a cross," said Watts.

I got back up and acted like I had somewhere to go.

"You're obviously on the track of something brilliant," I said. "I need those pages by tonight. Now, I appeal to you as a fellow garden-clubber to be elegant and witty and make us all proud."

Watts and Travers moved out the door in a soft-shoe routine, singing:

"Hear them calling . . . cross the sea! . . . For our sons of . . . Liber-ty!"

I fell back into my chair and Arleene brought me a cup of coffee and a stack of bills from Pelham.

Along about going-home hour, another visitor arrived. It was Julia, the lady I had met in Elaine's a few nights earlier. Julia had one of the nicest sets of tits you would ever hope to see outside of Beverly Hills or Sydney, Australia.

I suppose they were the whole explanation for why I had tried to meet her in the first place, or why I agreed to let her drag me off to explore a French restaurant right then, one of those places *Women's Wear* had gone mad about.

I did have to eat dinner somewhere, of course.

Julia had honey blond hair, was covered over with expensive jewelry, and looked like she devoted most of her time to shopping and screwing deck hands.

As I left the office with Julia, Arleene said, "How are you gonna get back down the hill?"

The French restaurant was one of those quaint places where your table was one inch away from four dress designers and your plate pressed up against your chest. Doves cooed in cages hanging from the ceiling. Wine only. And the entree selection was limited to garni-bone and cauliflower.

I told Julia to eat fast so we could go to dinner.

That Monday night I was now feeling the need for three things: love, affection and food. In moods like that, I usually asked Cooper to take me to Clarke's, my favorite bar.

Chapter
Seven

～～～～～～～～～～～～～～～～～

Pulling up to Clarke's in the Silver
Goblet hardly ever caused more of a stir than you
would find at your average Brazilian soccer riot. This
of course is P. J. Clarke's, at Fifty-fifth and Third
Avenue. Clarke's to a regular; P.J.'s to the tourist.

The saloon occupies the ground floor of an old two-
story red brick building on a corner. Once, all the
buildings in the neighborhood looked similar, and the
Third Avenue El rumbled above their roofs. Clarke's
sits there up against another minor skyscraper now.
Somebody bought all the air above it, but Clarke's
stayed—a landmark to the days when the Irish sang
more often than they threw bombs.

The place is in an area of Manhattan that has become crowded with modern bars and also with movies. At night the sidewalks are festive. You can find
people stumbling into an argument about subtitled art
films, or stumbling out of a marriage, or just stumbling. And there are these hordes of young apartment
dwellers wandering about, hoping to discover a mean-
ingful relationship behind the frost of the next daiquiri.

Cooper always let me out at the side entrance on Fifty-fifth, and then he would take the limo away and hide it somewhere, preferably underground. Or he would vanish into his own life, knowing he wouldn't have to come back and get me for at least four hours. Or six.

Marcie thought Clarke's was depressing. I, however, thought Clarke's had prevented a number of suicides, if the truth were known.

On the sidewalks people would stop to see who might climb out of the limo. It got to where I enjoyed their puzzlement when it turned out to be me—no one recognizable—instead of a talk show host or the star of a sitcom carrying a six-pack of Emmys.

Cooper said once, "If you'd drive and let me climb out of the rear of this thing, them folks would think they got their money's worth."

In Clarke's I sometimes liked to stand and drink for a while at what is known to an inner circle as "the garbage." This is a spot in the middle room at the end of the bar. It isn't really called the garbage because of the horse players, politicians, writers, detectives, actors and TV people who assemble there. It actually happens to be where the dirty dishes are stacked up in a pan and then taken away periodically by a couple of Oriental busboys we refer to as Wong and Wong-A.

The food is good, of course, the drinks come swiftly, and the waiters and bartenders not only know the scores of all the games, but what the latest polls show about the coming election and who the real thieves are. I guess I like the mixture as much as anything. Rich guys sit with Shylocks. Guys who wrote movies for Judy Garland sit with criminal lawyers. Ex-prizefighters sit with lyricists. I've sat with guys in there who said they invented the ice cream scoop, and I've sat with guys who said it could be profitable to kidnap Carlo Gambino's nephew.

Like any other New York bar with age, Clarke's has its share of lore. Most of the lore fans are the waiters. They can point to where Ray Milland stood in *The Lost Weekend*. A table in the darker and sometimes impenetrably chic back room is still known to many as "the Kilgallen table." The waiters like to point to where Ingrid Bergman sat with Lena Horne, where Vince Lombardi moved his chair over to join Hubert Humphrey, where Frank Gifford, Charley Conerly and Kyle Rote sat the night after the Giants beat the Bears for the championship, where Frank Sinatra told James Jones how to rewrite *From Here to Eternity* —or something like that.

They also like to point out this table by a window looking out on Fifty-fifth where Onassis ate one of his last hamburgers in America. The waiters were afraid Onassis and Jackie might get bothered by some drunks on that particular winter's night so they asked some regulars at the garbage to occupy a table next to them —to protect them from any possible intrusions from strangers or drunks. But the first thing they knew, one of the regulars who had sat down, a horse player named Billy, was leaning across Onassis's lap, saying, "Is it still snowing outside, Ari?"

It is said around the garbage that if the history of Clarke's is ever written, the title will have to be: *Is It Still Snowing Outside, Ari?*

We had one drink at the garbage waiting for Cooper to stow the limo. Then we were led by the owner, Danny Lavezzo, past a line of people waiting to get into the back room. We took a large table.

If there were fewer than the usual number of vicious remarks directed at me by the people in line, it was undoubtedly because of Julia's tits.

Our table in Clarke's filled up quickly, and not just with the two bacon cheeseburgers, cup of chili, and dish of hash-browns I requested for myself. We were

64

joined by a TV sports commentator from my old network, a detective, a guy who worked for the governor, a girl starring in a new cosmetic commercial, and the owner himself.

Much of the conversation around a table at Clarke's never changes.

"Chunk meat, not ground," I must have said at one point. "You can't use too much cumin seed. Throw out the tomatoes. You know who puts tomatoes in chili? Dinah Shore."

The detective said, "That kid with the dandruff who comes in here and drinks up all the Drambuie? His daddy owns the horses? I seen him at the track today. He gimme inside speed, but it was outside closers. I got drowned."

Danny Lavezzo said to Julia, "Frank seems to have a weakness for taking out deformed girls."

Somebody said, "In July he was the exacta king. In August he was living in a Queens Boulevard walkup."

Somebody else said, "How far is Monaco from Biarritz if you're driving?"

The girl in the commercial asked Cooper if he was an actor.

A little later, toward the end of what had been a lengthy discussion about the New York Giants' draft choices, another chair was added to the table. Norris, the director of "Satan Takes a Bride," sat down.

"I think I saw David Merrick out front," he said. "Or Hal Prince. Which one never smiles?"

I reached in my pocket and handed Norris some folded pages of script.

"Pete runs into a garbage grinder and gets chewed to pieces," I said.

"I appreciate this, Frank," Norris said. "It's a real boost to my career." He grabbed a waiter and asked for a triple Gibson.

"The girl tricks the witches into being locked inside

a mobile home and drops a match in the gas tank," I said.

Norris put the pages away.

Cooper said, "Old Watts and Travers are somethin' else. I'd take 'em with me anywhere I went for a day or so. Except to funerals, maybe."

"You mean Watts and Travers the writers?" asked the TV model.

"What do they write about?" Danny Lavezzo said. "Chili?"

Cooper said, "I thought Travers was goofier than Watts at first. Walked in Frank's office one day and Travers was standing on his head."

He was doing an imitation, I said.

"Of what?" Julia asked.

"Mussolini dead," Cooper said.

Julia yawned and looked out of the window.

The man who worked for the governor asked Julia a question.

"Is it still snowing outside, Ari?"

Cooper said, "That damn Watts, though. Frank had this party not long ago in the apartment. And Watts all of a sudden did a striptease. He was talking to a producer about a movie plot he was working on, and the next thing anybody knew, he didn't have no clothes on. And he started dancin' the hula, twirling his Pukka shell necklace around over his head."

"Did anyone punch him?" Julia asked.

"Naw," Cooper said. "Most everybody just figured it was another buckaroo headin' for the O.D. Corral."

There was a bit of commotion at the entrance to the back room, some loud voices and laughter. Herb Grant's voice was unmistakable.

Grant entered with two men and a girl. They followed Frankie Ribando, the maitre d' of the back room, to a good table. Grant stuck something in Frankie's tuxedo pocket. Judging by their blazers, patchwork slacks and fixed smiles I guessed the two men were ad agency types. One of them had already made his load. He fell into a coat stand before he sat down. The girl wrote something in a spiral notebook and put it away.

With his friends seated and drinks ordered, Grant came over to our table and shook hands with Danny Lavezzo.

"Looks like everything's under control here," Grant said. "I don't see any splints or slings."

Norris got up to leave.

"Thanks again, Frank," Norris said. "I do like surprise endings." He waved the pages at me.

"Hope it wasn't my cologne," Grant boomed.

"I think it was the conversation," Danny Lavezzo said.

Grant looked at me.

"You ought to take a minute to come over and say hello to a couple of guys from J. Walter," he said. "Bob Stervie's a hell of a guy. That's Styve Butler with him."

Norris disappeared.

"Which one's Styve?" asked the detective. "The guy who ain't had nothing to eat but peanuts?"

"Those aren't his good shoes, are they?" Danny Lavezzo said.

Herb Grant said they'd been at "the Numbers" all night. That's what Grant called "21."

I had already looked at the girl at Grant's table. To be keenly accurate, Marcie would have considered it a rather overlong stare. The girl had looked at me in return with what I chose to believe was a certain amount of curiosity.

I asked Julia to untangle her leg from mine and let me out.

"I'm ready to leave," Julia said.

I said I had to say hello to Scooper and Scuppy from J. Walter.

As I approached Grant's table, both agency guys hopped up in the tradition of agency guys to extend their grinding handshakes, give their names, list their clients, and tell me where they had sailed, played golf and skied lately.

One of them managed it okay, but the other, old Styve, knocked his chair over and poured most of a Galliano rocks on his Gucci. He straightened up his chair and sat back down and said to the girl, "Frick . . . Frank . . . Mmmmm Mackory. Tesh-o-vishin."

I heard it while the other guy, old Bob, who wouldn't turn loose of my hand, was saying:

"We must have met once back when I was with Bates and you were at CAU in Philly. Used to love to come in there and get Red and Bunky and Jumper and go around Merion. Hell of a bunch of guys in Philly. Hell of a town. *Hell* of a golf course."

I got my hand back and slid into the table next to the girl as I'd planned.

"Bob and I have had a few laughs together," Herb Grant said. "Right, Bob? How about that knitwear convention down at Greenbriar?"

"Oh, Christ," Bob said. "Just the thought of having to listen to your harmony again . . ."

Old Bob turned to me. He said:

"Hell of a track record in News, Frank. I mean, the space shots, the hearings, the whole bag of tricks."

Herb Grant said, "Let me tell you what this goose Bob did one day when he was handling Cadillac. He left the damn ninety-second opening commercial locked up in his office on a Saturday. And we were on the back nine at Maidstone when they found him. And he had to get some Pinkertons or somebody to break in and rush the damn can over to the broadcast center just in time for the spot."

"Fun days, Herb," said Bob. "Really were."

Bob came back to me.

"It's a pleasure to meet you," he said. "All that stuff from Nam. I mean, Christ. Here I sit with the guy who practically fucking invented Indochina, television-wise."

Styve woke up.

"How you feel about ficking Indichina, baby?" he said to the girl.

She smiled and said, "I hear they show it on real statues over there, just like pieces of sculpture or something."

I shifted toward her.

"My name's Frank Mallory," I said.

"I know," she said.

"If you had ever written a best-selling collection of magazine pieces, your name would be Sally Hawks," I said.

She looked at me through a pair of large, lightly tinted glasses. Her hair wasn't parted. It was dark blond, full, and it cascaded down past her shoulders. Even behind the glasses you noticed her eyes. She wore a snug silk blouse that stood open and exposed her neck and collar bones, and she fit it very nicely if you were talking about a league in which Julia would be ineligible. I had the height at five seven. And I had the age at twenty-eight but was willing to miss it by two years on the up side. For a girl, she was more than pretty. For a writer, she was a goddam show-stopper.

"You recognized me from the Carson show," she said.

"Book jacket," I said.

The agency guys struck again.

"Hey," old Bob said. "Guess you're getting some of the flab worked off now that you're prime-timing it, huh? Hell of a move this winter, by the way—*hell* of a

69

move—throwing 'Lopez' in the hammock on Wednesday night."

Agency guys love to use programming talk. To throw something in the "hammock" means to schedule a new show and maybe one you aren't sure of, between two shows with good shares that are roughly of the same nature. It's a device to keep the "audience flow."

For the second thirteen-week season I'd juggled some trash I'd inherited. "Lopez and Dusty" was rancid. A couple of hitchhikers finding mild adventure every week amid a repartee of ethnic jokes. The Big Guy liked it. He liked jokes about poor Mexicans.

I couldn't cancel "Lopez" and keep my limo, but I could improve on the taste of the scripts in the "second season." It had picked up higher shares when I put it in a hammock between "Murder Patrol" and "Woody Bean: Narc."

The Big Guy also liked "Patrol" and "Narc" because they taught kids how to kill and rat on their friends.

I had future plans for some members of the "Patrol" to get murdered themselves, and for the "Narc" to be suddenly stricken with a humiliating sense of guilt about his activities.

"Lish, Frank," said Styve, from a slump. "Biggie gosh you pishin in a purr smoll pan, doan?"

Herb Grant stopped a waiter and told him to bring Styve some beef barley soup, a hamburger and a glass of milk.

"And type up a new résumé for him," I said.

Styve hit himself in the chest with his chin.

An abnormal quiet swept over the room. Julia had risen and was walking toward the door. I looked around in time to receive her glare. Then I watched the waiters and customers admire Julia's heaving tits as they led her out.

Sally Hawks said, "I think your date is taking her two best friends home."

I moved my chair back as if to stand up.

I said to Sally, "Are you anything whatsoever like . . . reasonably easy to find some time?"

Her spiral notebook had reappeared and she wrote something in it. Those few seconds of madness passed when I thought she might be giving me her unlisted phone number.

"What kind of a piece are you working on?"

"A thing for *New York*," she said. "I do a TV and movie column twice a month."

Lowering her voice out of the hearing of Grant and his friends, she said, "It's sort of an offbeat piece on what kind of jerks buy participations on shows for their clients."

"You didn't know these people until tonight?" I said.

In the wildest of circumstances, she said, that wouldn't have been possible.

"I introduced myself to Mr. Grant on the phone and he arranged the evening. Actually, it's been very fertile."

I grinned and said, "It was definitely wrong of me, then, to assume that you and Styve had been lovers on a Club Med holiday."

She howled at that idea.

"You haven't answered my earlier question," I said.

Sally Hawks, writer, gave me a smile to remember, and said:

"I live on a small island in the North Atlantic. Manhattan."

Chapter
Eight

~~~~~~

The first time in my apartment most people did an obligatory glance at the spectacular view of Gotham. Then their heads snapped around and they stared at one wall of the den, and they said something like, "Holy shit, what is *that?*"

I would say, "Oh, that's my TV. Would you like to see it?"

By then they would have turned their backs on Gotham entirely and trotted into the den, where they would gape at eight television screens—a quartet of four-foot Sonys and four smaller nineteen-inch Sonys, all set into the dark wood paneling—and at the large clock with the second hand advancing around the dial in sudden regular jumps.

If the guest was somebody like Julia, you could walk up behind her, lift her dress and stick your hand down inside her panties, and she would just keep on staring at the TV wall. It beat the hell out of etchings.

What you could then do with your free hand was switch on the control box beside the big leather chair. For example, you might put four TV channels into action on the small Sonys, show a movie on one big set, a tape of an earlier program on another big set, a cassette of Olympic highlights on a third, and a Pete Smith Specialty on the fourth.

If the visitor was somebody like Julia, she might start to wiggle at that point. She might notice the Sony color videotape camera on the tripod. She might suggest that she whip off her dress and you shoot some tape of her and show it on one of the big screens so she can see what she really looks like naked.

In fact, that is exactly what Julia said. Then we heard a door slam and knew Cooper had come in.

Behind the kitchen downstairs there used to be four small bedrooms and a large bath. When I moved out of Pelham and Cooper moved into Park Avenue, we tore the walls out of the bedrooms and turned the area into a private suite for Cooper. Also downstairs were the living room, the dining room, another bath and the TV den. We used the dining room only to look out the big picture window at glorious sunsets over far New Jersey. Upstairs in the duplex was my bedroom, which was enormous, and a guest bedroom for when the kids stayed over or some old pal showed up from out of town. There were four fireplaces and five terraces. It wasn't an apartment that would necessarily cause the Queen of England to swoon with admiration, but she would probably go a little whacko at the sight of those TV screens.

Julia said, "Your driver will see us."

I said, "He won't come in here."

Which was true. When I had a guest like Julia, Cooper never popped in unexpected. If he had to talk to me, he buzzed me on the intercom.

Julia was playing with the control box. Before long, she had the same Abbott and Costello movie on all eight screens. She clapped her hands like a happy little girl on Christmas morning.

"You know something?" she said. "You're not a bit like my husband."

"Which husband?" I said.

"The husband I was with at Elaine's Friday night when you came over to our table," she said. "The man with the mustache? You knew him. At least, he knew you. He introduced us."

"Your husband didn't want to go to Clarke's with us that night, either?"

"My husband won't go to Clarke's. They were rude to him in there."

"They've never been rude to him in Elaine's?"

"Of course not. Nobody is rude to my husband above Eighty-sixth Street," she said.

"Why is that?"

"He's a gangster. His territory starts at Eighty-sixth on the East Side."

I said, "Oh? Where is he tonight?"

"At the trotters," she said.

"Where does he think you are?" I said.

"With you."

I removed my hand from Julia's panties.

"You don't have to stop," she said.

"I believe I'll have a cocktail," I said.

I put a stack of records on the stereo and made us a couple of drinks at the bar in the den. A ghost chased Costello across eight TV screens. Every time Abbott showed up, the ghost disappeared, and Julia laughed. I gave Julia her drink.

"Would you rather see a good movie?" I said.

"This is a good movie," she said. "I've seen it before."

I opened a cabinet beside the fireplace. Hundreds of discs and cassettes were neatly filed and labeled in there. Arleene came up and did that for me now and then. I had a collection of the classic movies. If a new film sounded interesting, I would get a black-market tape of it from a lab in L.A. and would see the final cut almost as soon as the director did.

It was kind of expensive, but a good way to check up on the talent. Cooper knew some guys who arranged for the tapes. Most of them, I didn't keep. But I had every Fellini, for instance. I had the Marx Brothers, W. C. Fields, Capra, Bergman, Hayworth, Gable, Grant, Wayne and so on.

I was admiring my movie library when Julia unzipped my pants.

"I'm not too sure if we ought to keep doing this, Julia," I said.

She said, "Don't worry about my husband. He's queer."

"A queer gangster?" I said.

"Gangsters have feelings just like other people," she said.

Julia unbuckled my belt, undid the button and knelt on a cushion.

"Tony knows the kind of sex he prefers, and he's man enough to get it," she said.

Julia took my shoes and socks off and tossed my trousers aside.

She was making some clever little noises when I said, "Why don't you quit watching Abbott and Costello, damn it?"

A few minutes later I knelt beside her and helped her remove her dress.

"I have to wear a bra because my tits hurt if I don't," she said.

I unsnapped the bra and her tits flew into my face.

"The funny movie's over," she said. "Do a movie of me now."

"My camera is busted," I said.

I lied. But what did I need with Julia telling Tony the gangster that I had nude pictures of his wife? I doubted if he was queer enough to laugh off that kind of news.

"What can we do then?" she said, disappointed. "I mean, you're all printed out, aren't you?"

I pulled down her bikini panties.

"Oh, that's wonderful," Julia said. "Could we see some kind of movie while we're doing this?"

I got up and put a cassette on one of the large Sonys. I turned off the other sets. Julia mounded up the cushions on the floor by the fireplace and lay back so she could see the screen. She spread her legs and reached up to me with her arms to guide me down to her.

I settled in the way Julia wanted, being an incurable old fantasist.

After a while, up on the screen, Bogart was saying:

"Ilsa, I'm no good at being noble. But it doesn't take much to know that the problems of two little people don't amount to a hill of beans in this crazy world."

Chapter
Nine

∞∞∞∞∞∞∞∞∞∞∞∞∞∞∞∞∞∞

At a table in a conference room on the twentieth floor of the Chambers building there were ashtrays, notepads, pens and coffee cups which Arleene had supplied for about fourteen people. I arrived in the middle of some laughter and a Stanley Coffman monologue.

"I turned it down on the basis that nobody gave a damn about watching a private eye operate out of a ski resort," Stanley was saying. "Who was the guy gonna investigate? Some Nazi who sold oversized stretch pants to Chicago vacationers? Jesus. Some fucking innkeeper who drove his Sno-Kat too fast? Well, the fucking thing's only been syndicated in forty-four different countries now. How the hell did I know they'd think up an avalanche every week."

Stanley glanced at me and lowered his voice to the others.

"Okay, cheese it, guys. Here comes Captain Success."

This was going to be a production meeting. No Big Guys or Herb Grants were invited. These were the people who were going to be primarily responsible for seeing if "Just Up the Street" could cost fewer lives than the eruption of Krakatoa. Except for Stanley. Network presidents don't get involved in actual productions, but they are kept informed of a show's progress so they can worry more.

Stanley was sitting in, as they say.

Among the people I'd called together was a fellow named Jack Nathanson. He was going to produce and direct "Just Up the Street." I'd thrown the whole project at Nathanson because he was the best News guy I'd ever worked against when I was with CBS. I wanted to go with a News guy on this instead of someone from Entertainment. I didn't need an artistic genius who edited singers and comedians on tape. Or a series director who knew how to shoot a Pete Stern gunfight in only two takes. It had to be someone accustomed to working live. We wouldn't have the luxury of even two takes. A good director from Sports might have been all right, but Nathanson was the best man I could think of in our building.

When I first talked with Jack there wasn't much I could tell him. The Big Guy wanted three continuous live hours showing real people in their homes. God knows what they'd be doing. Watching themselves watching television was a good guess.

"Well, first, we'll have to find a large family," Nathanson said. "A large family that isn't camera shy. A lot of people would give you subjects to cut back and forth with. Unless the intent of the show is to actually put the audience to sleep, which I'm not sure it isn't. Be nice if we could find some real Waltons who could get busted on cocaine during the first hour."

"Then John-Boy could get caught going down on his English teacher, and Mary Ellen could come clean that she'd been a hooker since the sixth grade," I said.

He said seriously, "What if we got two different

families in two different homes? That would give us places to leave and go back to. It would at least create a sense of action. Is this all going to be in one town?"

"It's your baby, Jack. You rock it," I said.

Not long after that, Jack asked me to join him for lunch at Mike Manuche's on Fifty-second Street so he could try something on me. What if we set up remote units in two different cities, he said, and we found some lively families and we simply let our best announcers go into their homes and interview them?

I calmly took a memo from my pocket that I had just received from the Big Guy and handed it to Nathanson. It read:

TO: F.M.
FROM: H.O.C.
SUBJECT: J.U.T.S.

I must tell you about the wonderful thing I saw last night on another network. I saw a pretty little girl on a show about a pickaninny. She was doing her homework and everybody sat around happy until the forest fire. I hope your show, J.U.T.S., can capture this wholesome atmosphere live with real little girls. Remember, I do not want interviews. They would be interruptive. It will be so much better if our cameras could sneak up on little Nancy. We can be there when she asks her Mommy, "Mommy, who blew up the bridge at Dorgenhorst?" We can be there when Mommy turns off her vacuum cleaner and says, "Why, I think it was the 2nd Armored, dear." Our cameras could even be there when Daddy asked for another dish of custard. I am very excited about the potential of your show, Frank.

* * *

Jack Nathanson said, "I wonder if it's possible that he thinks our cameras sneaked up on those Apollo space shots?"

"You've known him longer than I have," I said.

Jack said it was possible.

Then he said, "I gather money's no consideration on 'Just Up the Street'?"

None, I said.

"Let's just get drunk today and let me get back to you," Jack said.

Now we were back.

Everybody sat down at the conference table with me at one end and Stanley at the other. Besides Nathanson, there was a unit manager, an engineer in charge, some other directors and producers, and Arleene. Arleene liked production meetings. She got to do needlepoint.

Stanley said, "I sat in on a production meeting at that fucking bowl game we did last December. Jesus, who's that producer we've got in Sports? That guy who carries his clipboard with him to the toilet? He said, 'Heads up now, men. Remember not to zoom in close on the anthem.' We had that fat cunt who was gonna lip-sync the anthem, right? Then he said, 'Don't forget. On rockets red glare we cut to the jets overhead. Then we go to the balloons coming out of the floats. Then we go up to the booth to you, Kenny.' After that, he goes into this crap about the halftime and how we'll handle the majorettes who're gonna come out and jerk off the nigger band or something. He doesn't say anything about the game. Jesus, is this some fucking business?"

I asked Stanley if he would mind, terribly, if we got started.

"Sorry, guys," he said. Then he looked at Jack Nathanson and broke into a grin.

"Okay, Jew," he said. "Tell the little Wasp how

you're gonna keep this from being a real piece of shit."

Nathanson explained how "Just Up the Street" would not be technically difficult. You simply would have remote units out there near the homes with directors sending the best pictures they had into the New York control room where Jack would select what he wanted to put on the air. A normal remote.

As far as getting cameras into the homes, that would require laying some cable and building some mounts in some corners of their rooms, he said. But if the families were eager enough to be on television in the first place, then they would permit the work to be done and the network of course would pay for restoring things to order.

We would probably need to use at least one guy with a mini-cam in each home. Just to let him roam around and pick up things our mounted cameras would find out of range.

We could "mike" the homes, he said, but we would surely have a lot of trouble with the audio gains and levels and we would lose words if not whole chunks of dialogue when the people moved—provided, of course, we found people who could talk.

Nathanson suggested we also use "RF" mikes on the people. An RF mike—for radio frequency—is a tiny button on a wire attached to a battery pack and worn somewhere on a person's body. The battery pack might be in a man's hip pocket, for example, with the wire running up inside his shirt and the button, the mike, hidden near the collar or at the chest.

"When you're wearing a battery pack in your hip pocket, it makes you feel like your diaper's full, but you get used to it," Jack said.

Without all this preparation, he said, and without spending some rehearsal time with the families to let them get comfortable with the mikes and the cameras, the show was impossible to do.

"We can't just send a housebreaker with a mini-cam around to some neighborhood where the lights are on and get much more to televise than a guy calling the police," Nathanson said.

To do a show that is going to be on the air for three solid hours, we had to have cameras, lighting and audio, he said. The people would be able to move freely about, doing whatever they do, but we could manage it where we could both see them and hear them pretty well. We could put cameras in every one of their rooms, he said, only we probably wouldn't want to put one in any of the johns.

"Jesus, Grandma," said Stanley. "Come see this goddam turd. It looks like a fucking nuclear sub."

Nathanson said we wouldn't coach the people on what to do or say, naturally. But we would plan various ways for them to be more at ease. The hope would be, he said, that they conceivably could even forget they were wearing the RF's and wouldn't worry in excess about the cameras. We'd tell them that there will be a lot of time during the show when they *won't* be on. Just relax.

"If we're very lucky," Jack said, "we'll get some spontaneous conversation and some movement around the houses. Somebody doing *something*. The Big Guy may think we've sneaked in there to get it, but we'll have busted our asses for about two weeks beforehand."

Nathanson said, "I hope research can come up with two reasonably interesting families somewhere."

"Four," I said.

"Four?" Jack said.

"Makes it better," I said. "With four households and plenty of people in all of them, you won't have to devote more than, say, forty-five minutes of the three hours to each family. Gives you even more ways to throw it around. More illusion of activity."

"Absolutely, Frank," said Stanley. "When the fucking aunt answers the phone and says she can't make it to the Business and Professional Women's weekly meeting because of her virus, Jack can cut to the kitchen where some kid with acne is having a Twinkie spasm."

Stanley leaned back with a sigh.

"Jesus, I was happy as a station manager on the Coast," he said. "Had the Mercedes, the Bel Air membership. Guys begged to buy any shit you put in the window. Rich station. Ran itself. Guys couldn't find you. New York never knew what fucking time it was in L.A."

I said, "I think, too, we'll need on-the-scene commentators. They can stroll around out in the yard or in the neighborhood and we can go to them now and then, and they can talk about whatever is interesting about the family. We'll use our top News guys. They'll make it look important and they can vamp better than anybody."

"If we do that, we'll need some glue to hold it together. So our on-the-scene guys can have a continuity, you know, a transition from one town to another. Not mad leaps around America every few minutes," Nathanson said.

By the end of that sentence, Nathanson had figured out what I had in mind. He hooked a forefinger in the collar of his turtleneck and looked at me in a way that said: Oh, Mallory, is nothing sacred.

Nathanson scratched a kitchen match into flame and chewed on a cigarette waiting for me to say it. When I didn't say it, Nathanson said it.

"Hank Judson," he said.

"Great idea, Jack," I said enthusiastically.

"Thanks," Nathanson said.

Stanley said, "As your President, I'm going to order somebody else in the company besides me to tell Hank Judson he is anchoring 'Just Up the Street.'"

"I'll do it," I said.

"You guys heard that," Stanley said.

Hank Judson was the anchor man of our seven o'clock news.

There were flaws in the operation of *CBS News,* but in the public eye Hank Judson was the perfect American young grandfather. Honest, kind, patient, stern when necessary. The public didn't know or care that Hank Judson was the kind of reporter who if you assigned him a camera crew and told him to cover a buzzard fuck would come back with a scoop about finding the bones of poor dead animals in the desert, and there would be buzzard wings pounding the sand in the background of the film.

But Hank Judson could make you listen to his tale of the poor dead bones, and he might make you feel sad for them. Hank Judson looked like a man who went camping in the forest with his family and could be counted on to have coffee brewing in a pot on coals scraped from a cozy fire, while freshly caught trout wrapped in leaves baked in a pit of hot stones, and the kids and wife smiled fondly as Hank sat on a log playing his guitar and sharing his wisdom about past dwellers on the land and the maps of the stars in the sky.

Hank Judson was in his middle fifties, wore tweeds and kept his hair tidy.

We paid him $250,000 a year for being believable.

"Jack's got a great idea," I said.

"Hank's specials for the last few years have been interviews with world leaders," Nathanson said. "He may not go for this."

"I'll talk to Hank," I said. "Let's move to other problems."

I mentioned the four homes needed to be in the same time zone. Eastern. I didn't want to come on the air at eight o'clock and throw it to a city where it's an hour earlier and the guy's not home from work yet. Research, I said, had been told to come up with families in Tampa, Akron, Rochester and Washington, D.C. All on the same time, but a fair cross-section of the country in terms of regions, accents and interests.

"Right," Nathanson said. "We need everybody at home. Might help if some were cooking dinner, some were eating, and some had finished."

"Our subjects won't all be the same, either," I said. "Like everybody's not going to be upper-middle-income, and everybody's not going to be on welfare, and everybody's not going to be sick."

"Sick wouldn't be bad, Frank," said Stanley. "A lot of coughing and fever. A little retching. Ready Camera Two on the cough. Take Two."

Stanley was staring up at the ceiling with his hands clasped behind his bald head.

"Know what the little Wasp thinks?" he said. "I think we're going right in the old septic tank in the ratings. Nielsen's gonna put a fucking zero up so big you could stick Nova Scotia in it."

That, I said, despite all of the creative ingenuity at our command, was a very real possibility.

Chapter Ten

~~~~~~~~~~~~~~~~~~~~~~~~~~~~~~~~~~

To Cooper, if you stood in Texas and looked north, California was the Left Coast and New York was the Right Coast. Cooper was preparing to fly to the Left Coast a day ahead of me.

He said he had a friend who was opening as a singer at some joint in L.A., and he wanted to catch the act the first night. I asked if it had anything to do with talent scouting for the opening of his own Country & Western nightclub, where carpenters, plumbers and city inspectors had already made off with most of the capital Cooper had raised.

"Naw, this is just an old friend I'd like to see," Cooper said.

I asked if the old friend might be Cody Huber, a rock star in the late sixties. I had read in the trades that at the age of thirty-two, Cody Huber was about to make his second or third comeback somewhere in Orange County.

"Hell, I ain't seen Cody since he lost his hair. I guess I ought to look him up, but I owe him too much money, and right now he might need it."

Cooper used to hang out with Cody Huber. Cooper had appeared in Cody Huber's dressing room in San Antonio while Huber's band was touring. Cooper and Huber had got into a conversation about horses, the way I heard it, and pretty soon they were in Houston, and before long Cooper was living at Cody Huber's big house outside of Denver.

When Cody Huber showed up for a concert in Philadelphia, Cooper was in charge of security. Marcie and the kids and I had been in Philadelphia for about six months by then. I was head of News for WCAU–TV. Marcie was talking about getting a master's at the University of Pennsylvania.

A year or more might go between meetings with Cooper, but I generally knew where he was, and when I saw him again it was like we were carrying on in the same place we had left off, except Cooper was drifting into his profession and I was running at mine.

Cooper brought Cody Huber to our apartment as soon as the charter jet reached Philadelphia. Huber traveled with an entourage of sixty. While the rest of them were checking into the Marriott, Cooper and Cody Huber slipped off.

Marcie hated Cody Huber's music. As a music student and a singer herself, she said what the Huber band played was on the level of whacking garbage cans together. I hadn't paid attention to Cody Huber's music, but I had seen him on the news and in print.

In our apartment, Cody Huber was shy and quiet, twenty-two, wearing a white three-piece suit and burgundy necktie, and glasses with tortoise-shell frames. His notoriously long hair was bound into a neat pigtail held by a gold clip.

Cooper and I fell into old-timey talk about the hamburger stand where we used to gather in high school. It was a drive-in, and even in those days the parking lot would be two or three deep with cars on evenings and weekends. You could visit from car to car. Or you could sit in one car and get visited.

Cooper had a 1938 white Ford coupe with no doors. The right front fender was mangled from a collision with a cow, but Cooper had repaired the right front headlight. Cooper usually had a date when he showed up at the drive-in, which we called the Dick Dock. Since he drove a coupe, people would lean on the fenders or put a foot on the running board when they visited with Cooper and his date. I was one of the few whom Cooper allowed to make it a threesome in the car seat.

There were three of us in the coupe—Cooper and Clydene Jernigan and me—the night the crowd around Cooper's car suddenly scattered, and we found ourselves looking at twenty guys from Woodrow Wilson High School. They were wearing Levis and T-shirts and tight kid-leather gloves. It was plain that they were walking straight toward Cooper's car. In the lead was Booger Red McAfee, who was an all-district end and also a starter on the basketball team.

At that point we still didn't know if the guys from Woodrow Wilson had come for a general gang fight, or if maybe one or two of them were looking for one or two of us in particular and had brought along a band of bodyguards so they wouldn't be mobbed. Our school, Sunset, was Woodrow Wilson's chief rival in things like football and girls and ass-kicking.

So, many years later, while Cooper and I were remembering this incident, laughing and drinking in the apartment in Philadelphia, I realized Marcie was lecturing Cody Huber about music.

". . . *The Marriage of Figaro,*" I heard Marcie say.

"Cool, Mrs. Mallory. I really dig Mozart," Cody Huber said.

"Really?" Marcie said.

"In Act Three, the duet between the Count and Susanna, that lays me out, man," Cody Huber said. He

88

leaned forward excitedly, looking at Marcie. "When I was at Juilliard, I could sing that whole opera. I mean every part. Not good, of course. I was on a piano scholarship."

"You had a piano scholarship at Juilliard?" Marcie repeated.

The implications of that piece of information collided inside Marcie's head, and she would have lit the wrong end of her cigarette if Cody Huber had not turned it around for her.

"Just for two years. I was too much of a kid to appreciate what I really had," Cody Huber said. "When I was eighteen, I dropped out and started playing rock and roll. That was four years ago. I wonder what would have happened if I'd stayed at Juilliard."

I heard that much of the conversation while Cooper was in the bathroom. When he came back, he was laughing about how Booger Red McAfee had walked straight to the white Ford coupe at the Dick Dock that night and had said:

"Cooper, my ass is a watermelon patch. If you want some, wade right in."

"I don't recall having no argument with you," Cooper had said.

Once Booger Red McAfee had stepped forward, everybody understood the purpose of the Woodrow Wilson foray onto Sunset territory.

Cooper had knocked out Punk McAfee, Booger Red's younger brother, in the finals of the high school welterweight division of the Golden Gloves at the Sportatorium three nights earlier. On opening night, I had lost in the high school middleweight division to a guy with a Cherokee haircut. I fought in the Gloves because I was expected to, seeing as how I was a football player with a wise mouth, but I had never really cared for boxing. After I got my loss out of the way, I watched Cooper win five straight fights by knockouts to arrive in the finals against Punk McAfee. Cooper was a skinny kid with such elaborate ducktails and a pompadour that it was always a surprise how hard he punched. Punk McAfee, a year younger, won all his fights by knockouts, too—some opponents falling at the first opportunity from the pure terror of being in the ring with one of the McAfee brothers.

Ten minutes before their fight in the finals, Cooper and Punk McAfee were sitting close together on folding chairs in the back of the Sportatorium where the fighters waited.

Soon as Cooper knew Punk McAfee was looking at him, Cooper stuck his right glove up against his own right nostril and blew hard and a small garter snake flew out of his left nostril in a spray of snot. Or at least it appeared to. Punk McAfee stared at the garter snake as it squirmed under the folding chairs that clattered and crashed while fighters tried to stomp the snake.

Cooper said, "What the hell was that? You see that thing sail out of my nose, Punk?"

"I didn't see nothing," Punk said.

"That old mama snake must of had babies," Cooper said.

"You didn't have no snake in your nose," Punk said.

Cooper gagged and spat out a small frog.

"I guess the mama snake ain't hungry," Cooper said.

"Goddam a guy that would put a frog in his mouth," Punk said.

If there was one thing Punk McAfee was afraid of, it was crazy people. He had learned that fear growing up in a family that included homicidal maniacs. Punk was bullet-headed and built like a very young Marciano and was three inches shorter than Cooper. Punk liked to charge across the ring and knock people down without thinking about anything else.

Some say it was the snake and frog that caused Punk

to be cautious that night. Others say that Punk had watched Cooper's left hook and was wary of it. The result was that Cooper danced and avoided Punk's tentative rushes. Then Cooper hit Punk three left hooks in the face, Punk's head banged against a ring post and scraped the top rope, and Cooper won a first-round TKO and accepted the trophy while Punk was wobbling off to get twenty-three stitches in his right eyebrow.

So Booger Red McAfee came over to the white Ford coupe at the Dick Dock and said, "You and me the same age, Cooper. It ain't like you're picking on a little kid this time."

"I thought they handled those Golden Gloves deals on the basis of how much you weigh, not how old you are," Cooper said.

"Get out of that car, your chickenshit," Booger Red replied.

Cooper got out of the car and Booger Red McAfee blacked both of Cooper's eyes, knocked out a front tooth, broke his nose, cracked a rib and left Cooper sitting against the back wall of the Dick Dock.

The first thing Cooper said through bleeding lips as Booger Red McAfee and the Woodrow Wilson guys walked back toward their cars was to his date.

"Clydene, hon, let's skip the kissing tonight and get right to the juicy," is what Cooper said.

Cooper and I were laughing about that in the apartment in Philadelphia when we both heard Marcie say, "Count Almaviva sings":

> But why, why make me suffer,
> longing for your reply?
> But why, but why?
> Will you not tell me why?

Marcie sang it in English. Cody Huber said, "I remember . . . Susanna sang":

In time we women grant you
What we at first deny.

Still doing the Count's part, Marcie sang:

Then we shall meet this evening?

And Cody Huber sang:

You have my word,
I will not fail my word.

Marcie sang:

The sweet promise you gave me
Raises my hope so high.

Cody Huber sang:

All those who know what love is
Forgive me for this lie.

While Marcie and Cody Huber were singing *The Marriage of Figaro,* with Marcie as the Count and Huber as Susanna the maid, I was thinking about the end of the story about Cooper and the McAfee brothers.

When he recovered from the beating Booger Red McAfee gave him, D. Wayne drove his white Ford coupe over to the Woodrow Wilson tribal drive-in without mentioning it to anyone, and knocked Punk McAfee out. Then Cooper walked through the crowd, picked up Clydene and went back to the Dick Dock and still didn't mention what he had done.

After the news got out, it was agreed at Sunset and Woodrow Wilson that never in memory had there been such a display of courage. Booger Red McAfee put out the word that anybody who harmed Cooper would have to fight the entire McAfee family.

That night in Philadelphia, Marcie and I had gone to the Cody Huber concert and watched from backstage while Cooper moved around the auditorium checking on the security.

Cody Huber's hair was unclipped and swung at the hips of his tight red velvet pants.

Thousands of young girls clawed for the stage. When the Huber band hit what they called their "clit licks" on their electric instruments, the crowd shrieked and screamed and Marcie danced in the wings.

D. Wayne never told me exactly whom he was going to see in L.A. So I figured it was unimportant, or maybe too important.

Chapter
Eleven

〰〰〰〰〰〰〰〰〰〰〰〰〰〰〰〰〰〰〰

The morning after Cooper took off for the Left Coast, Arleene rescued me from yet another production meeting on "Just Up the Street" in time to make United Flight 5 from JFK to Los Angeles.

Around the CBC building in Gotham there was rising panic among everyone who had anything to do with "Just Up the Street." But with the taping of the Peggy Hanley special only hours away, and with the affiliates already gathering, for me to have worried about "Just Up the Street" right then would have been like brooding over the possibility of a nuclear holocaust and ignoring four muggers who were following me home.

United Flight 5 took off at noon. I went upstairs to the first-class lounge of the 747. I carried a couple of movie scripts under my arm. There is no better way of arousing the curiosity and affection of an airline stewardess than for her to see magical words like Paramount or MGM on a script cover. Sometimes I also read the scripts.

I heard a robot voice say, "Frank, what a pleasure. Sit down and have a drink with me."

The voice came out of one of those metal throat boxes. It sounded like a telephone connection in England.

I said, "Hello, Bobby."

Bobby Maitlow rearranged the white silk scarf around his neck. Bobby'd had his larynx operated on a year or so earlier. Considering all the throats Bobby had cut in his life one way or another, many people thought the operation was a form of justice.

Maitlow was a person you didn't want to know too much about unless you were the Mafia historian for the *New York Times*. The main thing I knew about him was that he owned, on the surface, thirty percent of the stock of the Wilcox Picture Corporation. Much of the Wilcox product was aimed at drive-ins, but occasionally a good film would somehow get made. Maitlow also had interests in trucking, hotels, liquor distribution and natural gas. Probably by now he had moved in on throat-box manufacturing.

I sat down across the table from him and asked for black coffee. The stewardess flicked her eyes at the script covers.

"Just coffee? Frank Mallory on coffee, hey, this ain't the guy I know," Maitlow said through his throat box.

"Got a long night ahead of me," I said.

"Business or pleasure?"

"Both, I hope," I said.

The stewardess brought the coffee and said, "Mr. Mallory, I'm Polly . . . a friend of Janie's? She had you on this flight two weeks ago? Sure I can't get you one of those five-olive martinis she said you liked so much?"

I said, "Polly, you ought to be in pictures."

It doesn't matter how often people are told they ought to be in pictures, they always believe it.

95

Maitlow laughed. A horrible sound. Maitlow was pale, with bluish cheeks and slick black hair. He had lost fifty pounds since the operation, and he had a new wardrobe of Savile Row suits.

"Treat this guy right, honey. Give him six olives," Maitlow said.

"Bobby, if you think I ought to have a martini, I probably ought to have a martini," I said.

Polly went to fetch the drink. Maitlow said, "I see what your pleasure's gonna be. What's your business?"

"We're taping a special tonight. Before a live audience of affiliates," I said. "Then tomorrow the affiliates' meetings start. Harley Chambers is going to tell them the wonderful stuff we'll fill their air time with."

"The Big Guy hisself? That's interesting," Maitlow said.

I took the martini from Polly and sipped it.

"Yes, it should be," I said.

"Between you and I, the Big Guy's wig has slipped," Maitlow said.

"He seems all right to me," I said.

"Frank, how long I known you? Ten years? Since you did that CBS story on the hassle we had with the Senate committee, right? Listen to me, boy. The Big Guy has got squirrels in his attic."

I said, "I know how you prize loyalty, Bobby. You wouldn't respect me if I sat here and told you my own boss is crazy as a pet coon."

Maitlow said, "I like you. Always have. There are people in the business who don't like you. They say you're impulsive. They say you make scars. Myself, I say a man couldn't come from them jerk jobs you used to have and go to the top being timid. I got no use for timid sons of bitches. I say a man has got to take big chances. You know what these timid bastards do now? They wire up theater seats that are supposed

96

to tell them what the audience is thinking every minute. Can you believe that? A man that claims he's got the guts to be in the movie business? He wires up theater seats?"

I said, yeah, I could believe it. In TV we did a lot of wiring and came up with numbers for everything. Want to know the top 100 best-known? The top 100 best-loved? If there is an audience for a show about Texas Rangers? And if there is, what kind of a show would the audience wish it to be? Guys were always coming up with numbers that were supposed to guide your thinking on how to put together future projects. If you listen to these guys, you couldn't miss. They say, look at these numbers, a show about a modern-day Texas Ranger with plenty of action in it has tested out at a 47, and that means a hit. They say, look at these other numbers, if you make the Texas Ranger a sixty-four-year-old redneck who lives in an old farmhouse and has problems with a bunch of hicks that ain't "Beverly Hillbillies," I mean they ain't funny, then you got yourself a testing out of 22, and so what you are talking about here is a built-in failure. In case you wondered what a failure was, they had numbers to let you know how you could tell whether a show on the air right now was a failure or a success.

I didn't say all that out loud to Bobby Maitlow. All I said was, yeah, I could believe it.

"He wires the goddam seats," Maitlow said in his awful voice. "Then he makes a movie that is shitola. It is shitola and it loses money, too. That's a crime. If you're gonna go broke doing shitola, why wire up the seats? Jesus, I could get a monkey in here and say do me a piece of shitola and I'd have as good a chance."

Maitlow's voice tailed off. It sounded like his battery had run down. But he was just resting. It must have been tough work to talk through that throat box.

"That clown we got now, he makes movies that

make my ass hurt," Maitlow said. "Worse than that, he insults me with his brains. He wires up seats. He knows what the people like. You know what he wants to spend $15,000,000 on? A remake of *Silver Chief, Dog of the North*. He says he did a poll that shows people are hungry for dog stories. I say, for $15,000,000 you're gonna make a dog picture? A dog picture costs no more than $200,000 tops for class. He says, well, this is a remake of a classic movie of all time, and it has got to be a big production with big stars on location up in Alaska where bacon and eggs cost twice as much as at the Beverly Hills Hotel."

"There never was a movie of *Silver Chief, Dog of the North*," I said.

"It was a classic, and people ate it up," Maitlow said.

Maitlow squinted at me and adjusted his silk scarf.

I said that it had been one of my favorite books when I was a kid. I said if it had been made into a classic movie, I would know it. I said even if it had been made into shitola, I would probably know it.

Maitlow said, "What does it cost to rent a dog?"

I said I didn't know.

"I don't mean to rent a stud to breed a world champion dog. I mean to rent a cute dog that is smart enough to throw a railroad switch but looks like a dog you'd see at the pound," Maitlow said.

I said Silver Chief was a hell of a dog.

"Yeah, he must be a hell of a fucking dog, all right, to make a bunch of big-dollar stars go to Alaska for three months. You know what the per diem is for a big star in Alaska? I could take a couple of broads to Monte Carlo for the same money."

Maitlow laid his head back against the seat.

"I got to sleep for a while," he said.

Polly had come back upstairs with an ice bucket.

"Okay, Bobby, I'll move to another seat and read these scripts," I said.

He shut his eyes.

"Hey, thanks for the tip, right?" he said.

Chapter
Twelve

~~~~~~~~~~~~~~~~~~~~~~~~~~~~~~~~~~~~

An indigo-blue Rolls limo, with Cooper leaning on the fender eating an ice cream cone, was waiting at the L.A. airport.

Polly had a shoulder bag and a little blue suitcase on wheels that she pulled with a strap. I had my under-the-seat Vuitton. So we walked past the crowd and straight to the indigo-blue limo.

"Polly, this is D. Wayne," I said.

"Far out," Polly said.

"Little bit unreal, ain't it?" Cooper said.

"I never saw a car this color," Polly said.

"It's a Left Coast kind of ve-hicle," Cooper said.

We were pulling out as Bobby Maitlow and his pearl-gray driver appeared and headed toward a maroon Bentley.

Cooper looked into the rear-view mirror and said, "Maitlow's gonna be buried pretty soon, I hear."

The heavy freeway traffic was just starting about 3 P.M. when we turned off Century Boulevard onto the San Diego Freeway. Orange smaze hung across from the ocean into the hills. Cooper chose the Sunset exit. It was nowhere near the closest route, but it took you on a climbing, turning road through Bel Air and Westwood and past the UCLA campus. The driveway of the Beverly Hills Hotel was stacked up with cars being delivered to women leaving the luncheon for the Photoplay Magazine Female Entertainer of the Year Award.

Cooper drove around to the side and parked the limo near the bungalow on the grounds behind the hotel.

"Come in for a cocktail?" I said to Cooper.

"Straight as an Indian goes to shit," Cooper said.

The carpet in the bungalow was like a pile of alpaca sweaters. Fresh flowers were in vases on the mantel over the fireplace. A large basket of fruit, a magnum of Dom Perignon, a quart of J&B, a quart of Johnny Walker Black, a quart of Wild Turkey, a quart of Beefeater and a quart of Polish vodka had been provided with the compliments of the management.

"They might of left an ounce of snort and a pound of weed, if we look in the cabinets," Cooper said.

While Cooper got the ice out of the refrigerator in the kitchen, I called the studio to inquire about Melvin, the director of the Peggy Hanley special. I had checked on him at least once a day and had been informed by Melvin himself that his battles with Peggy were now a memory. Melvin had sounded very cool and controlled. But I told the producer to keep the baby-sitter with Melvin anyhow.

Polly went into both bedrooms pulling her little suitcase on wheels. She came back into the living room, where I was on the phone.

"Which one?" she said.

I shrugged. She went into the room where I had thrown my bag on the bed. Cooper brought me a J&B and water while West Coast Production was assuring me Melvin was all right.

I hung up and said, "How did your friend's opening go last night?"

"Pretty fair," Cooper said.

"Critical approval and so forth?" I said.

"If there was anybody that didn't like it, they didn't tell me about it," Cooper said.

Polly returned, wearing a shorty kimono.

"Can I get you a drink, little lady?" Cooper said.

Polly was fascinated by Cooper. She kept staring at his long hair, Indian jewelry, boots, Levis, cowboy hat and weathery, wasted-looking face, like she couldn't imagine all those elements ever being combined in a single person.

"What's that you're drinking?" she said.

"It's a South Dallas martini," Cooper said.

"What's in it?" she said.

"Aw, it's just a regular martini," Cooper said. "Except I leave out the olive. And I don't put no lemon peel or cocktail onion in it. And I don't use no vermouth. My daddy used to make the best South Dallas martini a body ever tasted. It was kind of unusual for a preacher to be a expert at making drinks like this. But my daddy was an unusual man. He once knocked out a bear at a carnival."

Polly was watching Cooper prepare a South Dallas martini for her as he talked. He handed her the drink.

"Salud," Cooper said.

"Why, this is nothing but a glass of gin," Peggy said.

Cooper said he had to go meet his friend. From the look of Cooper's eyeballs, I would guess Cooper hadn't slept in two or three days. Being awake for two or three days was nothing special for the musicians Cooper liked to hang out with.

I told Polly I was going to shower and do an hour of jet-lag coma. She said she believed she would join me if it was okay. I told the operator to hold off on the phone calls.

"How hot do you like it?" Polly called from the shower.

About 5 P.M. I got dressed in my fine old well-faded Levis, my Charlie Dunn boots that were so soft you could roll them up like a belt, a white cotton shirt and my silk-lined lightweight leather jacket. I looked in the bathroom mirror, patted shaving lotion on my cheeks and said, "Self, you need to be very alert tonight, so let's don't take chances." I swallowed a green and white spansule and picked up the phone for a run-through on the messages.

Most of the messages were the usual urgent requests to call people I had never heard of or didn't want to talk to.

But one message said: *Will be in Polo Lounge from 5 to 6 if you can make it. Katherine.*

I told Polly I would be back to pick her up at six. I walked down the path through the jungle behind the hotel. Antoine, who took over as maitre d' after Dino died, was working the door at the Polo Lounge. Antoine looked like a French Foreign Legion colonel who had put on a tuxedo for a banquet in his honor.

"I 'ave your favorite ta-bul, Mistair Malloree," Antoine said.

He meant the corner booth in front near the bar. No, he said, no woman had asked for me. But certainly if one did he would conduct her to my table immediately. Not unless she says her name is Katherine, I said.

I slid into the booth and ordered a cocktail. The Polo Lounge was beginning to fill up with the usual traffic. A bunch of unbuttoned shirts with gold medallions hanging on hairy chests. Palm Springs suntans. Gorgeous women with their tits sticking out. Here and there a genuine beauty who wouldn't take barter for it. The women you see in Beverly Hills tend to make the women in any other city in the world, even New

103

York or Dallas, look kind of plain and unattended-to. The classier ones don't usually sit around the Polo Lounge at cocktail hour. When you get right down to the truth of it, the Polo Lounge is fairly shabby and smells like a whorehouse. But of course they keep it dark in there. And there are some of us who like the way a whorehouse smells.

Herb Grant, for example, wouldn't stay at the Beverly Hills Hotel unless he were kidnapped and would only go to the Polo Lounge if a big sponsor wanted to see the place. Grant always stayed at the Bel Air. Grant said the Bel Air was "civilized and European." By that he meant it was so quiet and dull at the Bel Air that even Grant could almost seem like fun to be with. Personally, I never went to Los Angeles looking to feel civilized and European. I went there to wallow in show business.

Another J&B and water. No Katherine as yet. She was usually late, except for work. It had been a couple of years since I had seen Katherine. I wondered what she wanted. While I waited I began to listen to the conversation in the next booth. One guy in a cashmere sweater and short haircut, an aging athlete like Hollywood is full of. The other guy in a brushed denim outfit with rhinestones all over it, smoking a pipe.

"Dustin doesn't have a backhand. You ever *seen* Dustin's backhand? He'll run off the court to try to reach his forehand side," the cashmere guy said.

"God, I wouldn't want him for *my* partner," the rhinestone guy said.

"I had him once at Palm Springs. Howard and Chuck beat us in the semifinals."

"God, how did you get that far? *You* must have played super."

"He's a nice kid, though. I wouldn't knock him," the cashmere guy said.

I took the telephone off the ledge between the two

104

booths, put it on my table and returned a couple of calls. I hung up and listened to the two guys again.

"The funniest thing was when they couldn't find the car for thirty minutes," the rhinestone guy said. "And it was the only brown Mercedes in the parking lot with a white dog in the back seat."

The cashmere guy said he had to go to Rome and guessed he would stay at the Excelsior again.

Then suddenly they were talking about me.

"I don't know how that girl got her own special— even as a summer replacement—unless she's been going down on Mallory," the rhinestone guy said.

"You ever met Mallory? I hear he's a prick," the cashmere guy said.

"It's funny. I was screwing this singer in Vegas who thought she was gonna marry him. But he dumped her and stayed with his wife," the rhinestone guy said.

Now they were talking about Katherine.

"Mallory can't possibly last very long in programming," the cashmere guy said. "He doesn't know a damn thing about it."

"One good fuckup and they'll bounce his ass and bring in somebody with experience and talent," the rhinestone guy said.

At that moment Antoine escorted Katherine to the booth and said, "Theese ladee is to see you, Mistaire Malloree."

"Frank, you look wonderful," Katherine said.

I stood up and kissed her.

I looked down at the two guys in the next booth. Because I was looking at them, Katherine looked at them, too. Clearly she didn't recognize either of them.

"Stay at the Flora in Rome," I said to the cashmere guy. "There's not so many loudmouth assholes at the Flora." The rhinestone guy stuck a handful of Fritos in his mouth and his pipe fell into a bowl of guacamole.

"What's that about?" Katherine said after we sat down.

"Just being helpful to the tourists," I said. "How did you know I was here?"

"I read it in the *Hollywood Reporter*," Katherine said.

A waiter helped the rhinestone guy wipe guacamole off the front of his outfit and clean up his pipe. The two guys paid their check and left without another word. I looked at Katherine. She had held up very well. I had heard she had gained weight and let her hair revert to saddle color. But she looked trim now, and her hair was blond, and she aimed that good soft smile at me. Katherine could smile at you and make you believe you were the finest, dearest person she had ever known.

"The timing is right. I'm finally getting divorced," I said. "Of course when Marcie's lawyers get through with me, I might decide to take off my shoes and walk across Africa."

Katherine laughed. "Don't worry, I'm not trying to pick up our romance again," she said. "The actual fact is, I thought it might be fun to have a drink with you and talk about old times. You've really gone to the top, haven't you?"

I brushed past that one and said, "You get rid of that sailor you lived with?"

"If you want to call a man who owns an eighty-foot yacht a sailor, yes I did," Katherine said. "He was a nice man. Very sweet. He took care of me. We did the big race from Newport Beach to Honolulu one year, and every year we spent three or four months cruising around the islands. He let me play princess. I could sleep with other people when I really wanted to. Nearly everywhere we went, he owned a house on the beach. He begged me to marry him."

"Why didn't you?" I said.

106

"The wind kept blowing sand in my Bain de Soleil," Katherine said.

We both laughed. Katherine sipped a Kahlua on the rocks.

"No, really, I couldn't go on living like that," she said. "I don't belong in paradise. One day I asked myself how come I was getting loaded all the time and turning to fat and saying motherfucker a lot. I decided it was because I just didn't fit in paradise. I needed to go back to work and be mistreated."

"Whatever you're doing, it looks great on you," I said.

She smiled and asked about my kids. She asked if Marcie had ever found out about us. I said Marcie believed I had been up to something serious sometime somewhere but didn't know any of it for sure. It was fantastic that Marcie could have missed feeling the heat of what went on between Katherine and me. But Marcie got so involved with herself, and being serious, that I was the guy in the suit who was always out of town when there was something she wanted him to do.

Katherine and I didn't talk much about Marcie, though. We talked about laughs we'd had together. Time passed fast when I was with Katherine. Suddenly it was 6 P.M. I signed the bill, tucked a twenty into Antoine's palm on the departing handshake, kissed Katherine goodbye in the lobby and ran for the bungalow. I never had asked what it was she really wanted.

Chapter
Thirteen

〰〰〰〰〰〰〰〰〰〰〰〰〰〰

The guard waved the indigo-blue limo through the gate at the studio in Burbank. I left Cooper and the stewardess in the executive parking lot and walked toward Melvin's trailer with the A.D., a kid named Stavros.

"We had an early dinner sent in for Melvin. Nothing too heavy," Stavros said.

The trailers were parked against a wall of the main building. Melvin's trailer was closest to the big sliding door which led onto the soundstage from the outside. You could drive a moving van through that door. I opened the door of Melvin's trailer and went in without knocking. In the indigo-blue limo, I had received a phone call that had touched my alarm bell enough to make a loud, distinct ping.

Melvin sat a table, idly tapping a fork in his chef's salad. Melvin was smiling and mumbling faintly. A stuntman named Dutch who had been acting as a baby-sitter leaned against the wall with his arms folded across his T-shirt.

"How do you feel, Melvin?" I said.

"Very relaxed. Very confident. We had a great rehearsal. I wish you could have seen it," Melvin said.

I said, "I wish *you* could have seen it. I heard you slept through it."

"I was seeing it in my mind. How many times do I need to see it with my eyes open?" Melvin said.

I looked at Dutch. It hardly need be said that stuntmen are tough, agile, fearless and more than half nuts. But stuntmen are usually short and compact, built more like rodeo cowboys than like pro football players. Dutch looked like a defensive end. Very tall, lean waist, California beach muscles in the chest, shoulders and arms. Full beard. Long hair. Maniacal eyes. Why the fuck would anyone have hired him as baby-sitter?

Pointing to Melvin, I said, "What have you presented me with, Dutch?"

"I gave him some downers like somebody said. I'm just bringing him back up. By seven o'clock, he'll be a tiger," Dutch said.

"If he's not, what's your price to do a gag off the top of the Hyatt House?" I said.

"Listen, goddam it, don't threaten me. I'm following orders. Somebody wanted this creep to be smoothed out right up to game time and then hit his throttle hard. That's what I'm doing, man, so don't get on my case, okay? I know who you are, and I don't give a shit," Dutch said.

I said I didn't see what could be accomplished by further discussion.

Outside the trailer, I said, "Stavros, who selected Dutch for this job?"

Stavros said, "I thought you did."

I said, "I told my secretary in New York to call L.A. and get Melvin a baby-sitter, not a terrorist. Who did she speak to?"

Stavros said, "Chick's the producer. Maybe him. But you know how these things get passed around.

Somebody probably told somebody. And Dutch was listening someplace and figured out he'd make a buck."

I made a mental note to trace it back so it wouldn't happen again.

"Melvin's been okay," Stavros said. "Really. He's done his work. He's been a little more docile than usual, maybe. Frankly, that's been a relief. He was tired this afternoon at the rehearsal. He'll be up for tonight."

I knocked on the door of Peggy's trailer.

"Miz Hanley ain't here rat now. Gone to the make-up room, ah speck," a voice said in a drawl out of *Gone With the Wind*.

I opened the door. Peggy was lying on a couch wearing cutoff Levis and a Mexican blouse and reading a paperback of *The Upanishads*.

Tommy Dorsey jazz was playing on the stereo. Peggy's hair was wrapped in a red bandana. When she saw me, she swung her long black legs off the couch. She got up and hugged and kissed me.

"Get you a drink? Carrot juice? Fresh peach?" she said.

I took a cucumber slice off her health food counter.

"I feel like my stomach is full of hummingbirds," Peggy said. "I can't remember a single song or dance step, or a word of the script. I've suddenly gotten very ugly. In the mirror I look like a deranged nigger."

I said, "My dear, you are not only beautiful and a genius, you are stronger than pig shit."

"And meaner than a broke pimp," she said. "I'm putting all my energy into living for two more hours and doing the best I can."

I said, "Peggy, here's what I think."

She listened carefully.

"I think you're gonna be sensational, you're gonna light 'em all up, you're gonna be the biggest star in the history of the whole crazy universe," I said.

"Oh, Frank, I love you," Peggy said.

She hugged and kissed me again.

"Uh, listen, Mr. Mallory," Stavros said as we walked through the big door into the soundstage.

"What?"

"You know, when you did that last line in Peggy's trailer, by the end of it you sounded just like Cagney," Stavros said.

"Forget it, kid," I said.

"John Wayne that time," he said.

In the next hour I had a number of things to do. One of them was getting Polly parked in a chair backstage where she would have a close look at the singing and dancing and all the cables, wires, lights, cameras, microphones and guys fixed up like telephone operators.

I was on my way to the control room when I encountered Peggy Hanley. She was in full costume. She paced quickly back and forth, with her hands clenched, listening to the orchestra tuning up.

"Stronger than pig shit, huh?" she said, holding out trembling hands. "I can't remember my name. Gloria? Betsy? Some good American name like that?"

I clasped her hands. "You're gonna knock 'em off like dead limbs, baby," I said.

Could it have been Gene Kelly creeping in there?

"If I'd known it was going to be scary, I'd have stayed in South Carolina and been a hooker like my daddy wanted," Peggy said.

"It's all on the high side now," I said.

That time I sounded like Frank Mallory. Almost.

Peggy hugged me again. Her eyes were glazed with terror.

When I entered the control room, the technical director, the associate director, the producer, the associate producer, the sound and lighting guys, the coffee kid, Dutch, all of them glanced around at me.

But only Melvin leaped up from his seat at the board and accidentally tore off his headset.

"Keyed up, Frank! Ready to smite a mighty blow! Here comes fun for the whole fucking Nielsen frozen chicken pot pea fuckers!"

I looked at Dutch. He wigwagged his thumbs to indicate all was cool.

Melvin yelled, "I go line 'em up, Frank! Stick their cute little asses all in a row . . . plup . . . plup . . . plup . . ."

Melvin patted the air with his palm, sticking the cute little asses all in a row.

"You ever smell a dancer?" Melvin yelled. "Football on the waterfront, that's what they smell like!"

Melvin rushed out of the control room, shoving people, half tripping.

"You got him pretty ripe, Dutch," I said.

I looked at the producer, Chick, who had done a terrific job of avoiding me so far. "I hope you haven't bought any new furniture," I said.

"Well, Frank, apparently what happened was . . ." the producer began.

Through the window I saw Melvin waving his arms as he sprinted up to Peggy onstage in front of the packed house of affiliates.

I leaned over and flipped a switch. Except for the first few rows, the audience couldn't hear what Melvin was saying to Peggy. But we could hear in the control room:

"Just show 'em what you are—a cunt! Slap old rosy on 'em! You know what's out there? Tits and cocks and balls and asses, but you got the only cunt that counts tonight, baby. Black as it might be!"

I ran out of the control room, jostled through a gathering crowd, hopped over a tangle of cables and approached Melvin as he was saying to Peggy in a suddenly calm voice:

"Peggy, darling, I know you're gonna fuck up. But that's okay, it's what I'm here for. We got an orchestra. We got singers who can really sing. Dancers who can really dance. If your spastic lurches get too embarrassing, I can simply cut away from your sweaty black body and do a closeup on your buck teeth."

The crew was absorbed by this little drama.

Peggy said, "Why don't you crawl up my ass and die, you hebe cocksucker?"

She started crying.

I said, "Melvin, go back to the board."

Melvin whirled and yelled, "Who said that?"

I motioned to Cooper.

"Frank, the goddam voice came out of the sky!" Melvin yelled.

Cooper took Melvin in a firm but gentle armlock and led him toward the control room.

"Stand by! Roll machines A through D to record!" Melvin yelled.

I gestured for a makeup guy to paint glitter under Peggy's eyes where tears made tracks.

"Within another hour, you will be the third most popular woman in my life," I said.

Peggy blinked and tried to smile.

"The other two are Billie Jean King and my mother," I said.

"You don't have a mother. You came out of an oyster shell," Peggy said.

In the control room, Melvin was back in the director's seat. The technical director sat on his left. The associate director, Stavros, sat on Melvin's right. Chick, the producer, was trying to drink a cup of coffee. Cooper stood by the door, near Dutch.

Into his headset Melvin said, "Okay, all you talented people, this is for real in ten seconds. . . . Rolling to record . . . gimme speed . . . One, stand by wide . . . bring up the fucking lights, Hal! . . . Hit it, Hermie!"

The orchestra conductor hit it.

Peggy started her number. It was a soul-modern, uptempo version of "I Can't Get Started."

Melvin said:

"Camera Three, start your dolly!

"Christ, Kenny, I said stand by for a waist shot! Go fuck yourself, Kenny.

"Stand by Two . . . Four . . . and Three. Take Two! Take Four!

"Put her in the upper left, Bobby . . . Slow dissolve to Two! . . . Hold it there . . . and . . . go . . . through to Two!"

Peggy was singing and dancing great enough to break your heart. And Melvin was doing his job like a pro. I began to feel that maybe I had been foolish to worry.

Melvin said, "Stand by . . . and fade to black!"

The number ended.

Melvin looked around at us. "Okay, that was a bag of wildcats. Clams and teeth. Plenty of fur," he said.

"Looked fine, Melvin," I said.

"Sweet," Chick said.

Melvin asked for a check on the tape. Then he flipped on the loud mike to the stage and said, "Peggy, let's pick it up some. A languid personality ain't gonna carry you for forty-six more minutes."

"Bite down on it, Melvin!" Peggy yelled.

"No need for naughty talk," Melvin said into the mike. "Just shove your sticky, chewy ass into the next setup. This is the one that makes you look like a horny ostrich."

"I don't have to take this shit! I can marry a dentist!" Peggy yelled.

I grasped Melvin by the collar and yanked him out of his chair.

"Peggy, this is Frank," I said on the loud mike. "Let's have fun on this one. It's for laughs . . . the number with Scotty and Jean . . . put Melvin clean out of your mind and lay your genius on us."

Jamming on a headset I said, "Roll A through F to record . . . and gimme speed . . . hit it, Hermie . . . and bring it up. . . ."

I looked at the monitors and quickly out the plate-glass window. I heard the chatter on the headset. Peggy was into a dance that would develop into a comedy skit.

"This number doesn't work. There's nothing fucking funny about it," Melvin said.

"Out of here, Melvin," I said. Into the headset I said, "Stand by wide, Three . . . dissolve to Three. . . ."

I was trying to study the shot chart.

"Boring number. Number's shit, Frank!" Melvin said.

Dutch poked me on the shoulder with one long finger that felt like the handle of a golf club.

"Hey, I got Melvin pumped up just right, like they told me. Give him his chair back," Dutch said.

I looked up at Dutch. His eyes glittered. His chest swelled. Veins stood out on his arms.

Dutch said, "Get your ass out of that chair!"

"Dutch, old buddy, you and me and Melvin is going to the cabin," Cooper said in a low voice.

Dutch jerked me out of the chair and threw me on the floor. I hit my head on the side of a machine and saw white worms for an instant. The producer moaned. I heard Stavros say, "Come back, Bobby . . . hold it there . . . take Three!"

Then I saw Dutch backed against the wall. Cooper was right up against Dutch's chest. Cooper's head tilted so he could look into Dutch's eyes. It was even money whose eyes looked the angriest and craziest.

". . . low-rent cocksucker if you're real smart or real lucky you might live long enough to leave town," I heard Cooper saying to Dutch in a quiet voice with a very hard edge on it.

Cooper's Binniss, the .32 snubnose Smith & Wesson, was half buried in Dutch's navel.

Cooper jabbed with the Binniss, and Dutch walked toward the door. With one arm, Cooper reached out and flipped Melvin sideways off his feet, so Cooper could drag Melvin while he prodded Dutch.

Leaving the room more or less on the back of his heels, Melvin clutched his genitals and screamed, "Here's your show, Frank! Right in the old crotcheroo! You'll never get a job in TV again!"

I said, "Take it, Stavros. You just got promoted."

Stavros gave me the old thumb-and-forefinger circle. The folks in the control room applauded. I felt good about everything then, and I knew the Peggy Hanley special would be what in the trade is often called dynamite.

It was.

After the show, the singers and dancers were running around kissing everybody. Two or three hundred of them kissed me. Melvin was right about the smell. I received eleven open offers of fellatio, nearly half of them from women.

Peggy kissed me and pleaded with me to come to the "wrap" party. It was in Holmby Hills, not far from the Playboy Mansion, at the house of some fan of Peggy's. I told her I would be there.

I found Polly the stewardess and asked if she had seen Cooper. I was a little uneasy about him.

"He went outside with some big tall wild-looking guy, and then he came back in. And just a second ago he ran outside again," Polly said.

116

I walked quickly through the huge sliding door in time to hear a loud *whang!* I saw Dutch beside the indigo-blue limo with a tire tool in his hand. I saw Cooper running toward Dutch, heard his bootheels on the pavement.

Blam-kawhiing! Blam-kawhiing!

Sparks flew up from Dutch's feet. Dutch could run amazingly fast, as he immediately demonstrated. Dodging behind cars, Dutch fled through the executive parking lot and could be seen windmilling toward the gate.

Cooper was pissed.

"Frank, look what that turd done," Cooper said. He pointed to a large dent in the left front fender of the indigo-blue limo. "If he'd done that to the Silver Goblet, I would of really lost my temper."

Cooper stuffed his Binniss back into his right boot. A guard came up and said he thought he had heard some shots. I told the guard a couple of big light bulbs had fallen off a truck. The guard was relieved. Polly and Cooper and I got into the limo and drove out the gate.

"What happened to Melvin?" I said.

"He burned out of here in a yellow Jensen, bounced off the curb and headed for Hollywood," Cooper said. "I believe he had as much speed in him as a man would ever need all at one time."

Polly was still in shock from the pistol shots.

"Does this happen on every show?" she said.

"If it had been live, you would have seen some real thrills," I said.

We were on our way to the party in Holmby Hills, but Cooper said when he got there he thought he would stay in the limo and listen to some tapes and maybe catch a few Z's.

It wore Cooper out to shoot at people. Always did.

Polly and Grant began playing electric Ping-Pong. I left them there and went back to the main house to get a drink.

On the way, I passed a pond full of goldfish two feet long and a monkey swung down out of a tree and fell in love with my leather jacket.

That was the only time in my life I ever kicked a monkey.

"Nice shot," a voice said from behind a bougainvillea vine.

No mistake about that voice. It was Bobby Maitlow. He stepped out from behind the bush zipping his pants and adjusting his scarf.

"Can't bring myself to piss in the house. The toilets are gold plated," Maitlow said in his metallic, squeeze-box voice.

"Who is Cotton Barstow?" I said.

"The guy mortgaged his brother-in-law's cotton farm for eighty thousand dollars and wrote, produced and directed a movie called *Swamp Fiend Women*. His brother-in-law did the photography and his sister did the sound. Movie grossed thirty nine million dollars. Cotton still can't read or write, but he must know something that ain't in the books," Maitlow said.

"How'd he write the script?" I said.

"Dictated it to his wife. She played one of the swamp fiend women. They got a divorce afterwards," Maitlow said.

We detoured around an animal that might have been a llama.

A tall man in a white suit came out of the house. He had a longneck Budweiser in his left hand and a two-dollar Jamaican cigar in his right. He had freckles and red hair and smelled of Vitalis.

"Hey, stud, how's it hanging?" he said to Maitlow.

"Cotton, I want you to meet Frank Mallory," Maitlow said.

"Glad you could make it, fella," Cotton Barstow said. He stuck the cigar in his mouth and pumped my hand. "How come you ain't got a drank?"

"I was on my way to get one," I said.

"Sheeit. Anythang you want around here, you jist give 'er one of these," Cotton said.

He put a little finger and a forefinger to his lips and blasted out a shrill whistle.

Immediately a waiter in a dinner jacket ran out of the house and took our orders. Through the glass doors along the porch we could see a hundred or so guests doing a mill-around in one room of the house. Probably seventy of them were female. Of that number, about half could make the cover of *Playboy* and half the cover of *Vogue*.

"What do you do with the ugly women?" I said.

"There ain't no ugly women," Cotton said. "Is they? You see one innywhurs?"

"Not here," I said.

"Whewsht, you had me skeert for a minute, fella," Cotton said.

He peered through the glass doors again.

"Closest thang to a ugly woman in there is that one with the sailor pants on and the sash around her waist," Cotton said.

"I don't think she's ugly," I said.

"I didn't say she was ugly. I said she was the closest thang to it in that particular room. If she'd undo some buttons so her tits could hang out a little bit, that would help. And if she wasn't so smart-looking, that would help. She kind of reminds me of one of them goddam women that's always trying to tell you what she learned someplace or what she thinks about some goddam thing or other," the host said.

The woman he pointed out was Sally Hawks.

"You want to see my helicopter?" Cotton said.

Maitlow and I said we'd rather wander around.

124

"Is they any niggers in the grotto?" Cotton said.

"Last time I looked there was," I said.

"Sheeit, that's what I was afraid of. Goddam niggers are scared of water, but they go in the goddam grotto all the time anyhow," Cotton said.

Peggy Hanley rushed out from some unseen door and kissed me wetly.

"Frank, sweet baby, wonderful baby," she said. She stuck her tongue rapidly in and out of my mouth. Then she turned and grabbed Cotton and stuck her tongue in and out of his mouth.

"Cotton, sweet baby. Frank is the man who made me a star," Peggy said, rubbing up and down on Barstow like a cat.

"I sure would like to take you to France or someplace," Cotton said to her.

"Darling, after the word gets out about tonight I'm going to be very busy," Peggy said.

"Well, sheet, look me up on your way down," Cotton said.

Arm in arm, they walked off into Cotton's own rain forest.

"The guy drilled one hole and hit a gusher. He don't know how hard it is," Maitlow said.

"He's the man who ought to run your studio," I said.

We walked through the glass doors into the big room.

"He don't go over with New York bankers," Maitlow said.

"Or the boys?" I said.

"Or the boys," Maitlow said.

"Excuse me a minute, Bobby," I said. "I want to talk to that ugly woman."

"Tell her she can dress up my house any time," Maitlow said.

Sally was standing by herself. You could tell she

was observing the room and making notes in her mind. She smiled when she saw me.

"You had some excitement tonight," she said.

"Yeah, Peggy was great, wasn't she?" I said.

"Peggy's always great. I mean the excitement in the control room when you dumped the director and took over yourself," she said.

"How'd you know that?" I said.

"Everybody knows about it," she said.

"Herb Grant doesn't," I said.

"Herb Grant wouldn't have known there was an earthquake in Peru last month if you hadn't told him," she said.

"You're sort of gossipy, aren't you?" I said.

"Herb himself told me that you told him about the earthquake," she said, laughing. "He wasn't all that impressed with Stanley's decision to put it on the air on a Saturday night, you know. He said you two were just trying to invent something else for America to worry about. He said America needs to smile."

I said, "Evidently Herb agrees with Harley O. Chambers on that last matter."

"I'd like a drink," she said. "Want to go to the bar?"

"Just give 'er one of these," I said.

I put two fingers in my mouth and whistled.

A waiter was at our side before the echo stopped.

"Scotch and water. J&B if you have it," Sally said.

"Same," I said.

Then I said, "I figured if you drank Scotch, it would be Chivas or Black Label or maybe some twenty-five-year-old brand that's largely unknown this side of Edinburgh."

"On my salary?" she said. "Do you have any idea what *New York* magazine pays for a piece?"

"No, but your book was on the best-seller list for a while," I said.

"How did you know that?" she said.

"It was a question on 'Hollywood Squares,' " I said.

She laughed again. Her laugh had a rich sound to it. Like she had thought about it and wasn't laughing merely to please you or because she was nervous.

She clinked her J&B against mine, to put it romantically.

What Cotton Barstow had called sailor pants and a sash was in fact a white silk jump suit by Valentino. It fit neatly around the hips and thighs and flared at the ankles.

Herb Grant walked up and said, "I hate to be the one to have to tell you this, Mallory, old man, but . . ."

"My date is fucking a basketball player in the grotto," I said.

"How did you know that?" Grant said.

Sally and I both laughed. Grant scowled and shook his head in disapproval, and moved away.

Sally pointed at Grant's head. His hair was wet.

We almost fell down.

"Have you got a date around here?" I asked Sally.

She said, "I came with a columnist from San Francisco, but he's probably fucking a basketball player, too."

Sally and I left the party. I offered her a ride to her hotel and maybe a quiet drink where we could discuss why Smerdyakov did it.

In front of the mansion, Cooper and Cotton Barstow were sitting on the dented fender of the indigo-blue limo.

"This old blue deal here don't hold a shuck to that Silver Goblet we got back in Manhattan," Cooper was saying.

"I tell you, D. Wayne, and it's a goddam fact, I got me four, five, maybe six of these limousines, and a Excalibur sports car, a mobile home, two pickup trucks, a Bentley convertible . . . let's see, now, . . . a jeep, a station wagon, a new tractor, and I'm thankin' about gettin' me a new sixty-four-passenger bus with a observation deck and dance floor. But it's come to where none of this stuff means a doodly shit. Only thang that counts to me now is my *ort*," Cotton Barstow said.

"Ready to hit it?" Cooper said to me.

I introduced Sally to Cooper. Cotton Barstow looked at Sally and frowned.

"I got a new movie out," Cotton Barstow said to Cooper as we got into the limo. Cotton closed Cooper's door and leaned on the window.

"It's about moonshiners and fucking," Cotton Barstow said. "Did a real risk on it. Put in four hundred thousand dollars and that sucker ain't did but nine million so far. That's the trouble with ort."

We said goodnight to Cotton Barstow and drove off. He yelled as we went down the driveway.

"Hey, D. Wayne," he yelled. "How come yawl didn't take no good pussy with you?"

Chapter
Fifteen

～～～～～～～～～～～～～～～～～～～～

On the way to the Bel Air, where she was staying, Sally mentioned that she had to get up early in the morning to play tennis.

I said I had to get up early and try to bat a few past the affiliates.

"I'm curious to see what you've done with the fall schedule," Sally said.

"Don't expect much," I said.

"I never do," she said.

"Then you're never disappointed," I said.

"Yes, I am," she said. "Television gets worse and worse. This year was the worst ever, but I expect next year to top it."

"Why bother to write about it?" I said.

"Why bother to write about a plane crash?" she said.

"As a matter of fact, television is better than it was ten or fifteen years ago," I said. "We do news and sports better. We schedule dramas and documentaries and even situation comedies that wouldn't have made the air ten or fifteen years ago."

"Not your network," she said.

"Look, let's don't argue about television. I can do that any time," I said. "Let's talk about your tennis."

"I have a Southern California backhand. When you grow up out here and learn young, you never lose your Southern California backhand," Sally said.

"You couldn't have grown up out here. You're not tall and blond," I said.

"I'm sort of blond," Sally said, smiling.

"It could be a rinse," I said.

"And I'm sort of tall," she said. "And I was born in Beverly Hills."

"Good god," I said.

She said her mother had been a film editor who had worked on a number of big pictures in the forties and fifties.

"T. Hawks?" I said.

"Her name was Thomassina," Sally said.

"I'll be damned. I never knew T. Hawks was a woman," I said.

"I'm pleased you've heard of her," Sally said.

"I'm the kind who reads the credits," I said.

Sally said her mother, T. Hawks, was dead. She said her father was Rodrigo Hawks. He had been a character actor and then a B producer in the thirties and on into the forties. He produced his last feature in 1947. It was called *Tomorrow's Darling*.

I said I had missed seeing *Tomorrow's Darling*.

So did nearly everybody else, she said. *Tomorrow's Darling* had stayed in a can on a shelf.

For several years Rodrigo Hawks kept saying *Tomorrow's Darling* would be released in the fall, she said. Or if not, then surely in the spring. Finally Rodrigo quit talking about it. He had other projects. Sally said Rodrigo kept borrowing money to option properties. He borrowed money to hire writers to develop the material. He called on old friends who were

130

actors and directors. He was always just about to put the big package together.

But Rodrigo Hawks never made another movie after 1947. Things never came together again. It was a common story in Hollywood. Sally said, thank god T. Hawks was in demand as an editor by then.

"Without T. Hawks, I wouldn't have grown up with a Southern California backhand," Sally said.

She said a short while after T. Hawks died in a car wreck on the Ventura Freeway while on some mysterious errand, Rodrigo Hawks sold the house on Cañon Drive and moved to a small apartment in Palm Springs. She said Rodrigo Hawks now told the story that he had been blackballed in Hollywood.

"I guess he was. But not for politics," Sally said. "I guess he was blackballed for being a loser."

"Some people out here build long and prosperous careers out of being losers," I said.

"Big losers do. Small losers disappear," she said.

I have never known a skillful way to ask an attractive lady about her prior love life, and I have never really known why a man would care. In my case, I chalked it up to a journalist's inquisitive nature.

"How many Southern California backhands have you been married to?" I said.

"None of those," she said. "A near-miss with a writer in New York. I type a lot, is what I mostly do."

Talking to Sally, I had failed to notice that we had already turned through the white pillars into Bel Air and were nearly in front of the hotel.

"One nightcap," Sally said.

"How about you, D. Wayne?" I said.

"I'll be along in a few minutes," Cooper said.

Sally and I walked over the bridge and went into the Bel Air Hotel bar. We were talking about movies when we walked in, and we got all the way to the bar and sat down before I realized what I was hearing:

"Frank-ly, I adore you . . . remind me to ignore you . . ."

That was a song Katherine used to sing, with emphasis on the *Frank,* when I was in the audience. There were songs she would change the lyrics to, or stress certain words, as a private message to me.

I looked over at the piano, and there she was. Katherine. In a white strapless gown. Now I knew where she was working, anyhow. In the Bel Air Hotel bar.

Katherine smiled at me. I lifted a glass to her.

Sally said, "Tycoons got cunt stashed everywhere."

I said, "What?"

Sally laughed. "I am quoting what a tycoon told me last night in explaining why it didn't matter to him that I refused to go to bed with him," she said.

"Cotton Barstow?" I said.

"No, he put it a different way. He said I'd probably be like sticking it in the tail pipe of a gravel truck," she said.

Katherine looked annoyed. One thing you did not do was laugh while Katherine was singing a ballad.

Cooper came in and sat at the other end of the bar. I motioned for him to join us. He indicated he would in a minute.

"That's a very interesting-looking man," Sally said. "Is he your friend, or your employee?"

"Both," I said.

"That must be a difficult relationship to maintain," Sally said. "What happens when the employee gets out of line and the friend has to be dealt with?"

"We get mad as hell at each other," I said. "If it's really serious, we play it off at Ping-Pong. Four out of seven."

Sally finished her nightcap and said she was going to put her head down. In the morning she was playing tennis with an L.A. *Times* columnist she wanted to beat.

132

"Let's get up a match back in Gotham," I said.

"You probably play at the Vanderbilt Club with people named after banks," she said.

"I do have two hours a week booked there," I said. Also I had two hours a week booked at the bubble on Fifty-ninth in the winter. It was pitiful how seldom I was able to use those hours.

"We'll play on my turf," Sally said.

"Where is that?" I said.

"The West Side," she said.

She gave me the address of the courts. We set a time and a date. Sally signaled the bartender for the check.

"What are you doing?" I said.

I seemed to ask her a hell of a lot of questions. She kept surprising me.

"You're expense account stuff to me, baby," Sally said.

If I had thought of it at the time, I would have said that it was good to meet a girl who liked Raymond Chandler.

Sally walked out swiftly. A couple of swishes of the white silk pants, and she was gone.

I called for another drink and applauded as Katherine ended her set. She smiled and curtseyed and came to the bar. Cooper moved down the bar to join us.

"You sound terrific," I told Katherine.

"You weren't listening," she said.

"Sure I was," I said.

"What tune did I close with?" Katherine said.

" 'The Flight of the Bumble Bee'," I said.

"Tell him, D. Wayne," Katherine said.

"Aw, now, it don't make a shit if he don't know what it was," Cooper said.

"I mean tell him what we've been talking about," Katherine said.

Cooper looked at the wall and said: "Taw-bah-gee-mar."

I thought maybe I understood him. I looked at Katherine.

"D. Wayne and I are talking about getting married," Katherine said.

I felt like dropping my glass, or falling off the stool, or striking myself on the forehead with a bladder and going inginginging.

Instead I said, "What for?"

"I was going to tell you this evening at the Polo Lounge," Katherine said.

"No you wasn't," Cooper said.

"D. Wayne is right. I wasn't going to tell you," Katherine said. She turned on the soft smile. "What I was doing was seeing how it is between us. If I still wanted you. Or you still wanted me. It was D. Wayne's idea."

"Wouldn't be no good to have somebody feel like they couldn't take a run at somebody because of somebody else," Cooper said.

"I saw how it is," Katherine said. "You're a nice guy, Frank. But I love D. Wayne."

"She can't hardly help herself, Frank," Cooper said.

They got quiet and waited for me to speak. My mind was a dark woods full of lightning bugs. Not the most worthy of my thoughts was that I didn't want Cooper to move out on me, but I didn't want Katherine living in the penthouse because something was bound to happen that in South Dallas leads to murder.

I said, "D. Wayne, you've been married four times to three different women."

He said, "It's five to three if you want to be real accurate. Remember that first time I married Nadine in high school, it didn't take."

I said, "Katherine, you married a trumpet player the first year you toured with a big band, and then you married a rancher in Nevada."

134

"I believe we already know these histories," Katherine said.

"Then why do you two want to get married?" I said.

"We love each other," Katherine said.

"So what?" I said.

"Frank," Cooper said slowly, "we want to do it, that's all. Ain't none of us can count on the sun coming up even one more time in their own personal life. So if we want to hire a preacher and have a lot of hugging and crying, well, then that's what we're gonna have to do. We'd like it if you'd like it, but we're gonna do it anyhow."

"D. Wayne, it wasn't all that long ago that you came and moved me out of my house," I said. Then to Katherine I said, "And it wasn't all that much longer ago that you and I were talking about what you and Cooper are talking about now."

"Life's a funny old possum, ain't she?" Cooper said.

"Gotta go to work," Katherine said.

She sat down at the piano. The spot flipped on. She went straight into a ballad. There's nothing quite like background music for serious moments.

Or an interruption.

Behind me, a voice said, "Get down here, guy. I want you to meet Lana Turner and Rhoda Fleming."

It was Stanley Coffman. He had come in and seated himself at the table nearest the bar with two women. They were too tan, too trim, too brittle and too pre-served to be wives of affiliates whose husbands had gone to The Strip to see a topless bottomless show. They were Beverly Hills housewives whose husbands were still playing gin at the club. They had cruised into Stanley, one way or another.

I looked at Cooper.

"Am I supposed to take a cab home, or what?" I said.

"Frank, it's your limo," Cooper said.

135

I got off the stool and sat down at the table with Stanley and his friends.

One of the women said, "Are you in television, too?"

I said, "Ah . . . ah . . . wall . . . ah'm gonna have to star at ya for a whall, Ma'am."

Could have been Jimmy Stewart.

"Talk fast, Frank," Stanley said. "I'm totally fucking in love with Charlotte and Emily Brontë."

Chapter
Sixteen

∽∽∽∽∽∽∽∽∽∽∽∽∽∽∽∽∽∽∽∽∽∽

I woke up without a Beverly Hills housewife in the bungalow. It was early but I still planned to run my two miles in a record for someone who had to spend the day with television affiliates.

Jogging in L.A. is like climbing inside a Texaco pump and taking a deep breath. I know people on the Coast who claim the smaze never reaches them in Beverly Hills. That it is only something they can see from their patios on a hilltop. A layer of something the color of Spanish rice—and way off in the distance where it belongs, down there where they drive Ford Granadas instead of his-and-her Mark IVs.

I never argue with them. Even as they sit in what could almost pass for sunshine around their swimming pools and tennis courts and claw at their eyes, I don't mention the headlights I've seen turned on at midday as far north as Malibu.

I sprang across Sunset Boulevard in front of the hotel. I thought of how nice it must have been when people rode horseback down the bridle path on the traffic island, and how they could always see the San Bernardino mountains.

I went through Will Rogers Park and angled out onto Beverly Drive. The tall palms on the street lead you to the township of Beverly Hills proper, where $1,500 denim was invented, and where you can sit in such places as La Scala and The Bistro and overhear talk about deferments and percentages of the gross before negative.

It was already stuffy. The rot had been held in overnight by the lack of a breeze.

Mansions with manicured lawns and finely edged flower beds went by slowly.

There must have been thousands of days in the past when a Japanese gardener didn't mind kneeling and crawling for eight hours because he knew he could look up through the palms occasionally and be forced to squint. Blinded by a sky bluer than technicolor. Squinting at the sun was different than a watery blink at the smaze.

There was definitely less old-fashioned squinting out here these days. Squinting, now, was something a producer did when he looked at a "literary" script.

Squinting was for affiliates from Scranton Pennsylvania, and Jackson, Mississippi, looking at one of my pilots for next fall.

I wondered if I would have looked foolish if I had tied a handkerchief around my face like a bandit. How could you look foolish doing anything in Beverly Hills?

Okay, you mugs. I've got a gat here. This is a stickup. Gimme all your denims.

At the first of the two Santa Monicas near the village I circled and started back up Beverly on the other side of the street.

I passed a huge white house with a driveway that could masquerade as a showroom for Cadillacs.

I hoped the air would be cleaner where that guy's wife would get her pedicure today.

I hoped his son got asked to pledge at USC.

I hoped his daughter married an executive in aerospace.

I hoped there was a closet Jew in Los Angeles Country Club.

I hoped everybody in California kept putting sour cream on their enchiladas.

Cooper was sitting on the steps of my bungalow.

"Order us some eggs while I get slick for the asshole affiliates," I said.

"What do you want with 'em?" Cooper said. "Bacon or armadillo?"

Chapter
Seventeen

~~~~~~~~~~~~~~~~~~~~~~~~~~~~~~~~~~~~~~

We were in a soundstage at a studio in the Valley. This was an intimate little luncheon for two thousand people. These were the affiliates and their wives, their general managers, programmers, sales directors, honored guests, reverend father, ladies and gentlemen.

An affiliate is a person who owns or runs a TV station that is affiliated with the network. If he owns an affiliated station as opposed to an independent station, a network pays him to carry the network's programming. If his station is located in a major market, an area of large population in other words, the network might pay him a great sum of money to carry the network's programming. But if an affiliate doesn't always like a particular program for some reason—let's say he finds it too "suggestive" or too "liberal"—he can substitute his own local programming for that half hour or hour and probably make even more money. Affiliates have it both ways.

There aren't many affiliates who wouldn't choose to run a Red Skelton movie everyone in his community has seen five times over a network news special exposing another political fraud. To satisfy his greed, the affiliate could sell so much clutter around the movie his viewers would think they were watching used car commercials instead of Red Skelton.

An affiliate has enormous power and he knows it. Sometimes he got to be an affiliate because he owned the only radio station or newspaper within a hundred miles of canned goods when the networks were formed. Sometimes he got to be one because his postcard got to the FCC first when people initially applied for licenses. Once in a while, an affiliate will be dropped and replaced by a station owner who has come to New York and bought a lot of dinners for somebody like Herb Grant, but that is very rare.

As much as they hate it, network people have to cater shamelessly to affiliates. The network needs the affiliate to clear his station constantly for things in which the network has invested millions. News, specials, documentaries, comedies, drama. All that.

When I was with CBS I used to have to appear before the affiliates and apologize for the rude manner in which our Washington correspondents discussed presidents.

Now I was with a different group of affiliates, but they wore the same maroon double-knits and white belts and white shoes as the CBS affiliates.

And I had to be cordial for a different reason.

The reason was, I had two new shows on the fall schedule that I wanted the affiliates to like, or at least tolerate. Getting the affiliates to clear their stations for prime-time shows in the beginning of a season is no problem. But keeping them on can be a problem if the ratings aren't overwhelming.

If you have a show that isn't getting the ratings after the first three or four weeks, you might look up to find that only 75 percent of your 180 affiliates are running it—and that means the show is suddenly being whispered around as "imminently cancelable" or "marginally renewable," both of which add up to dead.

It could be the most excellent and necessary show ever done, not to mention terrific, wonderful and hilarious, but if it doesn't have the instant ratings the affiliates will start scrapping for the life rafts.

One of the shows I had approved development of was about a happily married lady attorney who went around lobbing grenades at injustice without passing up any subplot chances for impersonal sex—a strong modern woman, in other words. The other show was about an ex-pro football player struggling to become a TV sportscaster despite his lack of familiarity with the English language. They weren't *Silver Chief, Dog of the North*. But I still liked them.

And I wanted the affiliates to give them a chance, even though they might not draw the 35,000,000 viewers Herb Grant would have personally promised General Foods and the Ford Motor Company.

If enough money was involved, a Herb Grant would cancel something like "The Mary Tyler Moore Show" any old day—and construct another Lawrence Welk from a roll of toilet paper.

And if the numbers improved, every affiliate on the line would be so delirious with the decision, he would throw a lei around his wife's neck and take her to the Sheraton Waikiki for a fortnight.

These are the stakes. You spend about $300,000 on a pilot. If you like it, you then spend another $1,500,000 on thirteen episodes. But today the sponsors are shrewd. They say if you don't deliver the audience you guarantee all the way, they get "make goods," which are commercials of theirs you have to drop into network newcasts or other prime-time programs, and that in turn costs the networks money. It is a form of refund.

Finally, the show is on the air at the mercy of the Nielsens.

It is strictly the Nielsen sample that determines whether any TV show is getting a good enough "rating" or "share," a rating being a percentage of the homes in the country, and a share being a percentage of the TV sets actually in use when your show is on the air.

If a TV series in prime time is not getting a good enough rating or share, wholesale panic ensues. From the leading actor or actress right up to the Big Guy. The stars will say the show is in the wrong time slot. Others will say it's the scripts. The Big Guy or Herb Grant might say it was a lousy idea to begin with. And the programmer and network president will say it's the Nielsens.

The Nielsens have defrocked many a network president and prime-time programmer.

It is easy to understand why. For me it is, anyhow.

When last counted, there were just under 120,000,000 TV sets in the country. There were over 200,000,000 viewers. There were TV sets in 70,000,000 homes.

But Nielsen was still wired into only 1,170 sets. One thousand one hundred and seventy out of a *hundred and twenty million*.

You like the numbers when they win for you over the competition, of course. The economics of the business is built on them. But what thinking person could ever accept them as truth or let them affect his judgment about what is good entertainment? Who really knows what people watch?

When I stood at the lectern and addressed the audience in that soundstage, it was after my two pilots and some of our other fall programs had been shown on a big screen behind me. The applause for all the shows was generous, but affiliates always applaud every show because they have been greeted at the luncheon by an armload of gifts from Tiffany.

Later, many of them will tell you, "Real fine gifts this year, boy. Damn handsome clock and pair of cuff links with the network logo on 'em."

Nothing I said to the affiliates was worth carving on the wall of a temple. I suggested that maybe the country had never been given an opportunity to develop a taste for class programming. That got a few mutters, I noticed. I said I was going to do the job my way and if this meant some surprises and experiments, so be it. I actually said that. Right there in my suit and tie. It is just possible, also, that I said I hoped our network next fall could become known as the one that truly cared about the quality show that might seem "marginally renewable" from a financial point of view.

I scanned the audience for a smirking Sally Hawks, and was relieved not to have spotted her.

If anything at all could be said for my sluttish performance, it would be that I never used the phrase "economically active viewer," I never said that CBC was more than just a network that delivered an audience to the next commercial, I never discussed whether a star's "recognition implied affection," I never said that with good programming you didn't need to "hype" the "sweep rating period," and I never used the word "demographics."

The applause wouldn't have dazzled a game show host, but the affiliates clapped.

Realistically, I think they just wanted to get on with lunch and move it on out to the log ride at Knott's Berry Farm.

One of these days a programmer may stand before an annual general conference of network television affiliates and say something like:

"You dummies are nothing but product sellers, so admit it. If any of you ever saw a drama that wasn't interrupted every six minutes by a commercial spot, you'd be so shattered you'd take off your white belts and beat your children. If you thought a comedy was something besides people slipping down on the kitchen tile, you might understand the problems of your own cities and homes better. I say you can have first-rate entertainment, either gripping or humorous, and still peddle detergent, cars and beer. But *you* can't be the judge of what's good, neither can the ad agency, neither can the sponsor, neither can the fool who owns the network by larceny or happenstance of birth, and neither can Nielsen. We the professionals will be the judge. Now bend over while we shove creative talent, for the good of our country, up your ass."

But in whose lifetime will any programmer say that?

TV is such an immense human pastime, with so many billions of dollars involved, it swallows us all. It can only be improved gradually from the inside of a network, if at all—if ever. Or so I reasoned.

Meanwhile, of course, it was fun to have a limo.

An affiliate meeting lasts for three or four days, until every show on the fall schedule has been unveiled, and every star and supporting player has been introduced to sing or tell jokes or lead a prayer. Until every game show host has broken his jaw smiling. Until every news anchorman, commentator or analyst has been paraded through the hall to answer charges about his liberal innuendo. Until every ex-athlete who has become a play-by-play announcer or color man has signed every autograph for every affiliate's son. Until every network executive from programming, news, sales, sports, research, promotion, marketing, stations, finance, corporate, lab, public relations, films, future projects, diversification, technical advance and frog-feeding has made his speech.

The affair then winds up, as this one did, with a

dinner dance in a massive ballroom two floors below the lobby of the Century Plaza Hotel, a place large enough to hold the Super Bowl if it ever has to retreat underground.

The center of the room was a buffet table so rectangularly huge it would not have fit in Forest Lawn unless you folded the corners. On it were ten towering ice sculptures of the Emmy statuette. Champagne squirted out of fountains and onto the maroon double-knits.

Hundreds of delicacies simmered in big chafing dishes. Cheese boards swayed from a tonnage of Brie. Loaves of bread seemed to be only slightly reduced replicas of the Goodyear blimp. Norfolk pine could have grown from the buckets where the Beluga caviar was exhibited. One hundred waiters circulated with drinks and steak filet, crab, lobster, pâté, oysters, lamb chops, ribs, shrimp and so forth.

Up on a stage a studio orchestra blended dance music with themes from many of our shows.

And moving around through all of this were roughly two hundred of the most adorable starlets, models and hookers any network could recruit, wearing their slinkiest, filmiest gowns.

I spent the early part of the evening trying to look like I wasn't looking for Sally Hawks. It did me very little good when I finally found her. She was with a former NFL running back who was now doing color for another network.

We met. Ricky Somebody. He was never all-pro.

"I believe you've topped them all," Sally said. "I thought NBC set an all-time food record last year, but this does it."

I said I relinquished all the credit to Stanley Coffman.

I was getting ready to suggest that we all go somewhere for a drink later when Ricky Somebody said they had to leave. It would have taken Cooper's Binniss to do anything about the grip he had on Sally's arm.

"Don't forget tennis," I said.

"You're penciled in," Sally said, looking back.

I got a fresh drink as Herb Grant marched up on the stage and went to the microphone. Grant tapped on the mike and said he had the great pleasure and privilege to make an introduction.

Grant said it had been five years since the man he was about to introduce had personally come before the affiliates.

This was a man of incredible vision, Herb Grant said. A pioneer. A great American. A friend of the needy. A counselor to heads of state. A man of wisdom. A father to us all, really.

I was standing watch on the Beluga when Stanley Coffman's voice behind me said:

"Here comes Moby Dick."

"Maybe they'll kill him throwing crab shells," I said.

"They're too drunk."

"They could pound him with their white shoes."

"They're shit-faced."

"They could throw bread. One of those loaves in the right place . . ."

"They're totally into cah-cahs and pee-pees," Stanley said.

"They could turn the fountains on him. Wash him overboard."

"They're full-limp, face-down, Chinaman, wacko, nigger," said Stanley.

"I guess you're right," I said.

"Look at 'em," Stanley said. "Half of 'em are crawling around on the floor looking for their cuff links. The others are throwing fifties and hundreds at the broads."

147

A man of taste, Herb Grant said. A man who had walked with kings. A man who knew Al Jolson, who knew . . .

"I think I'm in love," Stanley said. "See the redhead over there in the two-ounce dress? I gave her a little tongue-o, wham-o a while ago—on the back of the neck. Told her the little Wasp could eat his way out of the Paris sewers. I think she got a wide-on."

Herb Grant had several more file cards of notes to read, but he was interrupted by an explosion of outrageous cheering.

The Big Guy was on the stage and shuffling slowly toward the mike.

Herb Grant stepped aside. He put his hand to his mouth and whistled like Cotton Barstow, and he waved his other hand with the file cards above his head.

In an effort to dress "California" for the occasion, the Big Guy wore a bright yellow, polyester Dacron sports coat with his short gray pants, white socks and railroad shoes. He lowered the mike down to his little pink face and wispy white hair.

"Ladies and gentlemen, a plumber came into my home the other day and looked at me with contempt," he said.

And then he went on with it.

America needed to see America. Prime time. Three hours. Live. "Just Up the Street." Coming soon. Consult your local listings.

"A nation which can't see itself is like an ox with its foot caught in the tundra," he said.

Oh, how long, he said, since we've listened to the gentle sound of coats being hung in a closet? The carefree squeals of children being punished? The homey chit-chat of a man and wife balancing the checkbook together? The sizzle of liver in a frying pan?

148

He put his fingers to his lips, as if to ask two thousand people to shush.

"Rat-tat-tat-tat-tat," he said. "Burrraaang . . . Tow, tow, tow . . . We're pinned down here near the crest of a hill that's been a German stronghold for more than a week. . . . Our kids are tired and muddy, but their rifles are still cracking for Uncle Sam. . . . Get one for me, Johnny! . . . Overhead, the sky is a tumult of screaming patterns in death. . . . Mad Dog one to Blue Apple leader . . . Let's go, Marines! . . . Burrraaaang . . . *Eingin leeber stein. Nect bin swine der hagen!* Some of them will be dancing at the Savoy tonight, and some of them will still be in Germany. . . . Vroom . . . tow, tow . . . burrrooom . . . There'll be other grubby battles in this sordid war, and there'll be other GI's to fight them. . . . This was just one. . . . So for now, from below a burning, pock-marked hill outside a crazy little town in Italy, this is Harley O. Chambers saying . . ."

The Big Guy stopped and looked off.

"He never went to war," Stanley said. "The little sap might have started a few, but he never went to one."

A minute passed while ice jangled in cocktail glasses and throats cleared.

"Plumbers," the Big Guy said. "Plumbers who look at you with contempt are like rats locked out of the cargo. We can only guess what would happen if they all lifted their wrenches at once and angrily swung at our faucets. I daresay that Buffalo might float into Cleveland. Ah, but we have the medicine of electronics. We have television. And I have every confidence that our programming maestro, Frank Mallory, is going to fix the problem for us. His show, 'Just Up the Street,' is going to make our plumbers smile again."

With that, he said goodnight.

Applause went with him to the wings where two

military chiefs in full dress uniform took him by each arm and ushered him out of sight.

A maroon double-knit in a white belt and white shoes stumbled into me at the Beluga.

"What the hell was that thing you're gonna fix, Frank?" he said.

"Television. I'm going to adjust your fine tuning," I said.

"Shit right," the affiliate said. "Go get 'em, boy! and, say! That damn clock is a hell of a lot nicer lookin' than last year's desk set, don't you think?"

Chapter
Eighteen

∽∽∽∽∽∽∽∽∽∽∽∽∽∽∽∽∽∽∽∽∽∽∽∽∽∽

Cooper called it the Ghetto Racquet Club.

The limo, as instructed, stopped on Columbus Avenue between Ninety-seventh and Ninety-ninth streets, at the entrance to a huge outdoor tennis compound on the West Side.

The neighborhood was a symphony of horns honking, distant sirens, Spanish phrases being shouted, and Con Ed jackhammers sending puffs of dust into the air to join the soot.

"I'm goin' downstate to see if they got the tables put in my joint yet," Cooper said. "Pick you up right here in an hour or so—if you ain't been killed in a Puerto Rican dope war."

I had on a sweatshirt, Levis and the red Pumas with blue laces. I had my racquet and a can of new Wilsons.

A squad of black kids came over to admire the Silver Goblet as I got out.

"Hey, bro," one of them said, peeking in the window at Cooper. "You be Gunsmoke?"

"So dig this, man," said another. "Gunsmoke get hisself a space ship."

151

A black kid pitched me a rolled-up wad of wet toilet paper.

"Say, listen-s," he said. "You be got some balls you don't be needin'? We gots to get some run."

"You gonna get some run, man. We gots to get some run, too, you dig what I'm sayin'? Gimme ball, man."

I tossed the toilet paper back and went through the entrance as Cooper pulled away.

A guy sitting in the office who may have been the resident tennis pro was wearing Wimbledon whites with a Panama hat.

There were about twelve courts surrounded by urban-renewal apartment buildings and schoolyard fences. The courts were all occupied, mostly by Spanish guys chasing after the lobs of men with beards, glasses and dark socks. Some children raced about, yelling. There was a small area where people could sun themselves and read papers. An elderly lady who looked like everybody's grandmother pored through the *Racing Form*. A man with shoepolish sideburns, in a plaid jacket and turtleneck, who looked like he made collections for Julia's husband, studied the *Wall Street Journal*. On a far court next to an apartment building I saw Sally. She was rallying with a plump girl.

I couldn't help looking up and all around as I walked to Sally's court. It was tennis in a concrete canyon with the sound effects of a Viet Cong raid. And soot warfare.

Sally wore cutoff jeans frayed along the edges and they fit her like Marcie's short shorts. She wore white sneakers and those things women wear on their ankles that aren't socks. She wore a white headband and a wristlet. Her white T-shirt was as tight as a leotard and dark gold lettering was stamped across the front. BANANA CREAM PIE is what it said.

152

She used a Head racquet. And she was right about the backhand. She put it over low and hard with topspin.

"Hi," she said. "Get out here. Lisa has to go tutor."

The plump girl said she didn't have to go tutor for another five minutes.

"You two go ahead," I said. "I'll just hit a few up against Mrs. Garcia's window."

Sally whipped over a backhand that made Lisa chop at it like swinging a flyswatter at a drainboard. Lisa looked at the hole in her racquet as Sally came over to me.

Sally picked up a beige canvas shoulder bag off the cement and took out a pack of Winstons and a cricket lighter.

"Born to smoke," she said.

Her face glistened lightly with perspiration. She even knew how to sweat.

The plump girl said, "Was that your car?"

She wiped off her face and arms with a towel.

"This is Frank," Sally said. "Frank, Lisa."

"Your car's bigger than my apartment," Lisa said.

I supposed you smiled at that.

"A lot of water skiers complain that it doesn't turn sharply enough," said Sally.

And that.

"Play in the morning?" Lisa asked Sally.

"Typing," Sally said. "Maybe in the afternoon."

Lisa said, *"The Treasure of Sierra Madre* starts tomorrow on a double bill with *The Big Sleep* on Thirty-fourth Street. The whole week is Bogart."

"You're kidding?" Sally said. "They don't have *Sabrina,* do they?"

"No, but they've got *The African Queen* on Thursday."

"Fuck," said Sally. "Those editors from *Playboy* are coming in Thursday morning. I'm hung up."

153

A more compassionate man would have felt guilty about the movie cassettes in his Park Avenue apartment.

"I'll call you," Lisa said, as she slipped the cover over her racquet.

"Frank, about that car and all. What do you do?" Lisa said.

"I steal."

"Paul Muni," Sally said. *I am a Fugitive from a Chain Gang.*"

"Oh?" I said.

Sally said, "Lower the voice. More of a snarl. I *steal.*"

"Gotta go," Lisa said. And she did.

Sally dropped her Winston on the ground and mashed it with a sneaker.

"Want to hit some?"

"Yeah," I said, "if there's time before the tenement fire."

I won the first set 6–4, but not easily. Not without resorting to my arsenal of cut shots.

We were 5–5 in the second set when it happened.

I had served the first ball.

She hadn't moved.

"Long," she said.

"Long's ass," I had said.

"Long, *buddy,*" she said. "By six inches."

The second serve had been tossed in the air and I was going up with the racquet to put as much cut on it as anyone named Orantes ever had when the garbage hit my head.

The brown paper bag, consisting of coffee grounds, egg shells, orange peels, cigarette butts and soggy, uneaten cereal, struck squarely in my hair and top of my forehead.

I dropped my racquet and put my hands on my hips for a second.

I took an egg shell off my cheek and brushed some coffee grounds out of my hair.

Above and behind me, I heard a blast of Spanish.

A woman was on a balcony shouting at a young Spanish boy who was now running around on the court with a basketball.

I reached down the back of my sweatshirt and got an orange peel.

I looked over at Sally and she had collapsed on the court. She was sitting down, holding her sides, and shaking with laughter.

From the woman on the balcony above I heard more of the idiom of San Juan.

Two black kids double-teamed the Spanish boy with the basketball.

Sally staggered over to the net.

"Want to ace out the garbage? I live pretty close to here," she said.

The answer was yes.

She picked up her canvas shoulder bag, put the cans of balls inside it, and carried both racquets.

This left my hands free to continue raking the Hudson River out of my hair.

We went out the entrance of the Ghetto Racquet Club and turned downtown on Columbus. I hoped we might soon take a left and go as far as Central Park West. From there, I knew it would only be a short dash to the frontier—and freedom.

"I think I'm in a Fellini movie," I said.

"I like it over here," Sally said. "It's a lot more of what New York is really about than those fantasies you TV people put on the air."

"We don't deal in fantasies. Those guys in the mouse caps are real," I said.

"I haven't asked," she said. "Is your car a co-op?"

I kept walking.

"Really," she said. "The West Side is making a comeback."

"So is hepatitis," I said.

"You'll love my apartment," Sally said. "The bathtub's in the kitchen."

I said, "Hamburger Helper on the bookshelves? A radiator that plays Mick Jagger?"

"It's a country of choices," Sally said.

"The oven folds under and becomes a desk. Fire escape with a potted geranium," I said.

"Bromeliad," said Sally.

Ahead of us on the sidewalk a group of teenage kids, and some older, were standing around outside a store front.

"Did you ever live on the West Side?" Sally asked.

"In my youth," I said. "When I first moved up here as an A.D. in News at CBS. I'd come from the oh-and-oh in Philadelphia."

"It's amazing how many people jump to the networks from Philadelphia."

"I know," I said. "That's why I didn't mind leaving Dallas to get to WCAU."

We went past the kids.

"Where on the West Side?"

I said, "On Sixty-seventh, right across from Des Artistes. It was fun at first, but then I found out Chicken Delight only delivered in an armored truck."

I stopped suddenly and said, "Hey! That's my kid back there."

It was. It was Cindy. My sixteen-year-old daughter who lived in Pelham Manor and went to school at Rye Country Day. But she was standing on Columbus Avenue near Ninety-seventh Street in New York City around noon on a Thursday, and I did not know of Easter or any other holiday being moved into the middle of May.

I gave her a holler. She dashed over and we hugged.

She was wearing corduroy pants, Frye boots, and a tapered shirt with the sleeves rolled up to her elbows and the tail out. The boots made her taller. Her hair was long and seriously straight, parted in the center. Her eyes were by Maybelline but they were more surprising than gruesome.

Somehow my precious little virgin dumpling princess looked old enough for voter registration.

If this wasn't a field trip, I asked, what was the story on Gotham?

"Melody and I came in last night to go to the theater. It was for Music Appreciation. We stayed with Melody's aunt."

"No school today?"

"Well, . . . yeah. But I kind of like missed the train. We stayed up really late in the apartment. You know, just talking and stuff, but like really late."

I presumed she had called her mother.

"Not exactly," Cindy said. "I mean, I called her last night when we got back from the theater, but I didn't call this morning when I overslept. I called the school and told them about a sore throat and all. Melody and I were going to take the train straight to Rye and Melody's mother was going to pick us up and take us to school. Like, I guess you could say that's what Mom thinks I did. So if I catch the 3:17 then I'll get home about the same time I get home from school. I would have called Mom after I missed the train, but she would already be at the shrink. Melody's aunt lives in the Dakota."

I noticed down the street that Cooper had come back with the Silver Goblet.

"The Dakota's nowhere near here," I said.

"No, it's way down there," Cindy said. "We came up here to see some friends. Dad, you know Melody, don't you? Melody Foster?"

A few feet away, Melody waved from a group of guys.

"Hi, Mr. Mallory," she said. "Are those coffee grounds in your hair?"

I motioned for Sally Hawks to join us.

"Cindy, this is Sally," I said.

They exchanged hi's.

"Oh, and Dad," Cindy said. "This is Jeff."

I put my hand straight out and Jeff put his straight up, bent from the elbow. I obliged him by interlocking thumbs. I have never known exactly what that kind of handshake meant. I just always supposed that people who used it favored legalized dope, corner jump shots and not prosecuting urban guerrillas.

"Hey, all right," Jeff said, squeezing my hand.

Jeff was about twenty-one. He had blond hair that swept over a bit of his forehead and covered his ears, and it was the kind he could shake into place. He had a dark and well-cared-for mustache and teeth anyone might envy. Strong legs gave his faded jeans their shape. Bare feet were in his leather sandals. He was very well built and deeply tanned—the perfect surfer. His T-shirt said GO FOR IT. I judged the two necklaces he wore to be strung from the rarest of Niihau shells. He was bulletin board handsome. His smile reeked with sincerity and charm, and I was willing to bet that in moments of serious conversation he could manufacture a deeply attractive gaze.

Cindy, no doubt, would have agreed with a thought that came to me immediately. That if Robert Redford and Candy Bergen were to produce a son, he would look like a hunchback leper compared to Jeff.

"What part of California are you from, Jeff?"

It had to be San Diego.

"Near La Jolla," he said.

Close enough.

"But I winter in Hawaii. That's when the big sets hit the north shore on Oahu and Kauai."

"Jeff's a really good surfer," said Cindy. "He was in 'Get Tubed.' "

If it was a documentary, it wasn't in syndication yet.

"Yeah, we were pretty lucky to be out there when they were filming. It was far out. Lucas and Chamberlain and me. We were really stoked on this right curl outside Hanalei."

I asked if any of us had ever seen him on "ABC's Wide World of Sports." The Mokki Pocka championship at Makaha, or whatever it's called.

Jeff looked hurt. Then slightly soulful. Then hurt again.

"That's competition, man," Jeff said. "That's not surfing. Surfing's an art form. Surfing's where you just get it together, man, and you're out there. You're goin' for it. But like, really, you're just out there."

It always looked hard to me, I said. Like trying to stand up on a six-foot-long bar of Ivory.

"Jeff's surfed fifteen- and twenty-footers," Cindy said.

"Radicalness," said Jeff. "Like you can really trip out on a fifteen-footer. It's really radical."

I asked Jeff how he liked the waves on Columbus Avenue.

"I'm stoked, man. This is some town."

Had he been here long?

"About a month. The sets always leave the north shore in April. It was far out. There weren't even any swells over at Acid Drops by Poipu when I left. I've got a friend who's a bartender up here, so I came up to visit for a while. He lives right there."

He pointed at the store front.

"Jeff's a waiter at this place near Lincoln Center that sounds really groovy," Cindy said.

"I'm like mellowed out for the summer," said Jeff. "But when the sets start building up on the north shore in September, I'm back out there, man."

159

Sally Hawks said, "Do you work at Marble Arch Station?"

"Yeah," Jeff said. "Kind of a far-out name for a place but the food's good. I don't know where they got the name."

"I've been in," Sally said, looking at me. "It's really radical."

Cindy said she met Jeff last week when she and Melody came into the city to go to a dance at the Spence School and spend the night with Melody's aunt in the Dakota.

"We could have stayed with you but you were in California," Cindy said.

To Jeff she said, "You ought to see my dad's apartment. He can show movies and everything."

"All *right!*" Jeff said.

I told Cindy I would save her some train fare and run her home to Pelham in the limo.

"Can I sit in front with D.W.C.?"

"You'll sit in the back next to your old daddy. And maybe you'll figure out what you're going to bribe him with not to tell your mother you missed school," I said.

I took Sally aside for a second and said, "I could use some company for dinner. Want to do an Elaine's?"

She gave me an address on Ninety-fourth that was just short of Central Park West. Second floor walkup. The door with the Rita Hayworth poster on it.

Sally said her hair would be dry by 7:57. She handed me my racquet and the can of balls.

I said I hoped she wouldn't object if our game was in Palm Beach.

Cindy took a very good look at Sally, and I took another glance at Jeff.

Then I held Cindy's hand and we strolled toward the limo.

Chapter
Nineteen

~~~~~~

Entering Elaine's that night, Sally and
I plowed through the costumed crowd standing at the
bar in the front. Elaine saw us. We each kissed her
and commented on her new Moroccan jewels.

"The odd couple, huh?" Elaine said, leading us to a
table. "You never know about the pairings in this
joint."

On our way through the room, we couldn't miss the
usual quota of overheards.

"Peter wrote it as a musical and B-17's weren't
supposed to be in it anywhere."

"There's no question the New York critics have got
it in for Dennis Hopper."

"If he gave Styron a quote of *his* book jacket, why
wouldn't he give Larry one?"

"No, you go *past* Sagaponack."

"I'm sorry, but if you've got a skinny, black, bald-
headed model, nobody's going to notice what Halston
is trying to say."

For the fine restaurant and sit-around place that it
is, Elaine's looks no fancier from the outside than a

store where you might go to buy cheese or a bicycle. There is just a small yellow canopy and two plate-glass windows one doorway removed from a corner of Second Avenue and Eighty-eighth Street. I could understand somebody who might not know better wandering in the door of Elaine's to pick out a ficus tree.

When I went there, Cooper and the limo usually got a night off. Cooper always knew I would be late. And Cooper didn't like Elaine's anyway. He said there were too many pussys in there that would take the chrome off a trailer hitch.

Our table was in the rear by the door to the other dining room, Albania, and the johns. The other room was also where Elaine kept a wall decorated with framed book jackets, books written by authors she knew personally. Writers were among Elaine's first customers.

The table by the door was considered by Elaine and most everyone else to be a good place to sit. Anyone worth noticing or speaking to had to glide by eventually to do what a British actor once told me he had to do before his dinner was served. Which was "point old Percy at the procelain." I had dazzled more than one Texas visitor to New York with the sightseeing from that table.

Now Stanley Coffman was sitting there.

"This guy says he's big in commerce and knows you," Elaine said. "I sat him down before he had a chance to meet any royalty."

Stanley's hand was outstretched.

"Put it in the vise, slugger. This the new one?"

I introduced Sally Hawks.

Elaine turned away and dissolved into the chit-chat of art, backgammon and Gstaad.

"Jesus, is this place something?" Stanley said. "A total confectionary Swedish sperm-o sitting over there

162

with a guy in a five and a half shoe. Whole pack of high fashion broads doing three-foot handshakes. How 'bout the guy up front with twenty-eight pockets on the safari coat? Fucking guy's got epaulets on his ankles."

A waiter put drinks in front of Sally and me, and started off.

"Hold it," said Stanley. "The payee gets nervous when there's no backup stinger."

He continued to read the room.

"This fucking place is Homewreckers Anonymous," Stanley said. "I may do a full love shot on the wop chick with the tits. Soon as she gets the old piccata down and the choreographer jumps up to hug another one of those Noras or Glorias, the little Wasp moves in with his dough."

Sally said she took it that Stanley liked Elaine's.

"Yeah, which one's the Fat Lady and which one's the Big E?" Stanley said, roaring.

We had a pleasantly slow and drunken dinner.

"Know why I like mussels?" Stanley said during the appetizer. "They look like a clit."

Stanley went down on a mussel.

"How do you take this place on a regular basis?" Stanley said. "Ought to come up to New Canaan one of these weekends. Little change of scenery. Show you a hell of a mortgage. Couple of shitty kids. Asshole for a wife. We'll have some fucking laughs."

A writer stopped by the table and spoke to Sally.

The writer said he was pretty whipped. He had just finished a long piece for the op-ed page of the *New York Times* on Long Island potato farmers. He said he thought he could expand it into a book, but he was already two books behind with his publisher. One about sex life on the Alaska pipeline. And another about drainage zones in shopping mall developments.

An actor stopped to speak to Stanley and me.

163

He was a handsome, muscular black guy, a former All-American at USC who had become a star in a movie about a pimp who killed four thousand white cops. Being a life-long Trojan, Stanley had been largely responsible for the guy getting into the movies in the first place.

The actor's eyes roamed about the room as he gave us five. He wore a pirate shirt unbuttoned to the waist, and he had a gold object carved into the shape of a ram around his neck. He mentioned that he was getting ready to do another "now thing" on the Coast.

When he had gone, Stanley said, "Jesus, never take a fucking Zulu out of the high jump."

We were then joined at the table by Sally's agent, a young woman named Sybil Kafka Aynesworth.

Sybil Kafka Aynesworth ordered a glass of white wine and refused to look at Stanley or me.

Sybil Kafka Aynesworth asked Sally if she was interested in dashing off to Detroit to do a quickie profile for *People* on the happiest couple in data processing. Sally said no.

The agent asked if Sally cared to do a food piece on Cuban restaurants in Miami for Eastern Airlines' in-flight magazine. Sally said no.

Sybil Kafka Aynesworth wondered if Sally was interested in $750 and expenses to speak to a creative writing group at the University of West Virginia. Sally said fuck no.

Sally asked if Sybil Kafka Aynesworth had made any progress in peddling the foreign rights to her best-selling book. England? France? Nigeria, perhaps?

Sybil Kafka Aynesworth said she expected Sally's book to be published in at least forty foreign languages. There were nibbles everywhere, she said. Not only that, Hollywood had sort of become "unsprung." There was a renewed interest in three of the chapters. By four studios.

164

Sally asked Sybil Kafka Aynesworth why there was $678.47 worth of Xerox, telephone and messenger charges deducted from her last royalty check.

Sybil Kafka Aynesworth said she had to run. She asked where Sally could be reached tomorrow in case she got the good news she was expecting from Hollywood or London.

Sally said she would be sacking groceries at the A&P in the morning, and working in the gift-wrap department at Korvettes in the afternoon.

When the agent left, I asked Sally why Sybil Kafka Aynesworth was still her agent.

"What's wrong with Sybil?" Sally said. "She doesn't criticize my work and she returns my calls. You don't know much about literary agents, do you?"

After a while, I think the J&B was starting to take effect because I did Cary Grant's dog. Bee-ow, way-ow, wow.

I pointed out to Sally that she was no longer that funny, awkward little girl I knew. Overnight there'd been a breathless change in her.

She said that was because she was going to live, love, laugh a lot. Light her candle and burn a lot.

"I'm gonna write a show for you and we can put it on right here in Seaport," I said.

She said fine. Just put a star on the chart 'cause the song was coming from her heart.

"What's that you're humming?" I said.

"Oh, it's just a little something of my own." Sally smiled.

Stanley said, "Who the fuck am I, Polly Benedict?"

Sally looked across the table at Stanley, sipped her drink, and said, "You've come to Nottingham once too often."

I reached over and hugged Sally.

She said, "Take your mitts off me, screw."

Stanley said, "Jesus, both of you do me a favor. Don't fart."

Sally said to me, "He doesn't care. You think he cares about the guilt of Janet Ames? You think he's even inquisitive about the strange loves of Martha Ivers?"

"He's read the file on Thelma Jordan," I said.

"Sure," said Sally. "But he wasn't at the trial of Lydia Bailey. He hasn't called Nora Prentiss or Daisy Kenyon or Ruby Gentry or Esther Costello in weeks."

Stanley got up and told a waiter to "lay the old l'addition" on him.

I said Sally and I weren't leaving yet.

"Victor, don't go to the underground meeting tonight," Sally said to Stanley.

"I'll get the check up to here," Stanley said. "You can start a new one for the small talk."

He said he was going to take a run on the Junior League at the bar. "If you don't see me again, you'll know I found a lippy bubble gummer who likes it in the ass," he said.

The check came and Stanley glanced at it. "Jesus Christ, I didn't know I broke a fucking window."

Stanley walked toward the bar.

Sally and I agreed that we definitely needed another cocktail.

I asked Sally what she thought of my precious little virgin dumpling princess—my daughter.

"She's kind of spiffy. What's she interested in?"

"Everything," I said. "Books, sports, music, drama. I think surfing's about to move up."

"It could be worse," Sally said. "Jeff could be the first bionic guru. He could tell her about the Perfectly Enlightened Human Being in India."

I said, "And all about the harmony, purification and profound love that shines forth as pure light—if you get down with God."

166

"It happens," Sally said. "A lot of virgin dumplings get laid back with the Lord—and pregnant."

"Don't they usually wind up stoned on hash, sitting on a hill somewhere learning to play the sitar?"

She said, "Some of them change their name to Hsiao-ch'u, which means the taming power of the small, by the way. Then their hearts get purified out of sight. Really radical."

"Then?"

"Then they screw a lot and give their inheritance to the eighteen-year-old guru with a terminal hard-on."

Sally said she had done a piece on it once.

Compared to what she had just described, I said a surfer who had never heard of Marble Arch Station was not so bad.

"What is she, sixteen?" Sally said. "It's time to like boys better than field hockey, that's all."

J&B and me and Sally decided that Cindy was going to be plenty okay.

"I guess I haven't bothered to mention that I think you're not so terrible a writer," I said.

"Did you read my book?"

"As a matter of fact, I did. I liked the way you put it together. I'd read most of it before in magazines, but you gave it a point of view and it worked."

"It did very well," she said. "Collections usually don't."

"Ever think of doing a script?"

"I write *about* TV. Remember?"

"You could do a script with one hand while you were yodeling. And you could write about all those things women are interested in. Rape, abortion, venereal disease."

"Those are things men *say* women are interested in."

"That's because men are pretty much interested in love," I said.

167

"Poets are interested in love," Sally said. "By the way, is this the move?"

I laughed and realized I was sitting very close to her. In fact, our arms were touching.

"Women poets jump off bridges," I said, straightening up a little. "Women novelists wear tweed pants under a smock. Women TV writers eat breakfast at poolside."

She said, "You TV biggies don't have everything, you know. There's an ugly rumor going around, for instance, that your limo doesn't even serve buttered popcorn."

"I thought we said we owed ourselves another drink?" I said.

"We did," said Sally, rattling the ice in the bottom of her glass.

I looked around for a waiter and saw a Nicholson, an Altman and two Pacinos. A Bisset, maybe three Welches, and a Gifford.

And then I saw Thurlow Watts and Larry Travers. They stormed the table.

"Try this, Frank," said Watts, who was wearing a jellaba. "The principle character's with the IRS, but he's human. The world's first audit guy with a heart of gold. I call it 'Kaplan,' but that can be changed. Larry likes 'Pencil Man.' He says with 'Kaplan' we're stuck with a Hebe IRS hero and the demographics won't dance."

Travers wore carpenter's pants, a rubber snorkeling top, and a wreath around his head like Julius Caesar.

"Kaplan works in the field, right? So every week he does an audit in a different home. One week he exposes a maniac industrialist selling weapons to a foreign power. The next, he grabs an upholsterer bilking old ladies."

Watts said, "He never investigates a writer. That's do-do."

"His supervisor's a dame, like it?" said Travers. "I say we keep her as a principal and she looks like Dunaway. Thurlow says we kill her in a speedboat and she looks like cabbage."

Sally went to the john.

"Doesn't matter," said Watts. "Every week, Kaplan winds up filing an amended return for the mark. Something that tips the Feds. Like he puts the deductions in the depreciations, and he puts the depreciations where the deductions belong."

Travers said, "It blows out all the computers in Washington, and they swoop down like the chimps on Weissmuller."

Watts said, "I say it's dynamite. Larry says it's iffy. What do you think, Frank?"

I said it seemed to me they were still flying through some choppy air. They ought to change altitudes. Maybe sound out the passengers in the coach section.

"Got you," said Travers. "I'm glad you're sitting down. Here's the real killer. A show called—get this—'Cheat Stakes.' "

Sally came back and smoked.

Travers said, "I don't mind saying when I thought of it, I felt like the oilman in the dentist's chair who said, 'Keep drilling, I feel lucky.' 'Cheat Stakes' is America."

"All the ways for a guy to slip out of the house," Watts said. "Right now, we call him Ted and he works at the bank. Each week, Jane Ann, the hag, almost catches him. But he wriggles out with a story that the waitress wanted to discuss a personal loan in a motel."

"The hag keeps buying it—like true life—Ted cooks spaghetti al pesto, shoots baskets with the kids, and he's home free again. Next week, the manicurist. Sometimes he likes 'em old."

Watts and Travers stayed awhile longer. Then they said they had to go outside and look at the Chinese hospital. The Chinese hospital was an old apartment building on Eighty-eighth with balconies that made it look very strange when you smoked the appropriate herb.

They never returned.

Which was fine because by now there was nobody left at Elaine's but the hard stayers. Stanley had apparently scored. Daylight was about to crawl through the front windows and make your last glass of Scotch look like something in a black cape with a disfigured face.

I had sketched my four-napkin ranch.

Sally and Elaine were studying it.

"From this part here, you can see all around Taos," I said. "From that part there, you can see all the way to Crested Butte."

Sally said, "I can't envision someone like you retiring to a ranch. Even one like this."

"I wouldn't be retiring. Up there in the mountains with the animals and the Indians? I'd be the dirt mogul."

Elaine said, "When can I come riding?"

"Anytime," I said. "Here, I'll turn the whole place over to you."

I scooped up the napkins and put them in front of Elaine. I stood up and helped Sally stand up.

"Invite Ethel and the kids," I told Elaine.

Then Sally and I limped outside to do something really radical. Look for a taxi.

Chapter
Twenty

~~~~~~~~~~~~~~~~~~~~~~~~~~~~~~~~~~~

A day later I caught up with Hank Judson, America's most believable anchorman, at his hang-out bar a few minutes after the network news left the air. Hank went to the same bar near the office five nights a week, unless he was out of town to interview a world leader.

Hank always stood at the corner of the bar with his right shoulder against the wall. He would drink four or five martinis, straight-up, in about an hour, and play the match game with the boys, before a limo driver came in to deliver Hank to his apartment at the United Nations Plaza. CBC sent Hank a limo from a rental service, so the driver often was a stranger in uniform who would enter the bar and loudly say, "Mr. Judson?"

"With you in a moment, my friend," Hank Judson would say. Then he would turn to the bartender and say, "Chico, seeing as it is National Daffodil Day, I had best have a grand final."

Usually Hank Judson left the bar after the grand final martini. Sometimes he would have a grand-grand final, and then an *el último,* and then a "sleep-through." Three or four times a year, Hank would drink several "sleep-throughs," move on to a few "territorial imperatives" and wind up "on the beach," as he put it.

I said hello to the guys around the bar and they made room for me in Hank's corner.

"Ho, Mallory!" Hank said. "Chico, dear chap, could I buy my friend Mallory a drink?"

We drank and played the match game with the guys at the bar for an hour or so. In the match game each player conceals in his fist anywhere from none to three matches. The object is to guess the total number of matches. Hank Judson had learned the match game when he was a radio correspondent for CBC in London twenty-five years ago. Chase Morgan, our vice president for News, estimated that learning the match game had cost Hank Judson close to $100,000.

Hank did his grand-grand final and his *el último* and his first "sleep-through" and was about eighty dollars winner in the matches when the game broke up. The rent-a-limo driver in uniform leaned against the wall by the check stand. Hank and I got private and I told him what I wanted him to do on "Just Up the Street."

He studied a bowl of cheese crackers on the bar as he listened. When I had finished, Hank tinked his glass with a fingernail so Chico would set up a second "sleep-through."

"This is a little out of line, Mallory," Hank Judson said.

"You can make this show work for us, Hank," I said.

"I mean it is out of line to approach me about it in a saloon. You're talking an air-time thing. You're not asking me for a personal favor, like having lunch with your father-in-law from Houston. You're asking me

172

to work live on camera for three hours in a show that could hurt my image. I've heard about this blasted thing around the shop. Because I'm tasting a sleep-through, Mallory, don't think I'm so drunk I'll agree to spend three hours on the air looking like a fool."

"Hank, you're a News man. Look at this as a News show," I said. "What is news? It's what people do. News is people, Hank," I said.

"Mallory, please, I don't appreciate that kind of pep talk," Hank Judson said. "You're prime-time, dear fellow. I'm News. You were News yourself long enough to know how we look at you prime-time blokes."

"I promise this will be News," I said.

Hank smiled and said, "What people do at home on an ordinary Wednesday night is not network News."

"I want you to do this," I said.

"Then you *are* calling in a favor," Hank said.

If he wanted to look at it like that, I decided to let him. He was probably talking about something that had happened in Saigon. We got drunk in the Caravelle bar one night when Hank's interview with a world leader had just been canceled in reaction to a CBC–TV editorial comment written by Harley O. Chambers himself. Though dressed in fancier language, what the editorial said was that little yellow people had gone through ten thousand years of so-called civilization without inventing electricity and could hardly be expected to understand a modern world ruled by pocket calculators.

I cleared Hank's way back into the palace by calling in a favor from a Saigon politician who would have been shot if I had even attempted to do a CBS News piece on what I knew about him. It may sound like a violation of the principles of competitive journalism, but news guys often help rival news guys who are in trouble.

"I'm asking you to do it," I said to Hank in the bar. "Think of it as the Rose Bowl parade."

"I think of it as prime time," Hank said.

"I need you, Hank. It's a favor," I said.

Hank Judson placed his empty glass on the bar for Chico to refill.

"I'll do it for you," Hank said. "I hate to see a colleague—and I still think of you as a colleague, Mallory—in a hot spot with the brass."

"Appreciate it, Hank," I said.

"Glad to help. Tell me more about it," Hank said.

We talked about the show. It would have been out of line to mention Hank's special fee in a saloon. The next day at the office, the fee turned out to be $15,000.

You could look at that as about $850 for Hank Judson for each minute "Just Up the Street" would be on the air. And you could consider that during most of those minutes, Hank Judson would be sitting in our Manhattan studio watching television.

Or on the other hand you could call it prime time.

Chapter
Twenty-one

~~~~~~~~~~~~~~~~~~~~~~~~~~~~~~~~

I was spending an evening at home when the blue phone rang.

Cooper had gone to look at an apartment for him and Katherine, who was still singing on the Left Coast. He hadn't asked if Katherine could move into the penthouse. And I hadn't suggested it.

I was sitting in the den with André the cat in my lap. Dump and Ling, the Yorkies, were out on a terrace barking at airplanes. The networks occupied three of my small screens and the educational channel the other. The larger four-foot Sonys were programmed like this: *It Happened One Night,* Gable and Colbert; a new Hollywood musical; a tape of a tennis instructional; and a CBS sitcom.

I looked up and saw the educational channel was showing a special on space travel. I like space travel, so I switched the space show to a large Sony, killing the tennis.

On the table beside my chair were a bacon, lettuce and tomato sandwich with plenty of mayonnaise,

175

a quart of chocolate milk and a Colombian joint rolled to the size of a panatela.

On the same table were a half dozen scripts for pilots and TV movies.

I had my shoes off and my feet up on a hassock. The door to the den terrace was open, and I could see lights in the buildings far across the park.

You might say I was a fairly happy man at that moment.

Then the blue phone rang.

I looked at it. The number of the blue phone was unlisted. It was such a private number that most of the time I couldn't remember it myself.

I said, "Sorry, André." André had to get off my lap so I could walk over to the bookcase and pick up the blue phone.

"Hello?" I said.

"Frank, I'm worried about Cindy," Marcie said.

"What's wrong? Where is she?" I said.

"In her room."

"Is she sick?" I said.

"No."

"Then what's the matter?" I said.

"Have you noticed her development?" Marcie said.

"What are you talking about, Marcie?"

"Frank, that girl is developing enormous breasts," Marcie said.

"Come on, Marcie. They're not enormous. They're just very pretty," I said.

"Then you have noticed them," Marcie said.

"What's wrong with that?" I said.

"Don't be defensive. I'm not accusing you of anything," Marcie said. "I suppose compared to those movie stars you run around with, Marcie's breasts don't qualify as enormous. But for the Rye Country Day School, they are regarded as more than ample."

"Some of those young Jewish girlfriends of hers have got bigger tits than Cindy," I said.

"You do observe them pretty closely, don't you?" Marcie said.

"Marcie, I'm busy. Can you move along to whatever the problem is?" I said.

I took the blue phone on its long cord back to my chair and sat down. André at once hopped onto my stomach and began purring.

"Do you know how many times I've heard you say Marcie, I'm busy, what's the problem? That's what you told me the night Cindy was born," Marcie said.

"That's another story you tell about me that is not exactly true," I said. "Besides, I was covering Hurricane Beulah that night and was up to my armpits in a flood when I called you at the hospital."

"You didn't call me, you called Cooper," she said.

"I was calling you," I said. "A good friend happened to be there with you, because I couldn't be."

"Liar," she said.

"I was floating in a telephone booth down the street from the goddam Galvez Hotel," I said.

"No, you weren't. You were at the Galveston police station when you called," Marcie said. "And you did say you were busy when I got on the phone—*after* Cooper."

"It was a fucking hurricane!" I said.

"It was also the night a baby girl was born. A girl who's had to grow up practically without a father. Because her father was usually busy or out of town or both," Marcie said. "Well, let me tell you something that might turn your head around. Did you know the girls with weak or neglectful fathers are the ones most likely to be promiscuous?"

"Is Fornet over there? Has he been telling you this shit?" I said.

"Dr. Fornet doesn't come around any more. You

fixed that by pushing him into the rose bushes. After that, Frankie just laughed at the poor man and wouldn't listen to a word he said," Marcie said. "I don't need Regis to tell me everything. I can read books, and I can interpret what I have seen in my life. Regis wasn't my analyst, anyway. He was Frankie's. My analyst is Dr. Milligan."

I could tell Marcie was anxious, and it was starting to make me anxious.

"Frank, do you know how old I was the first time we made love together?" Marcie said.

"Sixteen," I said.

Lord, could that be true? I thought back and, yeah, it was true. Marcie's freshman year at the University of Texas. She had been double-promoted twice at Lamar High School in Houston. In college she never made anything below a B, and few of those. She could tell you a lot of facts about the Battle of Tours and how *Die Fledermaus* came to be written. But nobody asked her those things except on exams.

Sixteen. Lord, at sixteen Marcie's body was already a joy and a wonder. The first time we made love was behind a hedge at the far end of the intramural field, and I got her back to Littlefield dorm fifteen minutes past the 10 P.M. curfew. Which meant she couldn't go out at night again for thirty days. The first time we made love with all our clothes off was at a moonlight picnic on Mt. Bonnell. Marcie was slim and brown and had a body that I got dizzy looking at. And she was so young then.

Just about exactly as young as Cindy was right now, as a matter of fact.

"Marcie, I understand what you're saying," I said.

"What's that?" Marcie said.

"Cindy is pregnant," I said.

"Of course that's not what I'm saying. I'm sure Cindy is still a virgin," Marcie said.

178

"Like you were?" I said.

Marcie said, "You know there'd been only one other boy before you. And I was lucky to have a very strong, supportive father who gave me the security not to feel I had to make love to boys to gain their approval."

"And you were eighteen when we got married," I said, growing more alarmed, thinking about Cindy. "Are you sure Cindy is still in her room? She hasn't slipped out any place?"

"Frank, don't be silly," Marcie said.

I said, "Well, goddam, you call me up and suggest Cindy is screwing her way across Westchester County, and I'm not supposed to be worried about it?"

"I only suggested that Cindy is growing up and needs guidance," Marcie said.

"So we should call off the divorce and I should move back home?" I said.

"Certainly not," Marcie said.

"Then Cindy should come live with me?" I said.

"Frank, they would have to shoot me dead before I would allow that," Marcie said.

"What are you proposing, for god's sake?" I said.

"I am trying to tell you, in a gentle way, that Cindy hinted tonight, with Frankie sitting right here at the table, that perhaps she might go to the doctor and be fitted for an I.U.D.," Marcie said.

And Marcie started crying.

"I can't help it," Marcie said. "I can't help crying."

"If she thinks she needs an I.U.D., let her get one," I said weakly.

"Do you know if they'd had I.U.D.'s when I was Cindy's age, and if I'd had one, I probably never would have married you, and there wouldn't be a Cindy or a Frankie?" Marcie sobbed.

Marcie said wait just a minute, and she put down the phone.

Then she picked it up again and said, "I've got to go now. Rex is here. He knows how upset I am, and he's offered to take me to that little Italian restaurant in Mamaroneck."

"Rex, the tennis pro?" I said.

Around the club he was nicknamed Rex the Wonder Horse.

"I do have to run," Marcie said. "Bye-bye."

I thought about Rex the Wonder Horse for a minute.

Then I thought about Marcie's strong, supportive father. He was named Herbert. Herbert Gaines. He made a lot of money in construction. Among other things, Herbert's company built hundreds of roadside toilets. Marcie and her mother and her three sisters would stand in front of Herbert and talk about him like he wasn't there.

They would say, let's trick Daddy into buying a new Cadillac. He would blink and grin and buy a new Cadillac.

One year they said, let's trick Daddy into taking us and all of our husbands, kids and boyfriends to Aspen for skiing every Christmas.

I went to Aspen once with Marcie and her family before we were married. I also went to Aspen with Marcie and her family for the first two years we were married, and again on about the eighth year, and again on a total fluke on or about the fourteenth year.

One person you would almost never see around Aspen at Christmas was Herbert Gaines. He would have a big dinner the first night with the wife and the girls and the grandchildren and the husbands and boyfriends. The girls would laugh and say, look we tricked Daddy again this year. Then Herbert would get an emergency call and have to catch a plane. The girls would say, what a shame something comes up and Daddy has to work every Christmas. Then I started having to work nearly every Christmas. Except I really

180

did, for a long time. Maybe Herbert did too. The only words he said to me in his life were, "Har Yew, Frank?"

Anyway, after talking to Marcie I didn't care to watch my eight-screen lashup any more. I went upstairs and went to sleep. André slept on the pillow beside my head.

Chapter
Twenty-two

〰〰〰〰〰〰〰〰〰〰〰〰〰〰〰〰〰〰〰〰〰〰〰

We had the four families for "Just Up the Street."

Arleene thought the news called for a celebration so she gave me an extra English muffin with my morning coffee.

Jack Nathanson had phoned in from Rochester to say that he had approved of, and firmed up, the last family. As it happened, we managed to get all four families we wanted from the list of candidates supplied by the research department.

"I don't know," Arleene said. "Just because you're going to have actual human beings on the telecast instead of astronauts, that still doesn't mean you've got a fighting chance."

"Probably not," I said. "But it beats the hell out of pictures of living room furniture."

Arleene and I discussed the families who had agreed to let us string cable across their lawns, mount cameras in their homes, and wire them for sound.

In Rochester we had recruited Ralph and Ann Getz, who had a pretty teenage daughter named Roxie. Ralph worked for Xerox, and Ann worked for Kodak. Mr. Getz wasn't all that happy with the idea, but Mrs.

Getz had pushed it. Evidently her thinking was that this could be a show biz break for Roxie, who had all the requirements to become a future beauty queen.

"Thank god for stage mothers," Arleene said.

We had a black couple in Akron. Mr. and Mrs. Franklin Lincoln Perry. He was a foreman at the Goodyear tire plant. Pearl Perry taught school. Nathanson said they were good-natured and irresistible and promised to do something like charcoal steaks in the backyard and invite some friends over, if the weather was nice.

In Washington, D.C., we would be going to the Georgetown area and the townhouse of Bob and Dorothea Skidmore. The Skidmores looked like an attractive couple in their gloss photographs. They were in their mid-thirties and they had four children, all under the age of six. Bob Skidmore was a lawyer-lobbyist in Washington for a Houston oil company.

"It would be helpful if Dorothea Skidmore considered herself a rising young hostess in the power center," Arleene said.

Tampa was the prize. A plumber.

The plumber was Angie Rocco. A tough, self-made guy, he figured to be the least camera shy of all our subjects. Carmen, the wife, was considered the gourmet cook of their neighborhood. They had a son, Mario, who was practically grown.

Nathanson advised me that Carmen Rocco guaranteed such a spread on the dinner table for the show our remote directors would break down her door to get at the pasta.

"It would be fun if you could surprise the Big Guy with the plumber," Arleene said.

"It'll leak. Herb Grank has stoolies everywhere," I said.

"That reminds me," Arleene said. "You're supposed to see Grant before lunch."

I told Arleene our celebration over the four families had been rather short-lived, I thought.

The armed guard at the elevator bank on the thirty-fourth floor said, "Good morning, Mr. Mallory." Then he asked to see my I.D. card.

I took the part of the card which had not been worn away from carrying it in a money clip and held it up to the guard. On the card you could still see the left side of my face and read portions of my social security and employee numbers.

"Ought to go down to the fourteenth floor and get yourself a new card, Mr. Mallory. They can do it for you in five minutes," the guard said.

I was walking away when I said, "Don't forget, George. Whenever you get a psychotic assassin up here with a deer rifle, give News a call. They can have a camera crew on the scene in no time."

The thirty-fourth floor of the Chambers building was always ominously quiet and empty except for an aging receptionist, bent over the crossword in the *Times*.

Once past the armed guard, if you walked straight ahead as far as you could go, you would crash through a wall of glass and drop into midtown Manhattan like a Shriner.

If you turned left, you would enter an area I can only describe as part office suite, part museum and part Macy's Thanksgiving Day parade.

These were the quarters belonging to the Big Guy. Only he was hardly ever there. When the Big Guy wasn't home on his Connecticut estate, which was bigger than San Francisco—and known throughout the company as the Sanitarium—he was off on some sort of trip.

The Big Guy had a private, converted DC-10 I had seen once. Inside it, among other things, was a nine-hole Poly-Turf putting green.

Recently, the Big Guy had taken to going to Bangkok a lot, we understood.

"I know what he does," Stanley Coffman said. "He gets over there with his generals and admirals, and they all get naked on the plane. They run in a few little chink girlies. They hold the Far Eastern Regional Lick-Off, and the tired old fucker who squeals the loudest wins the gold-plated putter."

In the Big Guy's wing on the thirty-fourth floor, you could wander in and out of all kinds of rooms on thick carpet. The rooms were as spacious as a sculpture garden. They all had huge display cases filled with artifacts.

In the cases were old drilling bits, printing presses, paper scrolls, radio control boards, crystal sets, adding machines, ships' wheels, microphones, mortar shells, sun helmets, swords, jeweled crowns, model airplanes, Academy Award Oscars, dollhouses, anchors, spotlights, hand grenades, shepherds' crooks, consoles, TV sets, cavalry hats, machine guns, movie cameras and cash registers.

I think one day I saw a display case with nothing in it but the first experimental prophylactic.

If you turned to the right after leaving the elevator, you entered a long corridor of oil paintings largely depicting battle scenes. Then came a rotunda of fountains. Then an archway leading to the executive dining room.

If you went almost all the way to the end of the floor in that direction, you would come upon an Egyptian mummy propped up in a chair wearing a Princeton tie. That would be Herb Grant's male secretary.

Grant's office was impressive but it was nothing to send anyone sneaking around gathering up proxies.

Grant said to me, "I asked you to stop by, old man, because I wanted to chat about Juts."

"What?"

" 'Just Up the Street,' " he said. "I'm getting ready

to dictate my weekly report to the Big Guy and I wanted to be brought up to date."

Had he spoken to Jack Nathanson?

"Missed him by a day in Tampa," Grant said. "Missed him by a few hours in Washington. His secretary thinks he might be in Rochester tonight."

I said Jack worked too hard.

"Zeroed in on your targets yet?"

I said we had some subjects who were beginning to arouse our interest.

"The budget on this thing makes me cringe. What can you tell me about it that might help us sell some participations?" Grant said.

I said I thought the network was gladly going to sustain it.

"We are," Grant said. "Nothing wrong with trying to make a buck, though. Just thought I might be able to get old Styve Butler into a couple of tighteners at The Numbers and maybe pay for a few coats of paint. Can't hide your shingle when you're running fourth in prime time."

Grant lit a Vantage blue and unfastened his blazer.

"Coffee?"

"Black," I said.

Grant called to his secretary.

"Two cups of java, Blakey!"

Then he said, "I know you don't worry much about sales. We've been over that. But somebody has to play a tune on the old cash register or you can forget about making cherry sodas."

Grant's office had a clubby look to it. Old wood and leather, class pictures and pennants. The kind of room where the America's Cup could be left overnight for safekeeping.

He said, "It's not as simple as the old days when all we had to do was sell homes. Hell, nobody buys homes any more."

Blakey brought the coffee.

One thing I knew about Blakey. Whatever might be said of him, you could never mistake him for the guy who caught the winning pass against Yale.

"No, sir," Grant said. "Now they've got a study that tells them everything. Homes, viewers, women, kids, urbans, rural, old geezers. Who are you reaching? How many? When?"

He looked at his coffee cup.

"Know how to peddle this heartburn?" he said. "You find out what hours of the day and night the most dames between eighteen and forty-nine are watching the old tube. If the show you're buying skews old, you better be selling funeral plots. If it skews young, you better be selling toothpaste. If it skews eighteen to forty-nine, you can sell coffee."

Why didn't Herb Grant, I thought to myself, go skew himself?

"You know who had it knocked?" Grant said. "The guys at the place you came from. Back in the fifties and sixties the CBS boys sold from a damn priority list. I was with Doodle and Wimple then. You wanted to get your product on "Lucy" or "Godfrey," you had twelve or fifteen guys ahead of you."

I said I remembered some of the CBS people in those days standing around Toots Shor's discussing their yachts.

Grant said, "Well, if you can't tell me anything about the families, you can at least let me in on what you've worked out with the commentators."

I said I'd had no problems with Chase Morgan. Chase Morgan was the head of News for CBC. We were old friends and competitors. Chase had let me have Jack Nathanson in the first place as a director-producer. He understood my problems.

I gave Grant the rundown on the commentators. For a small fortune and the promise that I would never make such a request of them again, our four top Washington guys had agreed to handle the on-the-scene commentary. Jerry Cummings would be in Rochester. He covered the Pentagon. Rod DeRoache would be in Akron. He was our White House man. Tom Parsons would stay home and do Georgetown. He worked on Capitol Hill. And Robert Lewis would go to Tampa. Lewis followed the Secretary of State or whatever was hot outside the other beats.

Hank Judson was the anchorman, of course.

I said, "The only problem you ever have with commentators when you're working live is that they can't surrender the mike without a slice of their heart going with it. But it won't hurt anything if they're gabby in this case. We may need the fill."

"Hank will give it some dignity," Grant said. "He outrated Cronkite in the last affection study I saw."

I started for the door.

"Live remotes worry me," Grant said. "Never know when the audio might pick up something unfamilylike. Wouldn't want to call in a favor from Styve Butler and sell him, and then see us embarrassed by anything indecent on the air."

"Now that you mention it, there is one segment Styve might want to buy for Budweiser," I said. "We've found this typical American neighborhood where the mosquitoes are big enough to fuck turkeys. And there's this lovable old guy named Uncle Griff who has a habit of sitting on his front steps with a bottle of beer. We hope to come in close on him just when he says, 'Amy Jo, I believe it's hotter tonight than a preacher's prick in a mare's ass.'"

As I went out past Blakey, I noticed him looking at me as if he had just seen a live squid in his paella.

Chapter
Twenty-three

〰〰〰〰〰〰〰〰〰〰〰〰〰〰〰〰

Sally had been working for several days on a magazine piece about feminist politics for *The Atlantic Monthly*. She sounded tired on the phone. So I invited her over to the penthouse duplex to adore my eight screens and fondle my J&B.

I had invited Sally to the apartment at least every other day since our first dinner at Elaine's. But she said the invitation could be construed as an attempt to exercise undue influence on her performance as a television critic.

Then she would laugh to let me know that wasn't the reason she wouldn't come.

But this time she said, "Okay, Jack. Maybe we can pick up a couple of broads later."

Cooper dropped me at the Park Street entrance just before six and drove on down to the Village to see if he could catch the thief who had been stealing the nails out of the walls at the yet-to-open-increasingly-costly C&W nightclub.

Chester the doorman said, "A Miss Hawks was here. She'll be back in half an hour."

"Thanks, Chester," I said.

"She's a good looker. I fall for tinted glasses every time," Chester said.

Up in the penthouse, I hit the control box and lined up a spectacular array of news broadcasts. Then I fed André and Dump and Ling in the kitchen. I returned to the den and took Sally's book off a shelf. Pouring myself a cocktail, I looked at Sally's picture on the book jacket.

In a book jacket photograph the author is usually gazing across the Bosporus Sea with a look of wistful arrogance. Sally was photographed at her *New York* magazine desk, looking straight at the camera, with a cup of coffee in one hand. The biography underneath the picture said she was born in California and had attended Barnard. It said she wrote about a wide range of topics for a number of publications. That's all. Not a word about her Southern California backhand.

Sending Back the Entrée was the title of Sally's book. There was an essay on the portrayal of women in films of the forties, a profile on Leni Riefenstahl and these fun days in Berlin, and a discussion of how a woman could explain to her friends that she had just bought a garter belt.

The book had an interview with an African general as he lay dying on his palace grounds during a rocket attack. Sally had gone to Africa on assignment from *Sports Illustrated* to do a story on the village life of a woman who had won four Olympic gold medals. Being Sally, she had wound up at a coup.

Among the eighteen pieces in the book, only two dealt with TV, both of them expanded versions of the TV columns she wrote under contract for *New York* magazine. She wrote twenty TV columns a year. I thought maybe she got a touch too vicious in the TV pieces. But the reporting was as good as you could find anywhere.

I admit I was not disappointed in Sally's reaction to my eight-screen lashup.

When I showed her the TV den, she said, "I want it."

Sally uttered cries of delight and looked at eight newscasts while I brought her a J&B and also the copy of *Sending Back the Entrée* and a pen.

Contrary to the usual approach, I didn't stick my hand in Sally's pants. What I did was ask for her autograph.

She took the book but didn't sign it. She stared at the eight screens. I showed her how to work the control box.

"I wanted this the minute I was born, but I didn't know it until now," she said.

"Watch this," I said.

Deftly I operated knobs and switches and buttons.

And suddenly on the four large Sony screens we could see *Paths of Glory, Viva Zapata, The Maltese Falcon,* and *Yankee Doodle Dandy*.

"Frank, you big lug," she said.

I opened the cabinet doors and showed her the film library. She looked at the titles on the neatly stacked discs and tapes.

She said, "Okay, I'm yours. Fuck me."

It is hard to believe, but up till then Sally and I had not even kissed. It occurred to me that if I lifted my glass, twitched my lip and said, "Here's looking at you, kid," she might lapse into a dream sequence and dance across furniture and onto the terrace.

I thought if I just put my arms around her, we might fall in love.

So I kissed her. After a minute, she stepped away and said, "I didn't mean right this minute."

I myself was what you might call rocked by the feel of her.

It was very quiet while she sipped her drink.

"Why don't we sort of ease into it?" she said.

"I can wait," I said. Barely.

Chester the doorman buzzed me and said Mrs. Mallory was on her way up with Frankie and a gentleman.

Swell.

Sally laughed at the timing and said she was going back to her apartment to type some more about feminist politics.

"Don't leave," I said. "They won't stay long. Marcie probably wants to drop Frankie here while she's out with the gentleman. I'll put the kid straight to bed. No, I'll send him to El Morocco."

"I don't want to be in the middle of one of these marriage things," Sally said.

"I won't let them in. I'll block the door with my body," I said.

I had forgotten that Frankie had a key to the penthouse.

I was more or less blocking Sally with my body when Frankie opened the door behind me and let in Marcie and a tall man with swatches of white hair that mixed at the temples with a whooping head of black curly European hair.

"Hi, Dad," Frankie said.

"Hi, Frankie," I said.

We all looked at each other for a moment. The tall man wore a three-piece pinch-waisted suit that cost about six hundred dollars if you bought it in Rome. He smiled and put out his hand.

"Mr. Mallory, I am the doctor of your wife, Marcie," he said. "I am the doctor of her mind and a student of her mind. A curious thing, is it not?"

"Your name is not Milligan," I said.

"I am Dr. Bertolucci," he said. He smiled at Sally. "I hope we are not being awkward."

"Dr. Fernando Bertolucci?" Sally said.

192

"The same, I am afraid," he said.

"I'm Sally Hawks. I did a magazine story on your wife," Sally said.

"Ah, of course! The famous journalist Sally Hawks! What a pleasure!" Dr. Bertolucci said.

"This is Marcie and this is Frankie," I said to finish up the introductions.

I asked if I could offer them a drink.

"Yes, to be sure, you are most kind. An opportunity to discuss with the famous Sally Hawks is not to be passed lightly," Dr. Bertolucci said.

Dr. Bertolucci walked into the living room.

"How charming. What a marvelous view of the city. How clean the air up here," he said.

Marcie and Frankie followed him.

"He's a big international society psychiatrist whose specialty is rich women," Sally said. "He's married to Greta Thrisch, the ballerina who defected from Czechoslovakia."

"Please don't leave me," I said.

"Are you kidding? You think I'd miss this?" Sally said.

I poured drinks at the marble-top bar in the living room. Dr. Fernando Bertolucci opened the sliding glass door and walked onto the terrace. He spread his arms and stuck out his chest and breathed like he was sucking in the air at Madonna di Campiglia. I hate to think what tiny creatures flew down his throat.

Dump and Ling rushed in yapping.

"Thanks for the warning, guys," I said to the dogs.

Marcie had not yet said a word. She fiddled with her pearls, smiled coldly at Sally and asked for vodka. Polish vodka out of the freezer and over the rocks.

"Now, then," I said when we all had drinks. Dr. Bertolucci had arranged himself on the couch beside Sally, and Marcie still stood by the bar. "Now, I suppose Marcie and Dr. Bertolucci are on their way to a working dinner, heh, heh, and Frankie's going to spend the evening with his dad."

"Your supposition is dead wrong," Marcie said. "We *were* going out to dinner, yes, Dr. Bertolucci and I. As you can see, Cindy isn't with us."

I said I couldn't see Cindy anywhere.

"Where is she?" Marcie said.

"How would I know?" I said.

"Tell him, Frankie," Marcie said.

"Cindy's got a boyfriend in the city. You and Miss Hawks have met him, Dad. I heard Cindy telling Melody on the phone that you caught her on the street with her boyfriend," Frankie said.

"You know what happens to informers, kid?" I said.

"Don't accuse him of that. Frankie is worried about his sister," Marcie said.

"You ought to hear the stuff Cindy tells on me," Frankie said.

"Cindy was supposed to have left at noon today to come into the city to the Museum of Natural History. Then she was going to Melody's aunt's apartment for a while. She was to be home by 5:30," Marcie said. "When she didn't show up, I phoned Melody's aunt."

It turned out there had been no plans to go to the Museum of Natural History, and Melody's aunt couldn't remember the last time she had seen Cindy, or Melody either. Marcie put Frankie on the grill and he cracked.

"I had to meet Dr. Bertolucci, so I brought Frankie into the city with me to straighten out this matter," Marcie said.

I looked at Bertolucci. He smiled and turned up his palms. The poor bastard hadn't intended to get the kids laid on him tonight.

"Now, what is this young man's name that Cindy is seeing?" Marcie said.

"Jeff," I said.

"Let's go find him," Marcie said.

"Calm down," I said. "Cindy will turn up at home or over here."

"Frank, we're going to find that girl," Marcie said. "You're not going to slip out of your responsibility this time. You're not across the ocean in Viet Nam directing eight camera crews this time. You're not filming headhunters this time. You're not even taking pictures of a goddam moon rocket or burning Egyptian tanks. Let's go find Cindy."

Sally turned to Dr. Bertolucci and said, "What would you advise?"

"Ah, but I'm no authority in these little affairs," Dr. Bertolucci said.

"You're modest," Sally said. "You're famous as an authority on the psychology of marriage."

"Yes, marriage, to be sure," Dr. Bertolucci said. "I learned much about marriage from my father, the Count. He always had a wife and a mistress. If he lost a wife to illness or divorce, he would marry his mistress. That was his advice to me: marry your mistress if an opening arises. Then get another mistress who is young and pretty and devoted. If an opening arises and one does not marry one's mistress, it may lead to scandal or murder."

I glanced over to see how Marcie was taking this.

"Give me a cigarette," she said.

"With the greatest of pleasure," Dr. Bertolucci said. He lit a Gauloise for her with his Dunhill and then lit another for Sally.

"And all of the Count's wives and mistresses have remained good friends," Dr. Bertolucci said. "He gave a banquet for them last year at St. Moritz. There was a photograph taken. As one grows older, one appreciates the wisdom of the Count."

That speech of Bertolucci's rattled Marcie so hard that she began telling about the Christmas tree.

As she told it, she had driven for hours all over Westchester, looking for the perfect Christmas tree. The tree was required to have the perfect shape, the perfect color and fullness. And the tree had to be exactly the perfect height for our living room in Pelham Manor.

The star in the little angel's hands had to come within an inch of touching the ceiling.

After much hardship and a search that sounded comparable to locating the ruins of Troy, Marcie and her tape measure found the perfect tree on an Optimist Club lot outside of Scarsdale.

She brought the tree home and I cut a foot off the bottom to make it fit the stand.

"It was the most passive-aggressive act I've ever seen," Marcie said.

There was a loud gargle and a spew and a thunderous, reverberating laugh.

It was Dr. Bertolucci. He had just caught on.

"Ho, ho, ho. Really, this is wonderful. Could I have some more of that excellent vodka, Mr. Mallory?" Dr. Bertolucci said.

Frankie said, "One time Dad took Mom and Cindy and me to Mexico City for the Olympics. The hotel valet washed Dad's new suit. It shrunk up real tiny. Dad threw a color TV out the window. He tried to throw a chair out the window, but it got stuck."

Frankie shrieked with laughter. That Mexico City story didn't need to be relevant for Frankie to tell it, any more than the Christmas tree story needed to be relevant for Marcie to tell it.

The Mexico City story was a high point of Frankie's life.

I guess the same could be said for the Christmas tree story and Marcie.

"All right, Frank, if you won't go looking for your

196

daughter, you might at least tell me where I can start looking," Marcie said.

"I don't have any idea," I said.

I had decided I would head straight for Jeff's storefront the minute I could escape Marcie.

Maybe I could get Bertolucci aside and suggest he use his wiles to lure Marcie away. I wondered how much money he thought Marcie had. He could keep her occupied for hours if I hinted that she stood to inherit a fortune from the roadside toilet king.

And Bertolucci was the first of Marcie's analysts I liked.

Marcie suddenly had an awful thought.

"My god, Frank, what if this boy is a guru?" Marcie said. "What if he's one of those boys who talk girls into meditating and chanting and forgetting their religious upbringing? They can't talk to their parents ever again. They sleep on the floor. They wear funny clothes. They follow him anywhere."

"I don't think he's a guru," I said.

What I meant was not in the classical sense. By the way Marcie had just defined guru, she might be right about Jeff.

"I'm afraid of gurus," Marcie said. "I hate brown rice and astrology. I hate drugs. I stay up nights thinking about disasters that have happened to children of our friends. So many are dead or in the hospital or in jail. Or they've just disappeared."

Frankie yelled from the den to tell me I had a phone call.

He was watching the eight-screen lashup. He handed me the blue phone.

"Guess who," he said.

"Hi, Dad. I'm in trouble, huh?" Cindy said on the phone.

"Where are you?" I said.

"Home. I've been home for nearly two hours.

Frankie says Mom's at your place and she's really mad," Cindy said.

"She's not mad now. She's scared. She'll be mad when she finds out you're okay," I said.

"Well, you see, Jeff came up this afternoon, and I guess I must have gone riding with him on his motorcycle or something, and it got late, and Mom was gone when I got home," Cindy said. "Can you clear me with her?"

"I don't know. I'll try," I said.

"Thanks," she said

"Can you do something for me?" I said.

"Sure," she said.

"Use your head," I said.

I went into the living room and told Marcie that Cindy had called from home. I said there had been a little mixup. I said Cindy would explain it later.

"Thank god she's all right," Marcie said.

"Ah, these matters have a way of resolving themselves," Dr. Bertolucci said. "This is one of the joys of marriage. To have a family and dramas every day. Marriage is the golden ring that holds together the dramas of the man and the wife, the children, the lovers. You have wide experience of life, Miss Hawks. What do you think of marriage?"

"I think the need for marriage has vanished, and when that realization soaks in, marriage will vanish," Sally said.

"That's too bad," Marcie said angrily to Sally. "If marriage vanishes, a woman loses one of her biggest thrills—getting a divorce."

"No, no, ah no," Dr. Bertolucci said. "Marriage to a fine man is a woman's comfort, her protection against the world."

"You'll have to sell *that* somewhere else," Marcie said to Dr. Bertolucci.

Marcie almost accompanied her statement with the

198

old Italian gesture which roughly means: your cock should fall in the river and a turtle bite it.

Marcie looked at Sally and said, "If you were half as intelligent as you pretend to be, you would understand that the only reason you've never married is, the right woman hasn't come along."

"I don't consider that an insult." Sally smiled.

"You must, honey, or why would you think I did?" Marcie said.

Marcie could be pretty hard to handle when it came to effrontery.

To me, Marcie said, "You're really cute, Frank. And such a help."

Marcie took Frankie with her out the door.

Dr. Bertolucci stood up and put his empty vodka glass on the bar. He nodded to me and smiled.

"Mr. Mallory, I am charmed at your hospitality," he said. Then he looked at Sally. "Miss Hawks, I would so like to discuss with you your work. And I do have a dinner reservation for two at Grenouille tonight."

"Another time, Dr. Bertolucci," Sally said.

"Ah, then. A sadness but a dream," Dr. Bertolucci said.

And he departed.

Within a very short period, with nothing of consequence said, Sally and I were on the couch in the living room. Then we were upstairs on the bed, and we finished removing each other's clothes. We muttered and murmured and groaned. In the faint light from the bathroom door we saw incredible sights and felt sensations that cannot be described.

I hate to put it this way, but the earth moved.

Chapter
Twenty-four

〜〜〜〜〜〜〜〜〜〜〜〜〜〜〜〜〜

Arleene had been told to keep everybody out of my office and off the phones. I would take a call from an S. Hawks, naturally, or one of the kids, but I didn't want to be bothered by anyone on the Soviet Presidium or any of our friends among the Tupi tribesmen in the Amazon.

It was about a week before "Just Up the Street."

The show was scheduled for Wednesday, June 18, 8 P.M., Eastern Standard Time.

The publicity and promotional releases for *TV Guide* and all the newspapers and magazines had been sent out, and I had copies of them on my desk.

Arleene had read them and taken care to underline many of the phrases she felt had exceeded our literary expectations.

Her favorites were:

A heel-clicking inside salute to contemporary America . . .

A huggable, kissable suburban frolic . . .

A delightful progressive dinner with Old Glory for a tablecloth and lifted spirits for the wine . . .

Join with the rhythms and roarings of the hearts next door . . .

Come to a live picnic in the CBC backyard . . .

A joyful, boy-full, girl-full strum on the heartstrings of your neighbors . . .

A do-wacka-do, toe-tapping, rip-rollicking, flippity-jibbet of a clambake . . .

The heart-pumping-est, prime-time-ing-est, live, patriotic, celebration of the American theme since last year when Mary Poppins, Becky Thatcher and Mortimer Snerd went clang-clang-clanging on the CBC trolley . . .

The trouble with murdering people in Publicity is that you can seldom replace them with anyone better.

Sometimes when you do have a good publicist around for a while, he or she does not stay long, even with raises and bonuses. One day they have sold their novel to Hollywood and gone off to a shooting location in Portugal with Nicol Williamson.

A note was attached to the promo copy on my desk.

It was from Arleene. Two sentences.

Come clean. How the fuck did you really get into this?

I thought it might be therapeutic to answer.

So I typed the following memo:

TO: Arleene Maxson.
FROM: Frank Mallory.
SUBJECT: How the Fuck Did Frank Mallory Get Into This?

It all started many years ago in South Dallas. I come from humble origins, as you know. I was just a kid in rope-sole shoes.

I don't recall what it was about that particular

day as I stood in front of the Tivoli Theater. Maybe I had eaten too many chickenburgers. Anyhow, I bought a movie ticket with the dime I had earned selling 10,567 subscriptions to the *Saturday Evening Post.*

I knew my father didn't like movies. He was a railroad brakeman. He only liked Texas League baseball. Except he didn't even like that when Ed (Bear Tracks) Greer of the Fort Worth Cats struck out everybody on the Dallas Rebels.

He said Texas League baseball was better before the Galveston Buccaneers got replaced by the Shreveport Sports. He said Ed (Bear Tracks) Greer wasn't as good a pitcher as Ash Hillon of the Oklahoma City Indians, either.

When I told my father I spent my dime on a movie, he whipped me with a razor strop.

He whipped me another time when I was late coming home to eat my pork and bean sandwich for dinner. I was late because I was playing football on the vacant lot and the big kids stopped the game to look in a garage window. I asked what they were looking at. One of them, I think his name was Cooper, said, "The niggers are fuckin'."

I said that was why I was late in front of my mother, who was baking fried pies to sell to the men building a flight-training school in Grand Prairie.

In the kitchen, my father said, "You don't use no words like fuckin' in front of a Christian lady like your mother. They ain't nothing bad about fuckin' but you don't talk about it in front of women, unless they're women you're fuckin', and then it better be your wife."

My mother never said much. I liked her because she would let me play sick sometimes and stay home from school and hear how it all worked out on the radio with "Portia Faces Life."

My mother and I laughed together when we listened to "Vic & Sade." She said it would be nice to be like Vic and Sade and know somebody funny like Ike Kneesupper.

That would be better, she said, than being A. T. and Vera Mallory in South Dallas, although we had a lot to be thankful for, including me.

I asked her why my name was Frank instead of A.T., Jr.

She said I was named after Frankin D. Roosevelt, who had saved us.

The only time I saw my mother alarmed was when she heard a Catholic moved into the block.

Otherwise, strangers didn't bother her. Even niggers.

If a nigger or an old man without a shave came to the screen door, my mother would get him a glass of ice water and a potato pattie.

A Catholic never came to the door, but she knew there was one around.

I told my mother I liked movies. She said she didn't think she would like movies so much anymore because there was too much killing. I said nobody got killed except Germans and Japs on the whole.

I said my favorite movies were the ones where a newspaperman ran away with an heiress.

I said in the movies a newspaperman not only got to run away with an heiress, but he got to catch gangsters and go to war and not get killed.

My mother said working for a newspaper was probably a better job than being a railroad brakeman or cooking fried pies. She said if the Japs didn't invade California and make the war last so long that I would have to go, then maybe I

203

could learn to play football good enough to go to college and learn how to be a newspaperman.

This was another time my father whipped me.

"When you're old enough to be able to fix somethin' that's broke, you'll join the human race like the rest of us," he said. "A reporter don't lift nothin' heavier than his hat."

I decided I would definitely be a newspaperman.

When I was fourteen I was the ace reporter for the *South Dallas Bugle,* which was written on notebook paper and had a combined circulation—morning, evening and Sunday—of two. Me and Patsy Ethridge.

Patsy Ethridge was not an heiress. Her family had yet to get killed on the highway to Corsicana and leave her the poultry business. But she made me run away with her one night, anyway.

She took me to an empty two-story house that we all knew to be haunted. There was an old mattress on the floor in one of the upstairs rooms. Patsy Ethridge said she would bet that if we crawled around on the mattress and stuck our hands in some of the burned holes in it we could find the money the gangsters had hidden after they robbed O. D. Ware's cafe and filling station.

It was hard to find anything on the mattress because it was so dark, but Patsy Ethridge thought she came across something.

She said for me to be quiet, and give her my hand.

Part of the money was hidden in two mounds inside her blouse, but most of it was hidden between her legs. Patsy had plenty of room to hide money, if the gangsters didn't mind the rolls of bills getting soggy.

I wished they hadn't forced her to eat an onion sandwich.

I have wondered whether I would have kept on wanting to be a newspaperman if I had been a good enough football player at the University of Texas to play on the first team.

When I realized I wasn't fast enough and certainly not big enough to stay out there with the best eleven and had begun to listen to Marcie's music, my father said, "You ain't got a gut in your body."

Had he acknowledged the existence of fags, I think that's what he would have called me.

When he found out I was working on the *Daily Texan,* he told friends from the railroad who hung around Dace Mosely's Barbecue that I was a printer.

My mother was sad when I quit Texas before my senior year. But she said a high school diploma was probably all a family like ours could ever have hoped for in the first place.

My father never saw my first by-line in the *Dallas Times Herald,* which was a feature story about a one-legged police dispatcher named Toby Hunnicutt.

My father had been shot to death by somebody with a .22 in Dace Mosely's Barbecue one night. It was after an argument about who played third base for the 1937 Beaumont Exporters.

Marcie and I could have made room for my mother to live with us, but my mother said young people had a tough enough time as it was. She moved in with her sister on a farm that later became a supermarket in Richardson, Texas, and she lived there until she had a stroke one afternoon, not many years afterward, while she sat watching a game show on TV.

205

I have always been grateful to the ministry that my mother got to live long enough to see me star in Hurricane Beulah. That was her son, right there on the 6 o'clock local news, defying the gale winds with nothing but a KRLD–TV mike in his hands.

You may ask, Arleene, why a writer would grab a mike and wade into the swirling flood waters of Galveston, Texas, to square his chin and purse his lips against the howling gray death that was sweeping in off the Gulf.

One reason was because a Galveston telephone pole was wearing the KRLD announcer for a sweater. Another was because we worked for the same ownership and I understood company loyalty.

But the main reason was because I had seen all those goddam movies when I was a kid.

Why didn't I stay with the paper instead of taking the offer to move over to the TV station? Because I had a wife and a baby and I wanted to get me an air-conditioned Olds 88, too.

Guys on the paper who knew what the pay differential was stopped asking me to go eat Chili and rice with them. They thought I surely must have joined Brook Hollow Country Club.

Why did I switch into production from being on camera when I was obviously that rare combination of suave news reader and penetrating journalist? Because in front of the camera you had to read things other people wrote for you, and sometimes they wrote, "Councilman Rogers denied before the Dallas Public School Board today that he had any knowledge his dairy had been awarded the contract for all of the city's school cafeterias last year. He said, however, that he would certainly look into the widespread but so far unsubstantiated reports that literally hundreds of Rogers' Chocky-Foo ice cream bars had turned up poisoned."

Why would a man pack up his family in a lovely section of Dallas and move them to a crowded apartment in Philadelphia where they merely had to look off their balcony to watch his remote unit televising a demonstration?

Because KRLD in Dallas was only a CBS affiliate, whereas WCAU in Philadelphia was a company-owned CBS station—an oh-and-oh, as you people say in the trade—and the hallways of CBS in New York were teeming with oh-and-oh graduates.

I could have waited around in Dallas for the network to make an offer. I could have waited for another hurricane. Or another interview with Officer Tippit's widow.

But I was restless and I had done all I could do in Dallas.

And in those days I knew Philadelphia had wonderful race riots, their Eagles were competitive, and the city had a terribly interesting zoo parade.

You know how it works, Arleene. Once you've been exposed to the power and exhilaration of production, you're hooked. And you know the biggest ball games of all are played in New York City, New York, Gotham, Big Town, The Apple.

Now then.

The only good thing about "Just Up the Street" is that it will be live.

And when we are into the countdown in the control room, and Jack Nathanson is sitting in the director's chair with two cigarettes already lit,

207

and somebody shouts, "Ten seconds 'til air," I'll become a part of Jack Nathanson.

I will be up there with my squadron, Arleene.

And for those next three live hours I will be slinging my white scarf around my neck and adjusting my goggles and pointing my Spitfire into loops and rolls and turns.

And while I am doing all this, in those three live hours, I will be the only thing I probably really am.

Or maybe the only thing I ever could have been.

If you don't want to remember me this way, then think of the huggable, kissable, suburban kid I once had a chance to become.

Since my real name was signed to that confession of how I got into this, I moved on to the serious business of how I could survive it. Watts and Travers had started me thinking about the potential of their Mr. Kaplan. And something about the photograph of Bob Skidmore, the Washington lawyer with the pompadour and leisure suit, made me wonder how many stewardesses he had on scholarship.

Chapter
Twenty-five

~~~~~~

D. Wayne Cooper had a case of the opening-night jumps.

I could tell it soon after I parked the Silver Goblet at the entrance to the St. Regis and saw Cooper come out of the door with Katherine.

Because it was opening night of Cooper's bar and opera house, I was driving the Goblet and D. Wayne was riding in the back.

Because it was also Katherine's first night in Gotham after engagements on the Left Coast, I had thought a suite at the St. Regis stocked with Taittinger and Beluga would be a nice gift for the happy, engaged couple.

Riding up front with me in the Goblet was Sally Hawks.

Except when one or both of us was working, Sally Hawks and I had not been beyond groping distance of each other since the night the earth moved. Funny thing is, Sally and I had both thought of the "earth moved" line from *For Whom the Bell Tolls* that night. But neither of us had used it because it was true, and neither of us wanted to risk getting a laugh just then.

I, for one, was in love.

I loved Cindy, Frankie, D. Wayne Cooper and my job. I loved the Silver Goblet, anything live on television, tennis, J&B, chicken fried steak with cream gravy, colorful wars, my eight-screen lashup, André the cat, the Grand Corniche, country music and string bikinis.

I loved movies, Kona coffee, fireplaces, Arleene, thunderstorms, certain restaurants and saloons, a number of people I could mention, running in the mornings, Japanese baths, the Texas Longhorns, short par-fours with the wind behind me, tortillas, backrubs and Monte Cruz cigars. I couldn't help but love Marcie, too. I loved all these people, places and things on various levels.

But I was in love with Sally Hawks.

If she so much as brushed against my knee, it was like cranking up a six-volt battery and shooting the juice in me.

I loved to look at her and talk to her just as much as I loved to feel her. At odd times I would realize she had been on my mind. That day, for example, I had spent $400,000 of the network's money buying TV rights to the Russian ballet. Even while Herb Grant was telling me $400,000 was an absurd sum to pay Commies for hopping up and down, I was thinking how much Sally would like it. Of course, I didn't make my decisions based on Sally's opinions. That week I had approved $1,200,000 for six pilots of which Sally would probably detest four. But that was my effort to affect prime-time programming, and what was going on with us in the front seat of the Silver Goblet, that was love.

"Look at D. Wayne," Sally said when we stopped the limo in front of the St. Regis. "He's wearing a buckskin suit."

210

Cooper's new suit had fringes on the sleeves from the elbows down and on the legs from the knees down. I decided Katherine had brought him the suit from Western Costume in L.A. Cooper wore his Indian jewelry, his boots and his brown beaver hat. Katherine wore a denim outfit with a long skirt, and she clung to his arm.

The way I could tell Cooper was jumpy was he opened the front door of the Goblet and fell in on top of me while the St. Regis doorman held the rear door open.

The doorman helped pull Cooper to his feet.

Cooper pushed the doorman away and said, "Pass moff."

"It wasn't his fault, D. Wayne. Get your ass in the car," Katherine said.

Being at the wheel of the Silver Goblet was like steering with your brain. You thought about turning left, and the Goblet read your fingers and did a left so smooth and fast the smoke from Sally's cigarette would still be going straight ahead.

"Goddam, watch it, will you, Frank? You like to busted that old Buick," Cooper said.

"Yes, sir," I said. Which is not the way he would have answered me if he had been driving.

"You can't make every fuckin' light all the way down Park Street," Cooper said. "I'd rather get there alive than in a cigar box."

"D. Wayne, are you having menopause?" Katherine said.

"Pass moff, too," Cooper said.

"Oh, shut up. You know the damned club is going to be a sellout," Katherine said.

"Shit, it don't mean nothing to me anyhow. What do I care about a goddam honky-tonk? Fuckin' honky-tonks pop up like mushrooms in cow turds. Ain't that right, Sally?" Cooper said.

"I've never been to a country music nightclub before," Sally said.

"Well, they ain't none of 'em worth shit," Cooper said. "Just a pile of hicks and outlaws is all. Lot of fightin'. Do the cowboy two-step. Throw a beer bottle at the sanger. Puke in the parking lot. Goddam, I do love a honky-tonk! Hey, Katherine, I forgot to bring my Binniss. Naw, whewsht, here it is in my left boot. Frank! You damn near hit that Checker!"

"Let me fix you a drink," Katherine said.

"Maybe one little old South Dallas martini," Cooper said.

We went into the tunnel at Fortieth, cruised silently through the tube of streaking lights, came out at Thirty-third and stopped for a red at Twenty-eighth and Park.

Cooper had drunk a fast South Dallas martini and was working on a second. He had turned on the TVs in the back seat and was watching one of those college football all-star games they keep playing right on through the spring and summer. It was called the Last Chance Bowl and was made up of players no pro scout had ever personally spoken to. The game was played in Danville, Illinois. Our network's former vice president for Sports had bought it. My predecessor in prime-time programming had locked it into the schedule.

Cooper was describing to me that it was third and 14 at the Eastern Unknown All-Star 34-yard line. Western Unknown All-Stars had the ball, trailing 6–3 with a minute to go. Western Unknown quarterback threw a pass. The ball was in the air.

"Son of a bitch!" Cooper said.

"Touchdown?" I said.

"I don't know," Cooper said. "They all of the sudden put on one of them promo deals for your show about the saps."

212

Cooper turned up the volume.

". . . huggable, kissable suburban frolic . . . 'Just Up the Street' and just on CBC," I heard the announcer say.

". . . what a lousy break for a plucky kid," the football color man said. "The ball just seemed to leak its air."

The sign above the front door of the club said COOPER'S COUNTRY.

The marquee said JACKIE JACK SNOWDRIFT & THE DEAF COWBOY BAND.

Posters in the windows announced future appearances at Cooper's Country of Willie Nelson, Jerry Jeff Walker, Waylon Jennings, Dolly Parton, Tammy Wynette, Billy Joe Shaver, Patsy Cline, Charley Pride . . .

"I think one of those people is dead," I said.

"Don't let on," Cooper said.

I double-parked the Silver Goblet at the curb beside a black Cadillac limo. Cooper had hired two off-duty cops to keep order on the sidewalk and watch over any limos that might arrive.

It was still early, but the bar was almost full and the tables close to the stage were already occupied. We walked on red carpet, seeing ourselves in a long mirror behind the bar. Two guys in overalls stood on a stepladder working with screwdrivers on the baseplate of a chandelier.

"Stealing it, more than likely," Cooper said.

We went through a door at the side of the stage. A roadie in a cowboy hat sat on a folding chair guarding the amplifiers. He looked at us suspiciously as Cooper stomped through the backstage area to a gray door with HIGH VOLTAGE—KEEP OUT painted on it. Cooper knocked loudly, then pulled out a key ring and unlocked two locks.

A man in suedes with a fat beard and polished

glasses jumped up when the door opened and said, "D. Wayne, this is a bitching layout you got, bro."

Arranged around the musicians' backstage lounging room were Jackie Jack Snowdrift and the Deaf Cowboy Band. The bearded guy who jumped up was Lester Stagg, their manager-agent.

Cooper introduced everybody. Stagg shut the door behind us and double-locked it again.

Jackie Jack Snowdrift was on his feet. He smiled at us and his adam's apple jiggled as he swallowed from a bottle of tequila.

"Nice to know you all," Jackie Jack said. "D. Wayne, you put a sound system in this mother that'd make a harelip sound good. We threw our own stuff back in the truck."

The room was dark-stained plywood with mirrors and chairs and couches, and a shower and toilet behind another door.

The seven members of the Deaf Cowboy Band looked at us amiably. Three or four were plunking at guitars or mandolins. A couple plunged their arms into a plastic garbage can of ice and beer. Another was asleep on the floor with his boots on the arm of a couch. Four girls in pioneer-woman dresses wondered who we were.

Cooper and Jackie Jack Snowdrift did a cult handshake and then a hug that tipped Snowdrift's big white felt hat back against his neck.

"You old motherfucker," Jackie Jack said.

"You country pissant," Cooper said.

I had known they were friends.

"Love the double lock on the dressing room door," Stagg said.

There were bottles of J&B and Wild Turkey on a table by the shower. We all made drinks.

"You wrote one of my favorite songs. 'If I'd Listened,'" I said to Jackie Jack.

"If I'd listened, I'd never found the truth behind your lies, . . ." sang one of the Deaf Cowboys.

The Deaf Cowboys had long hair and wore cowboy hats and jeans. Except for one who wore jeans, boots and a Homburg.

"It's weird of you to say that," Jackie Jack said to me.

Jackie Jack was tall and had a turkey neck and big brown eyes. A pocket was ripped off his Hawaiian shirt. From his belt he took a container made from a polished piece of deer antler.

"I'm trying to recall how it goes," Jackie Jack said.

He unscrewed the top of the deer antler. The top had a bone scoop sticking down from it. Jackie Jack dipped the bone scoop into the bottom of the antler and came up with enough coke to cover a fingernail. He snorted that much in each nostril and passed the antler to me.

So I did a scoop in each nostril and passed it to Cooper.

I should point out perhaps that despite what Herb Grant thinks, cocaine is not the same thing as heroin. And cocaine is not what skinny little Chinamen smoke on wooden bunks in back streets of Singapore, either. Cocaine is what Sherlock Holmes and Freud used for a smartener.

Cocaine comes from the leaves of the coca bush which mostly grows in the Andes. Mountain Indians in Peru, Bolivia, Colombia and places like that chew the leaves or brew them into coca tea. This makes the Indians feel very zippy even when they don't make food to eat. Which is usually.

Forty years ago, cocaine was an ingredient in tonics and pills you could buy in any drug store.

It was thought then that cocaine was a good nerve

and brain medicine. A lot of people think so even today. But cocaine is illegal now. In New York they can put you in prison for life for doing cocaine.

Being illegal, cocaine has become so expensive that almost nobody can afford it except musicians, movie stars, doctors, politicians, lawyers, gangsters, professional athletes and dope dealers.

I don't do cocaine very often myself. But I don't turn it down when it is offered in amiable surroundings such as the dressing room of Cooper's Country on a gala occasion like opening night.

I will let drop a secret. Herb Grant takes speed. Only he calls it diet pills. Herb Grant says people who take speed should be flogged and locked up.

In his case, I might agree.

In the dressing room, Jackie Jack had picked up his guitar and begun to sing:

I'm gonna do it
Gonna leave this happy scene
I'm packin' up my outfits
One dirty
and one clean.
I'm goin' where the sweet life don't turn sour
where a man can drink and laugh,
forget about the hour.
She'll get the house and ever'thing else and
I'll get the albums of Willie Nelson.
Thought it was fine
but she called it hell.
It must have been bad,
she's still yellin'.
I'm gonna do it
Gonna leave this happy scene
I'm packin' up my outfits
One dirty
and one clean.

If I'd listened, I'd never found
the truth behind your lies.

The antler had gone around the room.

"Lord, I wish we didn't have that gig in Buffalo tomorrow," Jackie Jack said, mashing on his eyeballs. "I'd like to lay in the yard back home in Texas and play with my dog or my wife, either one."

Cooper said, "How long since you been to sleep, Jackie?"

"Five days, I believe," Jackie Jack said.

He snorted and passed the antler again.

"You took a nap at the table at that bar in Oklahoma City," a Deaf Cowboy said.

"Yeah, I forgot. That musta been yesterday," Jackie Jack said.

"That was four days ago," Stagg said.

"Ole Jody stayed up thirty-six days one time last fall," another Deaf Cowboy said.

Jody, the lead guitar player, grinned and blinked.

"I can go a week, but thirty-six days is hard to believe," Cooper said.

"Cost me seven thousand. What I can remember, it was worth it," Jody said.

Jackie Jack played a lick on his guitar and said, "I hate to sleep because I don't dream. If you ain't dreaming, there's nothing happening asleep. So I'd rather be awake."

Cooper grinned dimples at Katherine and said, "Jackie Jack don't dream because he don't really go to sleep. He stays up until he passes out."

"He must be trying to kill himself," Katherine said.

"Naw, guitar pickers don't think that far ahead," Cooper said.

"I didn't believe trumpet players did, either, until I married one," Katherine said.

217

Her first husband, Billy, played in the brass section for Kenton, Dorsey, Sauter-Finegan and several other big bands. When last heard from, Billy was at Bellevue.

"Trumpet players got good lips, godawmighty," said the Deaf Cowboy who had his feet on the arm of the couch. "Ever see one of 'em eat corn on the cob?"

"Their necks swell up," one of the girls said. "Dizzy Gillespie, his throat gets so big. Like a bullfrog."

"Well, fuck a cornet player," a red-bearded Deaf Cowboy said.

"You got to get an appointment, man," the Deaf Cowboys' horn player said.

"Don't mind me, keep on talkin'. . . . I'm just lookin' for my hat," Jackie Jack sang.

I whispered to Sally that Jackie Jack had just done a line from "Ain't No God in Mexico" by Billy Joe Shaver. She smiled and accepted this as a fairly important piece of knowledge. Which in fact it was. But you might be shocked at how confused some people could look when you told them something like that.

Sally and I both did another toot from the antler and passed it on.

One thing cocaine will do is make you want to pour J&B down your throat every time you notice there is a glass in your hand.

Another thing cocaine will do is make you consider how stupendously fucking easy it would be to get through lunch at "21" with the Big Guy. Which was what I had to do the next day.

"Jackie Jack, I appreciate you cutting in here for the grand opening," Cooper said.

The last two times Jackie Jack Snowdrift had played in Gotham, it was to sellout crowds at Carnegie Hall.

"D. Wayne, in my opinion you could stand flatfooted and shit in a dump truck," Jackie Jack said.

Cooper had worked for Jackie Jack Snowdrift off and on between Cody Huber and me.

"We get out of Buffalo without no serious diseases, I'll stop and play here awhile before I go home," Jackie Jack said.

"Uh, I don't know, Jackie," Stagg said. "You understand, D. Wayne. This has been a tough tour. Jackie's tired. He needs to go home from Buffalo."

What was understood without Stagg saying so was that Cooper also could not pay the Snowdrift price. Jackie Jack could get fifteen thousand dollars for one show at the Convention Center in Tulsa. That didn't put Jackie Jack in the Cody Huber rock star class. But it was a long way from what Cooper could pay him. Which I happened to know was expenses, scale, and a $2,000 ounce of coke for the band to split. Plus all they could drink. And that was heading toward a possible historical marker for eight musicians and one manager and three roadies and from four to twenty groupies.

Jackie Jack clawed at the torn pocket of his Hawaiian shirt, searching for a cigarette. His pack of Kools floated in the ice in the plastic garbage can.

"D. Wayne, I'll come back here to your joint any time, you old outlaw," Jackie Jack said. "If these cocksuckers don't want to," he said, indicating the band, "it don't make a shit because nobody pays to see them anyhow."

"Eat a pile of Viet Cong underwear," the piano player said.

Jackie Jack saw a long cigarette butt near the pointed toe of his lizard-skin cowboy boots. He bent to pick up the butt and fell across his fifteen-hundred-dollar inlaid acoustic guitar.

Jackie Jack lay on the crushed body of the guitar. He held the neck of it in his left hand. With his right hand, he put the cigarette butt in his mouth.

Stagg lit the cigarette butt.

Jackie Jack looked at the ruin of the guitar and said, "That fucker hit a bad lick."

Two of the girls in pioneer-woman dresses snatched pieces of the guitar to put in their memory books.

"There were only forty-eight guitars like that in the whole world, and Jackie Jack's busted seven of 'em," Stagg said.

Jackie Jack sat up and said, "I'll play that old Spanish wood guitar of yours tonight, Jody."

"I'll kill you if you touch that guitar," Jody said. "You know how Willie broke three of your ribs when you sat on his guitar? If you even touch my Spanish guitar I'll beat you to death with a brick."

"I didn't sit on Willie's guitar," Jackie Jack said. "I *fell* on it. There's a world of difference. Just like I fell on this one."

"You ain't touching my Spanish," Jody said.

"Fuck it then. I'll just sing. I'm a singer anyhow, ain't I?" Jackie Jack said.

Stagg had already sent a roadie to Jackie Jack's rented black Cadillac limo for another guitar. Stagg looked at me and smiled, tight and red-lipped, but with humor. You had to have a sense of humor, he was saying.

Somebody said it was time for the show. The opening band was doing an encore. The place was packed, and the opening band was a hit. Both bits of news were great for Cooper, because the opening band was the headline band for tomorrow night.

We had reserved a table near the bandstand. Naturally there were four guys in T-shirts sitting at our table. These weren't kids. They were in their middle thirties and had big arms, big bellies and crewcuts. One of them had eaten the RESERVED sign to educate the waiter.

Cooper slid in and sat down with the four guys.

220

Cooper in his buckskins and jewelry and wasted face and beaver hat. The four T-shirt guys with broken glass expressions and bulldog tattoos. Cooper mentioned the name of the man he had obtained his liquor license from. He mentioned the name of the vending machine company. The four T-shirt guys got up and went to the bar.

Cooper was a wizard in situations like that.

Snowdrift and the Deaf Cowboys did a first set that knocked the walls down. The crowd went goofy. Twice Jackie Jack shambled over and cut the volume off on Jody's guitar. Jody would cut the volume back up and play on top of Jackie Jack's vocals. The other Deaf Cowboys grinned, but the audience never noticed.

I had an arm around the back of Sally's chair. I felt her shoulder blades responding to the music.

Cooper would look at Snowdrift and the Deaf Cowboys, and then he would look at the screaming crowd, and occasionally his pale eyes would hit my eyes and he would do a grin that made me want to cry because I was so glad for him.

Another thing cocaine can do is make you want to talk to somebody like Sally Hawks even if she can't hear you. We were sitting close to a speaker the size of a phone booth. The sound vibrated my arm against her shoulder. I kept putting my lips to her ear and shouting things that I had to tell her urgently. She would turn her face toward mine and shout back. And we would kiss. A brush-of-the-lips-and-look-in-the-eyes kiss.

Jackie Jack got a foot tangled in some cables during a number and pulled off his right boot trying to get loose. The crowd loved it. He had on a dirty white athletic sock. He didn't bother with the boot because by then to his obvious alarm he had dropped a cigarette into a full pitcher of Sangria.

Jackie Jack sang a ballad:

> If I wander, is there far enough
> for me to go to make you leave
> my mind,
> and keep me thinkin' I'm not thinkin'
> of what I left behind.
> Or will I cruise the country
> like a clever old romancer,
> knowin' answers to other people's lines,
> and remember I'm forgettin'
> to love someone somebody else will find.

He had a husky, raw-gin voice that could make the room listen.

Jackie Jack sang:

> Runnin' is a means for me to measure
> what I used to treasure while I stayed.
> I hope some soul is deep enough
> to help me shake the feelin'
> that the two of us together had it made. . . .
> The two of us together, how we played . . .
> the two of us together should have
>   stayed. . . .
> We had it made. . . .

Jackie Jack walked off the stage. In one white athletic sock and one lizard-skin boot, Levis with shiny knees, a Hawaiian shirt with a torn pocket, a white cowboy hat with a feather band, and a middle finger thrust toward Jody. Applause and whistles and shots tore up Cooper's Country.

Back in the dressing room, Jackie Jack was stuffing the bone scoop into his nose, holding a beer in each armpit and pleading for an emergency blowjob.

He went into the shower with a girl in a pioneer dress.

People pounded on the dressing room door. Stagg peeked through the spy-hole and wouldn't open up.

"Plenty of cunt out there," Stagg said with his eyes against the spy-hole. "Plenty of fanatic dopers. Drunks. Fans. Nuts. I see some minor celebrities. Wouldn't be big ones at the door. Too packed."

Cooper was out in his joint mingling with his public. Jackie Jack had put the antler into my hand when he went to the shower. Sally and I dug in with the bone scoop and passed the antler.

Another thing coke can do is make you tend to dig in deeper as the night goes along.

I heard Sally asking Jody what he found to do while he was staying awake for thirty-six days.

"Visit folks," he said. "Pick. Play golf. Drove back and forth from Austin to Phoenix three times. Every time I'd get to Phoenix I couldn't remember what the hell it was I wanted there."

Sally and I stayed in the dressing room during the second set. I locked both locks on the door. I believe I admitted once again that I was in love with her.

"Say that sober in your real voice," she said.

"I already did," I said.

"Say it again," she said.

I said it again.

She opened her blouse, pulled off her pants and lay down on the couch. She had on tiny brown silk panties. She had them on for about another minute and a half, anyhow.

After Cooper's Country closed, we had a few nightcaps at the bar. D. Wayne counted up the take. He didn't say how much it was, but it filled three bank bags. Stagg watched Cooper put the bags in the safe. Jackie Jack refilled the antler and passed it. The Deaf Cowboys, the girls and the roadies got up a game in the dressing room. They called it Cluster.

Katherine asked if D. Wayne had spoken to me about being best man at the wedding.

I said no, he hadn't.

223

"I assume he will," she said.

Jackie Jack said he had written a new song he wanted us to hear. He sat on a bar stool and played and sang the new song for us:

> Buford and Roy were buddies
> They lettered playin' ball
> Buford in the backfield,
> Roy in the forward wall
>
> Married Joanne and Alma
> Took up the arts
> Buford fixed your sink
> Roy sold auto parts
>
> Made the suburbs what they are
> With cars, boats and kids
> America loved Roy and Buford
> And all what they did
>
> Admired their wives, they said
> Had real good homes
> Buford flushed your toilet
> Roy sold you chrome
>
> Cooked in the backyard a lot
> Went down to the lake
> Danced at the club
> Drove to the Homecoming game
>
> Yeah, Roy and Buford did their best
> America tipped her hat
> Til Roy finally died
> And old Buford, he got fat
>
> Thought about Paris, London
> Things they might have tried
> But Buford, he got fat
> and Roy upped and died.

Jackie Jack said it was a song he owed to America. Stagg told him he had a hit.

I was thinking it was funny that Jackie Jack Snowdrift had written a song about a good American who was a plumber. The Big Guy would banish that song from the CBC radio network if he ever learned of it.

Thinking about the Big Guy, it occurred to me that we had a lunch date at "21." I needed to go home and sleep a few hours.

Another thing about cocaine. It can make you wonder how the whole night just went by.

I looked out the window of Cooper's Country and saw sunlight. Not any dawnlike sunlight, either.

It was more like 11:30 A.M. sunlight.

I told Sally what the problem was as I ran toward the door. She ran with me. So did Cooper. Seeing us running, Jackie Jack jumped up and ran for the door, too. When Jackie Jack ran, Stagg ran with him.

The five of us arrived at the Silver Goblet at the same time.

Cooper bounced off a parking meter. His eyes looked like fire ants.

"Where we running to?" Jackie Jack said.

I said I had to meet the Big Guy. I said I would drive the Silver Goblet and drop Sally off uptown. I said why didn't D. Wayne just hang around his joint and have fun.

Cooper at once took this to mean I thought he was too loaded to drive.

"I don't hear no music to go along with that two-step *you're* doing," Cooper said.

I said I didn't give a shit what he thought about it, I was going to drive.

"Frank, I love the Silver Goblet," Cooper said. He did a penguin totter backward and collided with Katherine, who had come out to see what we were doing.

225

"I love the Silver Goblet more than almost any goddam thing in the world," Cooper said. "But the honest truth is, I could take that old black rented Cadillac limo over there with the foreigner in the front seat, and I could run the rubber off this silver son of a bitch with you driving, Frank."

I said did he expect me to laugh at that, or what? I said did he remember the summer when I had a blue Studebaker and he had a black and yellow Chevy? I said did he conveniently forget how we used to meet for breakfast at the Toddle House every morning? I said did he conveniently forget that after breakfast we used to race to the construction job where we worked? I said did he conveniently forget that not only did I usually beat his ass in the car race, I also forced him into two wrecks?

"Well, now, let's see what we're talking about," Cooper said. He reached into a boot and pulled out a fold of green money. "Does five hundred sound about right to you?"

I said five hundred sounded fine.

"I'll put five hundred on the silver deal myself," Jackie Jack said.

"You got it down," Cooper said.

By then I was behind the wheel of the Goblet and had started the engine.

Sally jumped in beside me.

I saw Cooper grab the chauffeur and haul him out of the black Cadillac that Jackie Jack had rented.

"First one to pass them little iron midgets out front of '21' picks up the cash," Cooper yelled.

As I steered the Goblet away from the curb, Jackie Jack Snowdrift tumbled into the back seat with his guitar and said, "Don't show D. Wayne no mercy."

"No, no, get out of there!" Lester Stagg screamed at Jackie Jack.

Stagg clawed for the door handle but missed. He

226

did manage to hurl himself into the back seat of the black Cadillac.

I had a quick glimpse of Katherine in the doorway of Cooper's Country. And of the Deaf Cowboys looking out. One of them was naked.

Chapter
Twenty-six

∿∿∿∿∿∿∿∿∿∿∿∿∿∿∿∿∿∿∿∿∿∿∿

The first light was green. But in Gotham the traffic light coloring code has no more effect on pedestrians or taxicabs than if you hung a neatly lettered sign on the pole that said: FUCK 'EM.

The Silver Goblet slid through twenty jaywalkers at a good speed and didn't hit a one, but a man in a black turtleneck crammed his nose against the windshield for an instant. Behind us, the black Cadillac burst through a magically parted crowd and was gaining.

"People up here are crazy," Jackie Jack said, snorting from the antler and looking out the back window.

For a few blocks I kept a tight lead on the black Cadillac.

Then I hit a red at Twenty-first Street that some tourist in a rented car had stopped for. A mere toe on the brake of the Goblet stopped us so suddenly that we flew out of our seats and Jackie fell about halfway into where Sally had been.

Cooper squealed the black Cadillac to a stop close to us. He was behind a truck.

"Get out of there! Get out, Jackie!" Stagg yelled from the black Cadillac.

Stagg started to open his door, and two taxicabs shot through the space against the light and disappeared into the pedestrians.

We pulled around the car and truck ahead of us when the light changed and suddenly we were side by side going up Park Street at about fifty miles an hour a few minutes before noon.

"I never thought I'd die in such a stupid way," Sally said.

"Hell, I knew I would," Jackie Jack said.

He had turned on the televisions and picked up a phone.

"Operator, this is Jackie Jack Snowdrift, and I want to call my old lady and sing to her one more time," Jackie Jack said. "Hurry, will you, hon?"

The Goblet and the black Cadillac approached Thirty-third Street.

"My god," Sally said, realizing what was about to happen.

At Thirty-third Street the tunnel goes underground to Fortieth. Or you can take the street around the tunnel and rejoin Park later.

But because of the traffic only one lane was open, and the Goblet and Cadillac couldn't go through the tunnel at the same time.

I mashed the pedal and the Goblet surged a half length ahead and reached the tunnel first. At an even fifty, Cooper swerved right and skidded between the outside tunnel wall and a delivery truck.

There was a whining, singing, spacy noise in the tunnel, going fast.

I thought Cooper was probably dead.

"Operator, I think who I'd rather talk to instead is Darrell Royal," Jackie Jack said. "I got the number here in my shirt pocket."

229

The Goblet sailed up out of the tunnel and missed by inches crashing into the black Cadillac.

Wheel to wheel, we went up the ramp that goes through Grand Central Station and curves around by the Commodore Hotel and comes down onto the real Park Avenue at Forty-sixth Street.

Maybe I don't need to mention that there were thrills connected with this. Honking. Quick turns. Near head-ons. Distorted faces. Screams. Flying briefcases and shopping bags.

"That's right, I don't have a fucking pocket," Jackie Jack said. "I wish we were goin' down to Chinatown to see a sword fight."

The next time we had to stop was for traffic and a light in front of the Waldorf Hotel.

There was a third limo between us. It was black with Japanese flags on the front fenders. The driver was Japanese. A Japanese man in a gray suit sat in the back with his wife. The man had a small mustache and glasses.

"Operator, forget about Darrell Royal and call the Navy Department in Washington. We done trapped Hirohito," Jackie Jack said.

With a grand slalom through trucks, cabs, pregnant women and marchers with signs protesting the soil bank, the Goblet and the black Cadillac did incredible left turns onto Fifty-first Street. St. Patrick's Cathedral and then Rockefeller Center spun past.

We arrived at the corner of Fifty-first and Sixth. Radio City on the left. Tall gray buildings full of loonies. Sam Goody's record store on the right.

"My album's in the window!" Jackie Jack shouted.

We arrived at that corner going twenty-five miles an hour, which on a crosstown Gotham street is like doing a hundred and thirty on a highway. The light was against us. The northbound traffic had started up Sixth.

230

Cooper had the inside lane on me. He wheeled onto Sixth and did a screaming right just ahead of the northbound traffic. I twisted the Goblet into the traffic and we caromed to the right off an air pocket or something—I would never attempt to explain it—and we reached the corner of Fifty-second and Sixth with the black Cadillac ahead by maybe five feet.

But this was the final block of the race. I might as well lose by the length of Manhattan as by five feet.

Cooper made a great sharp turn onto Fifty-second, hugged the right side of the curb and struck through an opening between a United Parcel truck and a bunch of Hare Krishnas.

The left side of Fifty-second was blocked. If I followed Cooper through the right side opening, I was beaten.

So I said hidy, Lord, and took the Fifty-second Street turn wide left.

I mean wide enough that the Silver Goblet ate up sidewalk in front of the CBS building for a few yards before we cut back onto Fifty-second with a four-foot lead on Cooper in the black Cadillac.

Then I saw the Big Guy walking across Fifty-second Street in front of "21." The Big Guy had parked his Plymouth at the opposite curb. Two military chiefs walked with him. The Big Guy was waving his two index fingers. He was leading a band. I assumed he was singing, "Consider yourself . . . one of the family."

They say if you rise to a top job in an important corporation, you ought to be able to make decisions.

The Big Guy didn't notice the two limos roaring straight at him. The two military chiefs, however, scrambled for the south sidewalk.

I jammed the brake on the Silver Goblet and we made a noise like a 747 taking off, and we tumbled all over the inside of the car.

Also we stopped two feet past the little iron midgets.

Cooper swerved to avoid crashing into the Goblet and wound up on the sidewalk beside the military chiefs.

Waving his index fingers, Harley O. Chambers walked down the steps into "21."

He walked past Stanley Coffman who was at the doorway observing this arrival with a cigar in his mouth.

I looked at Sally.

"It's biggies on the go," I said.

I felt like an acre of swamp water.

"Frank, I think maybe I wish you weren't in love with me," Sally said.

"Operator, I want the Soap Creek Saloon in *Austin* . . . not *Boston*," Jackie Jack said into the phone.

Alive
with pleasure!
Newport

©Lorillard, U.S.A., 1976

18 mg. "tar", 1.2 mg. nicotine
av. per cigarette, FTC Report Dec. 1976.

Newport
20 CLASS A CIGARETTES
Newport
MENTHOL KINGS

Warning: The Surgeon General Has Determined That Cigarette Smoking Is Dangerous to Your Health.
True lowers tar to only
5 MGS. TAR
And has a taste worth changing to.
TRUE
FILTER CIGARETTES
5 MGS. TAR 0.5 MGS. NICOTINE
TRUE 5 MGS. TAR
Regular: 5 mgs. "tar", 0.4 mgs. nicotine, av. per cigarette, FTC Report Dec. 1976.
©Lorillard, U.S.A., 1976

Chapter
Twenty-seven

Purely out of a sense of duty, being a part of the business and all, I thought I should go straight to the men's room in "21" and test some products I had seen advertised on television.

First, I wanted to try one of those electric shavers guaranteed to transform a field of unharvested grain into something smoother than the top of a Formica table.

Instead of following the Big Guy upstairs to a private dining room where Herb Grant and Jack Nathanson were already sure to be waiting, Stanley Coffman chose to go with me.

"Jesus," he said. "Would that be a fucking headline? Right there on the front page of the *Daily News*? Network Biggie's Limo Kills Tycoon."

Ahead of the electric shaver, I selected an attractive mouthwash.

"Rocky dies yellow," I said, with my head over the basin.

Stanley said the Big Guy was in a good mood.

"He's the happiest little dildo you ever saw," said

Stanley. "Been around the office all morning long. Doing his little whimper-smile and his stumble-dance for the secretaries."

"How much law has he got with him? Just those two?"

Stanley said, "They wear so much of that fucking braid, I'm surprised nobody's ever asked 'em to park their car."

With the electric shaver I started cutting a path through the Everglades.

"What's he so happy about?"

"His new TV set," Stanley said. "Let me take it from the top. Grant found out you've got that plumber lined up as one of the four families on the show. The guy in Tampa, right? So Grant couldn't resist telling the Big Guy there was gonna be a plumber on 'Just Up the Street.' "

"I'm sure Grant said *he* found the plumber."

"I think he might have said it was Nathanson's idea, but he initialed it."

Stanley said the Big Guy was so excited about the plumber, he sent his DC-10 to Zurich to bring him back one of those $250,000 screens for the den of the sanitarium in Connecticut.

"The forty-footer?" I said.

"I don't know what they call the thing. The Stroganschleiger 35-MW, or something," Stanley said. "It's forty feet and total color. The Big Guy says it works perfectly. And all he had to do to make room for it on his wall was take down the painting of the Arizona doing a full zappo at Pearl Harbor."

I had heard of such a thing being under development as a TV set with a forty-foot color screen complete with equipment to record shows. I was delighted to hear that it worked.

"It's a steal at $250,000," I said.

I think I might have meant it.

I was now into sundry bottles of lotion.

"Got a tie?" said Stanley. "I don't want you to get hit by a sniper."

There was a tie in my coat pocket.

"Jesus, you're starting to look like a guy I know in television," Stanley said. "Couple of swipes at the hair, dump a little green-and-white on the tongue—just to eliminate the doubt—and you'll be ready for a fucking conference with Jesuits."

Stanley wanted to take the scenic route through the bar with all the junk hanging from the ceiling and the corporate guys hanging onto the Dewar's. And then go upstairs.

Everyone looked the same at the bar, even though they represented different networks and ad agencies. It was the usual convention of dark suits, white shirts, striped ties, big smiles and elbow leans.

Stanley had a glad-handing, good-natured line for all of them.

"How's it going, Timmy? Still got the same old ten million tied up in twenty-eight pilots?"

"Hey, Burt! Still trying to sell that sensitive Polack schoolteacher series? Do yourself a favor, guy. Put it right in the bowl."

"Good news, Vance. They're gonna counter-program the brusque Irish cop and his little nigger sidekick into your idealistic intern. Your guy's gonna kick ass and take names, fella."

Somebody accidentally stepped on Stanley's foot.

"Oh, I'll tell you what, Bruce," Stanley said to the guy. "You walk on the tops and I'll walk on the bottom."

He nudged me.

"Old Hollywood High gag," Stanley said. "Jesus, did I run with a slick fucking crowd."

Stanley acted like he was going to stand on a chair.

"Wait up a minute, Frank," he said. "I want to say something to the team."

He burst into laughter.

Then he left his pals with a bit of good news.

"Got the hand right there on the old lever, guys," he said. "Sales are up, costs are down, and morale's at an all-time high."

We were almost to the private dining room when Stanley said:

"Big deal. Lunch at '21.' Wish I had a dollar for every time I've thrown up in here. The little Wasp would own the corporation instead of the fucking nit-wit."

Chapter
Twenty-eight

∞∞∞∞∞∞∞∞∞∞∞∞∞∞∞∞∞∞∞∞∞∞

The military joined us for lunch, so we were seven. Four of us were Stanley, Grant, Nathanson and me. We all faced the Big Guy at the head of the table. On the Big Guy's left sat Rear Admiral Cletus (Barren Down) Boynton. On his right was Lieutenant General Merle (Shotsy) Stovall.

Other than to reminisce at some length about Iwo Jima, Salerno, Bataan, Normandy, Tobruk, Leningrad, Guadalcanal, Calais, the Rapido River, the Coral Sea, the Bulge, all the great one-liners that came out of Hiroshima, the way Ike liked his steaks cooked in the London headquarters, and how we gave it all away at Yalta, the General and the admiral did not say much.

Inevitably, the Big Guy rapped on his buttermilk glass with a spoon.

He told us about the forty-foot Stroganschleiger 35-MW that was now covering a wall of his den in Connecticut. Those who had already heard about it in detail did their best to appear fascinated.

This wasn't hard for Herb Grant.

The Big Guy said to Jack Nathanson, "I hope you

didn't mind Herb letting your little frog hop out of the campfire?"

The plumber.

"Marvelous inspiration," the Big Guy said. "Shall we drink to our Herb and our Jack?"

We raised our wine glasses and Nathanson said, "Actually, it was Frank who . . ."

That was as far as he could get before Herb Grant decided to cough up part of Newark.

Not that it mattered. The Big Guy wasn't listening, anyhow. His eyes were closed, his wispy white head was tipped back, his glass was up to his little pink face, and two tiny rivers of buttermilk were trickling down either side of his little pink neck.

The Big Guy put down his buttermilk and dried off with a napkin.

He asked if there was something more that any of us could tell him about the plumber.

"He lives in Tampa, Florida," Grant said.

"He has a wife and a teenage son," said Stanley.

"His name is Rocco. Angie Rocco," Nathanson said.

It may well have been my imagination, but I could have sworn the Big Guy bounced up and down in his seat with a whimpering smile.

As far as I knew, no porno filmmaker had touched on the theme of people getting off on the thought of an Italian plumber.

"I must have a little gathering to watch the show on my new gadget," the Big Guy said.

The general and the admiral took out pens and notebooks.

"Whom shall I invite?" the Big Guy said. "Shotsy and Bat, of course. Herb, you'll come, naturally."

"The Roccos are tied up," Stanley said. "But they send their best."

"So am I," said Nathanson.

238

"Me, too," I said.

"Stanley?" the Big Guy said.

"Working, Big Guy," Stanley said. "I'll be right there in the old trenches. Watching the numbers on the Electro-Check."

The Electro-Check was the name of one type of electronic scoreboard a network could lease in order to keep up with instant ratings. Ours was a large board carrying the outline of the Greater Metropolitan area. Within the outline were hundreds of small light bulbs that flickered in red, green, blue, yellow, orange and white.

The board was wired into Nielsen's homes. Rather, the TV sets in Nielsen's homes in the New York market which is the biggest in the country. Four hundred bulbs.

If your show was one with the red bulbs, for example, you could look at the board in any given moment and see how it was doing against the other shows.

We were green.

It was sometimes gratifying to see the board monopolized with green lights, if you approved of the show in the first place. It could be depressing to find only a scattering of green in the red and yellow.

I never paid that much attention to the board. At CBS we didn't have one—or need it, for that matter. We were always up there. And I believe I stated my opinion earlier about 1,170 sets confirming the tastes of 120,000,000.

But network presidents and others enjoyed the cheap S&M thrills of watching the board. Stanley was assuredly going to be in the trenches on the night of "Just Up the Street."

"A party can chase the gnats into the sponge," the Big Guy said.

His guest list was enlarged.

He was inviting Burch and Kitty Klinersparing. Burch, as we knew, was chairman of the board of UniCork. He was asking Gunther and Fatemeh Trask. RXP Industries. The Robertsons would probably come up from Hobe Sound. Packey and Deeny. Tuck Meeker, the P-41 ace, would be there with his new wife, Helena. The Moleclares from Newport. The Seatons from Easthampton. Dipsy and Olivia from Bronxville. The Von Klammers from Dusseldorf. And others.

Same old crowd.

Most network lunches have a habit of concluding with somebody saying, "Good luck, guys. And good show."

Ours ended with the Big Guy saying, "Gentlemen . . . as the bombardier said when he waved goodbye to his little batch of incendiaries . . . *Eect bin oberdongin der schwine das plumbers!*"

Chapter
Twenty-nine

∞∞∞∞∞∞∞∞∞∞∞∞∞∞∞∞∞∞∞∞∞∞∞∞∞∞∞∞

No limo of any color or design was waiting for me when I walked out of "21." I got in a cab and told the driver to drop me off at my apartment or a rehabilitation center, whichever came first.

I halfway expected to find Jackie Jack Snowdrift passed out on the marble floor of my entrance hall, and maybe some Deaf Cowboys playing wheelbarrow with the girls in pioneer dresses, and possibly Cooper and Katherine taking a bubble bath together, but Sally was the only person there.

Sally was curled up asleep in a chair in the den.

André, Dump and Ling were watching "The Mortal Storm" on all eight Sony screens.

I woke Sally up with a kiss.

She said Cooper had brought her to my place after the finish of the Limo Grand Prix, and Cooper had gone to his joint with Jackie Jack to continue celebrating the opening.

She also said the following things:

1. She intended to sleep for the next forty-eight hours.

2. She was starving to death.
3. She was on deadline for a piece.
4. Buford he got fat and Roy upped and died.
5. She was going down to the kitchen and make herself a Glug.
6. A Glug was as much vanilla ice cream, chocolate syrup and sweet milk as you could get into one big glass.
7. Did last night mean the final deluge had begun?

And:

8. She thought she might be in love with my cat.

In the kitchen I drank coffee and I watched Sally make her Glug, and then make half of another one. I also watched her make a BLT which expanded to include bologna, onion, cheese and relish, and we talked.

She asked how it had gone at lunch. I said I wished I'd had a Glug and a BLT–BOCR instead of whatever it was that "21" called sole meunière.

"I meant with the Big Guy and the show and all that," she said.

"Just Up the Street" was coming along, I said. Our remote crews had confirmed that all four families in Tampa, Rochester, Washington and Akron spoke fluent Norwegian and were either crippled or infirm.

"What do you really expect?" she asked seriously.

I said it was impossible to predict. I made no mention of what our researchers were hoping to confirm in Georgetown, or of my devious variation on the Kaplan project.

"You're not going to get much out of Tampa with the plumber except dinner and maybe some recipes," she said. "The teenage girl in Rochester is cute—if she'll talk and do something. Akron's the backyard thing, right? Maybe something will click in Georgetown."

God willing, I thought.

"You may be surprised at the response to this," Sally said. "Your promos are selling the hell out of the idea that CBC is doing something wholesome and American. The old departure-from-crime-and-violence crap."

"We'll see," I said.

I was finding it increasingly difficult to let Sally Hawks get out of my sight or my grasp, but she insisted she wanted to go home to her own apartment.

She said she had some typing and sleeping to do —she really did—so she would very much appreciate it if I did not tempt her with anything intriguing for the next couple of days.

She suffocated me with a kiss at the front door and left saying, "I don't want you to take this the wrong way, Slim, but you sure give good Glug."

Chapter
Thirty

〜〜〜〜〜〜〜〜〜〜〜〜〜〜〜〜〜〜〜〜

Cindy was missing.

That was the word from Marcie on the blue phone a few nights later. At this very moment, Marcie said, Cindy was probably being ravaged on a flea-ridden bed in the East Village. A gang of powerful, disoriented, dope-sick revolutionaries had punctured her arm with needles and they were having their way with our lovely sixteen-year-old daughter.

I was alone in the penthouse when Marcie called. I was working on a shot rundown we hoped to be able to stick close to on "Just Up the Street."

Which was only twenty-four hours away, as every proud American knew.

Sally was home working. Cooper was down at his joint reminding his bartenders that he carried a Binniss just in case any of them had it in mind to play some bartender games with the receipts.

Katherine had a singing date at the Concord.

"Frank, it's eight thirty," Marcie said. "Cindy told Frankie this afternoon that Melody's aunt had been rushed to Lenox Hill with a chest pain. She said Melody's mother was driving them all straight to the hospital. When I came home from the club I naturally called the Fosters. Melody is home with her parents! Do you know where Melody's aunt is, Frank? She's playing in a bridge tournament in *Aruba!*"

Cindy had let me down and I was pissed off about it. But I wasn't concerned about her safety. I knew where I could find her.

She would be at Marble Arch Station watching Jeff wait tables. Or, if he had the night off, she would be hanging around that store front on Columbus Avenue where Jeff bunked with two or three other healthy, white, virile, male welfare cases.

"I know you're distressed, Marcie, but give me a couple of hours and I promise you I'll round her up. She'll be just fine," I said.

With a free hand, I picked up the white phone and dialed Cooper's Country.

"Two hours," Marcie said. "I'm expected to sit here and be calm for two hours? Frank, you astonish me. You always have. You are a rotten . . . selfish . . . thoughtless . . . son of a bitch."

In our marriage it had somehow been predetermined that Marcie was the one who got to have all the fun indulging her temper. I was permitted to placekick inanimate objects every so often, but not if they came from Parke-Bernet.

Throughout the past two years, however, I had taken to doing something Marcie said was worse than anger. When she launched an attack I would sometimes retreat into song, sort of like Cooper.

"Walkin' is better than runnin' away," I sang just then, "and crawlin' ain't no good at all."

Willie Nelson.

"One hour, you bastard," Marcie said. "I want a phone call from you in one hour. I'm not going to sit here and be worried to death without hearing anything."

"She'll probably come walking in there in five more minutes, and then you can have the pleasure of making her cry," I said.

Nothing.

I said, "Marcie, why don't you get one of those analysts to come over and keep you company?"

"Dr. Ridley is here now."

"Dr. Ridley? What happened to Dr. Milligan?" I said.

"Clayborn Ridley is far more advanced than Felix Milligan could ever hope to be," Marcie said.

I told Marcie I would call her.

While I was waiting for Cooper and the Silver Goblet in front of the building, I tried to think of how I was going to handle it with Cindy.

A weird part of me felt some kind of disappointment that Cindy could have told such a dumb lie. Where was her creativity? Would I say *that* to her? Hey, kid, in the future, here's how to trick your old mom and not get caught.

She obviously wanted to see Jeff so badly that not another damn thing mattered. I could give Jeff a face he could take back to Hawaii that would make the other surfers laugh, but what would Cindy think of that?

Well, I would say something worldly and persuasive and loving, but firm. But first I had to find her.

The waiters at Marble Arch Station were asked to dress like guards at Buckingham Palace.

A fast look told Cooper and me that Cindy was not among the clientele. So with Cooper on one arm and me on the other, we lifted up a Buckingham Palace guard and carried him out to the sidewalk.

Jeff's fur hat fell off on the ground. A black kid grabbed it and started running toward Harlem.

"In Hong Kong, Jeff, they televise executions live," I said. "It's a fairly new thing but it's getting good ratings. We're going to pretend we're in Hong Kong now. Do you have any final words about where Cindy is?"

Jeff had only to look at Cooper to believe this was a serious conversation.

"Hey, I was really stoked on that chick, man," said Jeff. "But I thought she was older. Like I thought she was nineteen, you know?"

"That little old girl is just on the outside of sixteen," Cooper said. "She just finished the eleventh grade two weeks ago."

"Wow," Jeff said, softly. "It was lookin' good, too, man. Really."

"Where is she?" I said.

"I don't know, man," said Jeff. "Like I talked to her on the phone and told her I was thinkin' I might split. I've got this buddy in Ft. Lauderdale and he told me it was righteous down there. I didn't think it would get heavy, man."

"So she came in?"

"Yeah, she came to my pad about four hours ago. We were all laid back there, you know. I was gettin' my head fixed to go to work. And all of a sudden, this chick comes in, man."

"Her name is Cindy," I said.

"Right," said Jeff. "All of a sudden Cindy's there. She's lookin' good at first. We were talking. Then she starts in on Ft. Lauderdale and how if I go down there she's never gonna see me again. I tried to cool her out. Like give her the water pipe to get straight, but she starts crying, man. Then she follows me down here. Full on."

"How long was she here?"

"She ate three cheeseburgers," Jeff said. "Like she was taking up a whole booth by herself. And this cat I work for in there, man, he's giving me looks. So I finally asked her if she had some cabfare. She did. So I told her to go back to my pad, and when I got off, I'd come up there and we'd just lay back and listen to some moon rays."

"That's where she is?" I said.

"Far as I know, man," Jeff said. "Hey, like I'm sorry, you bein' her dad and all. Like we never did anything you'd be ashamed of her for. That was kind of radical on my part because I was really stoked, man. But it's true."

Cooper said, "I think if I was you, cousin, I'd get on down to Ft. Lauderdale quick as I could. Otherwise, them feet of yours might have an accident and you wouldn't be able to scuff on no more scuff boards like old Duke Kacooney-mackey."

Cindy was not at the store front.

In fact, there was no one at the store front but a grizzled derelict asleep on a cot.

When I shook him, he said, "Doughnuts!"

I asked if a young girl had been in there recently.

"Jeezy place got doughnuts," he mumbled. And he rolled back over to dream of better days.

Cooper said Cindy might have taken a taxi home. Pelham wasn't that far. And this late, she would have sense enough to get a taxi instead of the train.

I said I wasn't sure how much sense she had exactly.

I also knew that if Cindy had not gone home, I didn't know where she was. If I phoned Marcie to see if Cindy was home—and she wasn't—well, I didn't need that, either.

In the limo I phoned my apartment and let it ring ten or twelve times, just to make certain Cindy had not gone to my place while I was interviewing Jeff.

Nobody answered. Not even the service.

Terror is too strong a word for whatever I was feeling. Worry is too weak. Alarm? Maybe something like that.

248

"D. Wayne, run me over to Sally's," I said. "I need to talk to somebody smart."

On the ride to Sally's apartment I did a very fatherly thing. From the bar in the limo, I poured myself a hell of a drink.

Even though the Rita Hayworth poster on Sally's door was clearly identifying me as the same Glenn Ford she knew in *Gilda,* I banged on Rita's gown anyway with my fist.

Cooper stayed in the limo. He had an idea that *he* might call Marcie and say that he and I were looking for Cindy in different places. That way, he would take the heat, but we would find out whether Cindy was back home yet.

Music came from inside Sally's apartment.

James Taylor was apparently helping Sally type.

I heard several bolts turning and chains being unhinged, and the door opened. In a long yellow nightshirt, Sally smiled at me with a glass of white wine in her hand.

"The trouble with the world is, a sixteen-year-old girl can't even believe in her goddam, motherfucking, phony-ass, cocksucking heroes," I said.

"Daddy!"

Cindy's head was poking into Sally's living room from the walk-in kitchen just off of it.

She raced over and grabbed onto me with a can of 7–Up in her hand.

I had any number of questions, but the one I thought of first was, "You okay, babe?"

"Sure," Cindy said. "I mean, I am now. Like I probably wasn't so okay a while ago, but now I'm cool. Only, wow. I'm in big trouble this time, huh?"

"You won't get life, but you'll do some time," I said.

Cindy said, "It isn't like I robbed a bank or anything, Dad. All I did was, I wanted to see Jeff, you know?"

I said, "Kids have a hard time learning two things. You get in more trouble than ever if you lie. And always let your parents know where you are."

Cindy said she guessed she thought she could come into the city, see Jeff, and get back to Pelham in a taxi before Marcie came home from the club.

"Mom usually stays late on Tuesday. Sometimes she even calls up and says she's going on to dinner with friends and she tells Frankie and me to find something to eat in the frozen food thing," Cindy said.

"I hope seeing Jeff was worth getting caught," I said.

Cindy wrinkled her nose and said, "Yuk. Jeff. Blaaah."

The recuperative powers of a young girl always amazed me. If Cindy had been crying, you couldn't tell it. In college, Marcie could sob for twenty minutes over TCU upsetting the beloved Longhorns, and then in an instant she could look ready to go to the Lake Austin Inn and sing Tri Delt songs.

I said, "Your mother is borderline frantic."

Cindy said, "I should have called her, but Sally and I got to talking about life and things, and I didn't know how to tell her where I was. We tried to call you. Your service didn't even answer."

Cindy added, "Sally decided the best thing was for me just to stay here. She said you were bound to call."

Sally said, "Hi, sailor. How about a champagne cocktail?"

I said Scotch would do.

While she made my drink, Sally spoke of destiny's role in our lives. Sally said she was typing when she realized her thesaurus was missing. She had loaned it to Lisa. So she walked over to Lisa's apartment to get it, and that was how she ran into Cindy on Columbus Avenue.

"What were you doing?" I said to Cindy.

"Nothing," Cindy said. "I mean, just standing outside the store front. And maybe crying. I was waiting for Jeff, but I knew he wasn't coming. Jeff, yick. Daaah."

Sally said, "We've had a good time. I've told her about all the other Jeffs she'll meet along the dusty old trail."

Cindy said to me, "Some boys take all they can get and don't give anything back. And some girls are so determined not to get robbed by that they're never willing to give anything."

"Which are you?" I asked Cindy.

"I want to give," my daughter said. "Only I've got to learn how to pick my spots better."

Sally raised her wine glass in a toast.

I went to the phone. It sat on the floor next to a stereo and some scattered albums.

Cindy was fine and she was with me, I said to Marcie. Cindy had done a stupid thing but maybe she had learned something from it, I said. She didn't seem to be addicted to anything but 7–Up. Since it was late, I said, Cindy would spend the night with me.

Cindy tugged at my arm and said, "I want to see the show in the studio tomorrow night, Dad. Ask Mom."

I asked Marcie if that would be all right.

Marcie said, "That child is not going to terrify me and then get rewarded for it."

I said, "She's interested in television, Marcie. She likes being in the control rooms. And this show is going to be a little something different."

"She has piano tomorrow," Marcie said.

I said, "Cooper will have her home before noon. You can beat her up. Then he'll take her to piano. Then they'll come to the studio. And Cooper will bring her home tomorrow night after the show."

"Very well, Frank," Marcie said. "Are you home now?"

"We're in a restaurant," I said. "Are you going to watch the show?"

"If I get back from dinner in time," Marcie said. "We've had these reservations at La Crémaillère for over a week."

"That place up in the country that serves fat duck?"

"It's excellent," Marcie said.

I asked who her dinner companions were.

"Eddie Burns," she said.

Eddie Burns?

Eddie Burns was the assistant golf pro at the club. Compared to Eddie Burns, Rex the Wonder Horse was a gerbil.

"May I speak to Cindy now, please," Marcie said. "I want the satisfaction of telling my child that after tomorrow night she is *grounded* for a month!"

Cindy took it like a trooper and hung up.

I told Cindy to run on down to the limo and wake up D.W.C. I would be there in a minute.

Cindy gave Sally a hug and left.

With the front door standing open and Rita Hayworth looking on, I kissed Sally and held her.

"Did I hear you say you were in a restaurant?" Sally whispered.

"Unfortunately," I said. "Why the hell was I afraid to say where I was?"

"I don't know," she said, doing things to my ear. "Why was Anna Karenina?"

I looked down at her.

"If you came to the broadcast center early enough tomorrow, I could take a break and kiss around on you for good luck," I said.

"Darn right," Sally said. "Half the fun is watching you matadors kneel in front of the crucifix before you get your asses gored."

PART
THREE

but there know we were really going through with it.

Chapter
Thirty-one

～～～～～～～～～～～～～～～～～～～

"We're 'Just Up the Street' in Ak-
ron, Ohio . . . and inside this pleasant four-bedroom,
three-bath ranch-style house, Mr. and Mrs. Franklin
Lincoln Perry are working out on their Exer-Genies
before sitting down to a dinner of . . ."

Rod DeRoache, the commentator in Akron, glanced
at a card in his hand and bent his mouth into a horrible smile.

". . . fried okra, sweet potatoes, cornbread, navy
beans, hamhock, beets and raisin pie. God almighty,
are they really? Listen, Jack, do I have to say this?"

Rod DeRoache was speaking from Franklin Lincoln Perry's frontyard in Akron. We were seeing
DeRoache on monitors in our biggest and newest control room in the CBC broadcast center on the eighth
floor of the Chambers building in Gotham.

It was twenty minutes before air time for "Just Up
the Street."

Jack Nathanson was doing a whip-around of the
four cities, checking the hookup and letting the crews
out there know we were really going through with it.

"What's the matter, Rod?" Nathanson said into his headset.

"Nobody could eat a meal like this. It turns my stomach," Rod DeRoache said.

"You don't have to eat it. Just report it," Nathanson said.

There were pictures on all twenty monitors in the control room. Jack Nathanson sat in a leather chair in the middle of the front row with the monitors covering the wall in front of him. Four assistants sat in leather chairs on each side of Nathanson. All nine wore headsets. Nine more leather chairs on the second row, one step higher than the first, were occupied by people connected with putting "Just Up the Street" on the air.

Unless you wore a headset and had access to the right switches, you couldn't hear what the people were saying on the twenty monitors. But you could see them.

The way you could tell which picture was appearing on America's TV screens was to look at the monitor labeled Air Screen.

The Air Screen was in the high panel to the right of Nathanson. Another large monitor was labeled Line Screen. That one showed the same picture that was on the Air Screen but without the commercials.

Next to the Line Screen was the Preview Screen. The Preview Screen showed the picture Nathanson was preparing to move to the Air Screen and thus into the homes of our audience.

If that seems confusing, remember also that machines were whirring, people were talking about tapes and levels and feeds, others scurried in and out carrying clipboards, telephone lights flashed, and a half dozen technicians pointed urgently at different things that might go wrong.

On the Preview Screen we had a lovely color picture

of Hank Judson digging a finger into his nose and studying the script for his opening.

Once Hank had agreed to do the show as a "favor" to me, he never complained or expressed doubt or criticism of anything involving "Just Up the Street." He never did say he enjoyed it, either. To Hank, in his field a pro was a person who said what was supposed to be said when the red light came on, and said it clearly and convincingly. Hank could be humorous when the story called for humor, but he didn't believe an anchorman ought to joke with his colleagues while on the air. "Some of these fresher blokes, they josh the weatherman about being wrong, and they ask the political reporter who's going to win the primary, and they even allow themselves to be kidded about their golf scores. In other words, dear fellow, they appear to be victims of the news rather than authorities on it," was what Hank said when Herb Grant suggested CBC try a lighter news format.

I walked around the control room sipping coffee, putting down the cups and losing them.

Actually I wasn't any more frightened at that moment than I was when our helicopter got shot down near the Cambodian border.

Sally approached with a notebook and a Pentel in her hands.

"You understand, Frank, that as a journalist it is my responsibility to report honestly to my readers on what happens here tonight," Sally said. "Even if it means describing the humiliation and ruin of a man I could have loved."

I knew she was trying to amuse me and smooth me out.

Also I knew what she said was true.

If Sally decided to write a *New York* magazine column on "Just Up the Street"—as any columnist with any sense at all would do, especially given an inside look at this monumental act of insanity—she might fry me until there was nothing but a grease spot where once had parked a silver Rolls limo.

To my mind, Sally would be doing the right thing if "Just Up the Street" turned out to be as stupid, ill-conceived, trivial and monotonous as the daily newspapers had been predicting.

The *New York Post* had said, "What Frank Mallory is doing is saying, look at CBC, America, we're going to cross our eyes, stick our tongues out sideways, and blow spit bubbles on our lips."

If the *Post* had suggested that earlier, I might have been able to do something with it.

On the other hand, if "Just Up the Street" turned out to be as wonderful as our promotion department predicted, then Sally might write something nice about me and fling herself into my arms and beg me to take her.

So I wished to think.

"A crack reporter can't afford to go soft on nobody, baby," I said.

"I only cry at weddings," Sally said.

D. Wayne Cooper came in with Cindy.

Cindy said to Sally, "Have you ever heard D.W.C. explain television?" Cindy was grinning.

Cooper said, "All them screens are showing pictures from cameras in all them different towns. The director picks out a picture he wants the folks at home to see. So he tells somebody to move that picture from one of them little screens to this big screen here. That's about the main thing there is to television."

"But tell Sally how television works," Cindy said.

"I just told her," Cooper said.

"Tell her how a picture gets from Akron to New York," Cindy said, "and stays in the room for a while and then a director sends it to your home."

Cooper said, "The picture flies through the air and

sticks in all them tubes and wire deals in the back of the set. You unscrew the back of a set sometime and look in there. You'll see what I mean."

Cindy laughed and was pleased that Sally laughed.

"It's dangerous to unscrew the back of a TV set, though. You can get electrocuted," Cooper said. "That's how come you ought to leave the picture flying stuff to the scientists and just stick with what I'm telling you."

Cindy hugged Cooper.

I edged past them and went into the next-door VIP room.

Behind me I heard Cindy say, "Daddy just patted me on the head and said nice doggie."

"Your old daddy's got a lot of electrical do-dads to think about right now," Cooper said.

Stanley Coffman, a public-relations girl and a bartender in a white jacket were the only people in the VIP room.

Stanley stared at the Electro-Check board. The board was ten feet high and ten feet wide. The tiny electric bulbs glowed red, blue, green and yellow on the map of the Greater New York area. There were a fair number of green lights for CBC. We might even have been out front.

That was because I had talked Stanley into ordering an extra half hour of news specials on the schedule that week. On the theory that many people would rather keep watching news than those shows that usually come on right after the news, from 7:30 to 8, and are aimed at the car-up-on-the-blocks-in-the-frontyard crowd.

I figured an extended early evening news would give us a sizeable leading audience to "Just Up the Street" and would arouse their voyeuristic curiosity about human behavior.

And I also hoped they might consider "Just Up the

Street" as news, which was what I had told Hank Judson it was.

"It's gonna be a hell of an awesome sight," Stanley said, looking at the board.

"What is?" I said.

"In seven minutes, all those green lights are gonna turn off," Stanley said.

On the twenty-five-inch color screen built into the wall, a skier swooped down a mountain at seventy miles an hour, caught a tip in the ice and did cartwheels in the forest.

We had been running clips of great sports action on the sports segment of the extended early evening news. We had run film of tornadoes in Kansas and nude bathers in St.-Tropez on the weather segment. The news itself had been a circus of civil wars, cute puppies at the pound, world leaders nodding at airports, lingerie fashion shows, killer whales, babies for sale, a Con Edison scandal, highlights of the day's fires and murders, a two-minute piece on how to open a Swiss bank account, whither bears and wolves, etc. At no time all week did we have three or four CBC experts sitting in plastic chairs discussing the economy.

Stanley held out his empty glass to the p.r. girl.

"It's lonely at the top but nobody has to stay long," he said.

We hadn't invited press or sponsors or special guests to the VIP room for "Just Up the Street." We had liquor and hors d'oeuvres in the event some insisted on coming anyhow. So far they hadn't.

I left the VIP room and walked up and down the hall. In one studio they were taping a Girl Scout chorus singing songs about America. In another they had been spending the day knocking off a week's worth of celebrity game shows. In a third, the tail of the news was fighting the clock. Perspiring writers whose faces would never be seen on camera sat inches away from our not-as-famous-as-Hank-Judson-but-still-worth-$200,000-a-year substitute anchorman. His face shone a rich beige color from the pancake makeup. It was a fast-breaking story, and the writers wore earphones and typed big letters on sheets of paper they shoved in front of the anchorman, who looked into the camera and recited the words. It took him twenty seconds to read a page. The main writer had about a thirty-second lead on the anchorman. If the main writer toppled out of his chair dead, the anchorman would have no idea what to say next.

It was kind of exciting.

Two minutes till air for "Just Up the Street."

I had been staying out of the control room as much as I could, so as not to intrude too heavily on Jack Nathanson.

Marcie was partly right about some aspects of my personality. I do have an inclination to take charge and run everything. There have been times of emergency when I knew at the bottom of my soul that I could handle the situation better than anyone else, that I was in fact the *only* person who could handle it. Like at the political convention when the riot started, and our floor men were getting crushed. I took over the board that day. My action caused certain people to call me a megalomaniac, and the replaced director to threaten suicide. But anybody in the business will admit our coverage was the best.

That was just about the last working trip Marcie made with me. She said she couldn't stand the way I behaved after the convention riot. She said I acted like I thought I was a hero. She was partly right about that, too. I wasn't a hero like our guys on the floor who were being punched and having their equipment smashed. But I felt I deserved a rush of pride and pleasure. Because pretty soon in the TV news busi-

261

ness I was bound to hit a screw-up, and I would feel just as low as I had felt high.

I slipped back into the control room just as Jack Nathanson was saying into his headset:

"Five seconds, gang . . . and— Go Hank!"

"Just Up the Street" was on the air.

If you were watching CBC television somewhere out there in America, you saw Hank Judson sitting at a rolltop desk in what appeared to be his study. Hank looked into your eyes and said:

"Good evening. Tonight we are going on a journey into the heart of this country. You will be an eye-witness to history . . ."

As Hank Judson spoke, Nathanson called for the picture from Rochester to be put on the Preview Screen. I slipped on a headset and flipped a switch and heard our man in Rochester saying, "Get away from me. I don't need any more hair spray." America didn't hear that. America was still watching Hank Judson, if America was watching CBC–TV.

Hank finished his opening by saying, ". . . so sit back and let's travel together . . . and maybe learn to love each other a little more."

Next on the Air Screen was the face of Jerry Cummings, our man in Rochester. Jerry was six-feet-six and had a jaw like Basil Rathbone.

"This is Jerry Cummings, 'Just Up the Street' in Rochester, New York, at the home of Ralph and Ann Getz and their daughter Roxie. Mr. and Mrs. Getz have both put in a hard day of work on their respective jobs at Kodak and Xerox . . ."

In the control room, on the Preview Screen, Nathanson's next shot was ready. It was an interior of the Getz home. Mrs. Getz wore a party dress with risky cleavage and was rushing around the living room, dusting tables, straightening cushions. Ralph Getz was fiddling with the battery pack on his hip and glaring

262

offscreen at our guy with the mini-camera, whose shot was showing on another monitor in the control room.

The teenage daughter, Roxie, sat at a table doing her summer school homework. A black Labrador dog gazed at the activity and thumped her tail on the floor.

"Looks good, Jug," Nathanson said into the headset. He was talking to the director in the remote truck in Rochester. Through my headset I heard the Rochester director say, "Getz is hot about something."

"We're coming to you anyhow, Jug," Nathanson said.

To the technical director on his left Nathanson said, "Take the living room," and swept a finger through the air like a musical conductor.

The Getz living room now appeared on the Line Screen and the Air Screen in the control room at the CBC–TV broadcast center, and in the homes of all who were watching.

Nothing was happening except Mrs. Getz nervously skipping around. Ralph Getz sat down on the couch, scowled and shifted his weight off the battery pack and studied the floor between his bare feet. He had on Madras Bermuda shorts like I had not seen in fifteen years.

Ann Getz fluffed the cushions behind her husband's back and said, "Did you have a hard day in assembly, dear?"

Ralph Getz said, "What do you care?"

"Come on, Roxie, do something," I said.

On the hope that she might, Nathanson cut to a mini-cam closeup of Roxie. She was a cute little rascal, and she did put the pencil in her mouth and chew on it in a kind of suggestive manner.

I flipped through the biographies that research had prepared on our four American families.

"ROXIE GETZ—age fifteen; twirler in high school band, average student, popular with boys. Hobbies: dancing, archery. Wants to be a paramedic when grows up, or else a dance instructor. . . ."

By the Big Guy's rules, our on-the-scene commentators were not allowed to ask the families questions. But the biographies gave Hank Judson and the commentators something to say when we cut back to them to fill time.

Roxie looked at her mother and smiled.

"Mom, where are we going on our vacation this summer?" Roxie said.

"I'd like to visit Samoa," Mrs. Getz said.

"Samoa! You think money grows in a cabbage patch?" Ralph Getz said. "Who the hell put Samoa in your mind?"

"One of the TV men told me about it. He said it would be just our kind of place," Ann Getz said.

"Yours and his, or yours and mine?" Ralph said.

"Why, yours and mine, I think," Ann said.

"What would I do in Samoa?" Ralph said.

Ann Getz squinted, thinking hard.

"I don't know what you would do in Samoa, Ralph," she said. "Maybe he did mean him and me."

And Nathanson moved "Just Up the Street" to the Georgetown area of Washington, D.C.

Tom Parsons, the Georgetown commentator, stood on a cobbled street in front of a narrow, three-story townhouse.

". . . and here in historic Georgetown, the Skidmores' four children . . . all under the age of six . . . are snugly in their beds . . . while Bob and Dorothea Skidmore await the arrival of their dinner guests. . . ."

Parsons dropped his eyes quickly to the card in his hand, looked up and said:

". . . dinner guests, um . . ."

Parsons glanced at the card again.

". . . dinner guests, ah, ah, . . . Dorothea's amusing

sister and brother-in-law who own a chain of car washes . . ."

Parsons started laughing on America's TV screens. Nathanson cut to the inside of the townhouse.

"I don't remember that bit from the biog," Nathanson said into the headset to the remote director in Georgetown. "Oh, you just learned it? Believe me, you guys had better get serious."

I had been stepping up and down between the first and second rows of leather chairs. I noted Sally, Cindy and Cooper looking at me from the doorway to the VIP room. I walked over to them.

"Not bad so far, huh?" I said.

They said it was interesting.

As a one-word critical expression, "interesting" is death.

On the Line Screen, Dorothea Skidmore walked across the room with her chin raised, her shoulders thrust back and her arms at her sides with palms out. She wore a white silk gown and pearls and a fifty-dollar coiffure.

"I do hope Gladys and Phil like the Chablis I picked out today," Dorothea said.

"Oh, I'm sure they will. Phil can drink anything, the old soak," Bob Skidmore said with a smile. "Darling, don't be cross. It was only a joke."

I knew from the bios that Skidmore was a thirty-seven-year-old lawyer on the Washington staff of an oil company that had its headquarters in Houston. Skidmore's wife, Dorothea, five years younger, did in fact aspire to replace the Iranian ambassador as the city's leading party giver.

I bent over and whispered to Nathanson. I said for him to have Parsons give out basic Skidmore information in a voice over, in case anybody had missed it at first, like I evidently had.

Dorothea smiled and kissed Bob lightly on the lips.

She turned to the camera and let her gaze drift on over the lens as if she hadn't noticed any camera but was listening at the window for the arrival of Gladys and Phil.

"Mmmmmmm. Just right," Bob Skidmore said, lifting a bottle of wine out of a bucket of ice.

"Darling, don't take the wine out yet," Dorothea said.

"I was only feeling it," Bob said.

"When you take it out of the bucket too soon, it interferes with the chilling process," Dorothea said.

"I should have known. Sorry, love," Bob said.

"That's all right, darling," Dorothea said gaily. "How was the golf at Burning Tree today?"

"Two over par. Not bad, not good," Bob said. "On the sixteenth I hit what I thought was a super shot, but I must have caught it a tiny bit thin, because . . ."

Stanley pushed through from the VIP room and said:

"That's it. The little greenies are just about gone. It's reds and blues and yellows from here on, guys. In a few more minutes, there's a real chance we'll be actually feeding a show to a hundred and eighty stations that nobody in the fucking world is watching except the Big Guy."

Nathanson checked with the Franklin Lincoln Perry location in Akron and decided to go there, after first letting America see Hank Judson relaxed and smiling in his simulated study, and hear Hank say, ". . . to our friends in Ohio . . ."

This time Akron commentator Rod DeRoache did the intro quickly, like he was trying to hold his breath, and Nathanson cut to the inside of the house.

The house was filling with people. They were coming in the back door. Two guys wore softball uniforms with LEROY'S AUTO PARTS on the back. The crowd was

266

mostly black. Our mini-cam guy got jostled into view on the air and ducked out of sight again.

"Naw, it ain't plugged into no socket," Franklin Lincoln Perry said on the air to a friend. "Just sticken this hunk of a thing in my pocket and this wire comes up under my shirt and this little microphone they got taped under my collar."

Perry unbuttoned his shirt to show America how a battery pack works.

"You want to say something anybody?" Perry said, pointing to the mike.

"Hey, is we on the TV?" asked a man with his hat brim turned up. "Where you TV set, Franklin, so I can see?"

It had been my idea to remove all TV sets from the four "Just Up the Street" homes. Certain critics later picked on this as dishonest, because three of the four families on our show would probably have been watching TV on an ordinary Wednesday night. But if we left the TV sets in the houses, all four of our families would have been watching themselves.

And you could have said removing the TV sets was an honest attempt to see if four American families "Just Up the Street" could go through a Wednesday night being watched instead of watching.

You could call it real life if you ignored the trucks, lights, generators, cables, cops and crowds out in the yards of these four American homes.

If the four families would forget the concealed cameras inside the house, and the mini-cam guy creeping behind the furniture, and the mikes and battery packs, it was just about like real life. Except for no TV to look at.

"They taken away my TV," Franklin Lincoln Perry said.

"That must of been it in that truck out in the drive-way. I'll go get it back," the man in the hat said.

Nathanson said into the headset, "Hear that, Jug? Got a cop handy? And can you plug that leak at the back door?"

Inside the house Pearl Perry looked at the dishes on her dining table.

"Hey, look at this, we got plenty of fried okra," she said to the people pouring into the house.

Nathanson read my mind and had Rod DeRoache, the commentator, lay in more biography: Franklin Lincoln Perry, forty-six, was born in Georgia, fought in Korea, was a union official and a foreman at Goodyear. Pearl's occupation was elementary schoolteacher.

"I tell you this, man. You don't look at me like I was no bug, man. You dig? I see you lookin' at me, I stick beans in your eye, man," a guy in a softball uniform said straight into the live camera.

Nathanson tried to switch to our fourth location— Tampa.

Line trouble caused Jack to delay the move to Tampa. Hank Judson filled with background on the Florida West Coast.

The picture was still not perfect on the Preview Screen. But the Big Guy himself had phoned the control room to ask when he could see Tampa.

Tampa was the home of Angie Rocco, the plumber.

Also Angie's wife Carmen and fat son Mario.

It was a whitewashed house built on concrete blocks. The house had a screened-in swimming pool and a boat in the driveway. The boat was a twenty-eight-foot cabin cruiser.

Lewis, the Tampa commentator, did a quick bio on the Roccos: Angie had worked his way up through the plumbing ranks to become a specialist you called for tough jobs.

Angie was a brain surgeon when it came to crawl-under jobs and elbow-bend pipes.

"To his fellow plumbers," the commentator said, "he's known as King of the Hard Reach."

Then Lewis looked at his bio card again and said, ". . . Angie Rocco calls his boat *Eduardo*. Most ships, or boats, if you will, are named after women. But Angie Rocco named his boat, he said, after a friend's pizza that doesn't go down so easy."

A feeble smile strained on the face of the commentator.

On the Preview Screen was a picture of Angie Rocco in his living room, cleaning and oiling a 16/0 fishing reel on the coffee table.

Mario Rocco was eating ice cream out of a mixing bowl and reading *Penthouse* magazine.

Carmen Rocco was nowhere to be seen on any of the monitors.

"Nothing . . . it's nothing," Jack Nathanson said.

"Stick with it for a minute, Jack," I said.

"Stick with what? It's nothing," Jack said.

On the monitor for the camera covering the front-yard, we saw a Chevrolet park at the curb. A man got out, showed a cop some sort of I.D., walked across the lawn and rang the bell.

Jack told his technical director to punch up the Air Screen as Angie Rocco wiped Three-in-One oil on his khaki pants.

"If you got trouble in your pipes, come back Monday," Angie said, looking through the screen door on CBC–TV.

Carmen Rocco backed into the room from a closet where—research turned up this item—she hid a plastic bag of Snickers candy bars.

According to research, Carmen weighed 265.

"What's the guy at the door?" Carmen said.

"He's a guy that's got to come back Monday," Angie said.

"Mr. Rocco, my name is Kaplan. I'm here about your income tax," the man at the door said.

"You said *what?*" Angie said.

"Sorry to come so late, but we have to work all hours keeping up. I guess you understand that in your business," Kaplan said.

"What about my income tax?" Angie Rocco said.

"I won't know for sure until I see the records, will I?" Kaplan said.

Stunned, Rocco backed away from the door.

"Get tight on Rocco's face," Nathanson said into the headset.

"Look at old Angie, he's about to pass a kidney stone," Cooper laughed in the control room.

There were a few other laughs in the control room.

Stanley yelled from around the corner of the VIP room, "Wops and Jews, how can you root?"

"Get outta here! Go away from this house!" Angie shouted at Kaplan live, on television.

"Angie, if the man wants to see our tax records, we got to show 'em. He's the government," Carmen said.

"Don't be alarmed. Think of me as your accountant," Kaplan said.

Carmen Rocco opened the door for Kaplan, who came in, put his briefcase on a table and rubbed his hands together.

Our mini-cam got a good shot of Kaplan's squinty eyes behind rimless glasses.

"The records, please," Kaplan said.

"I did the taxes myself. I'm no criminal," Carmen said.

"Sure, Carmen might of made a mistake in arithmetic, but she ain't trying to swindle Uncle Sam," Angie Rocco said.

"You helped me, Angie!" Carmen said.

"I didn't help her," Angie Rocco said to Kaplan.

"Mario, the slob, he helped her. He ain't even my kid. Carmen had another marriage."

Mario got up with his copy of *Penthouse,* opened what was clearly a bathroom door, went inside, slammed the door and loudly locked it.

"This ain't no time for that! Come out of there, kid, and tell Mr. Kaplan what you done about the income tax," Angie Rocco said.

Mario turned on the water at the bathroom sink.

"It isn't just you, Mr. Rocco," Kaplan said. "We're tracking down every plumber in the United States."

"I've got a cousin in Detroit that can take care of you," Carmen Rocco said.

"No threats! Don't threaten Mr. Kaplan!" yelled Angie. "You want the records, Kaplan? I know where she hides 'em."

Rocco opened the closet door, dived inside and reappeared with the bag of Snickers candy bars.

"It's a big surprise you gained thirty pounds on your diet!" Angie Rocco said to his wife.

Carmen Rocco waddled into the kitchen.

Angie Rocco sat down and looked at Kaplan.

"Kaplan, I'll come clean. I got no records," Angie Rocco said. "Here's what happened. God's truth. The niggers took my records. Yeah, eight or ten niggers stuck me up and stole my tax records."

"Could I have a description of them?" Kaplan said.

"What description? I said niggers," Angie Rocco said.

"A description of the tax records, Mr. Rocco," Kaplan said.

This all went out on the air on CBC–TV.

Scanning the monitors, Jack Nathanson guided Hank Judson into Akron, where the party had spilled into the yard and there was a melee near the remote truck.

Rod DeRoache, the Akron commentator, appeared on the Line Screen.

271

"There is a misunderstanding 'Just Up the Street' at the home of Mr. and Mrs. Franklin Perry," Rod De-Roache said.

DeRoache coughed and covered his mouth with a hand for a few seconds before he continued:

"A neighbor believes Mr. Perry's television set is inside our CBC remote truck. The man is being forcibly restrained by the Akron police and our crew. This seems to have put the Perrys and their guests in a nasty humor."

DeRoache coughed again and gagged.

"And back to you, CBC Central," DeRoache said.

"Rubber fumes are getting DeRoache," we heard the Akron director say on the headsets.

Nathanson had been examining the monitors. He switched the air picture to Rochester, where on the porch of the Ralph and Ann Getz house, commentator Jerry Cummings had stopped a teenage boy.

"Could I ask your name, please?" Cummings said.

"Larry Wilkins," the boy said.

"And is that a bandage on your wrist?" Cummings said.

Before he came to the News Department, Cummings was a veteran of post-game locker room shows for sports. He was best known for having asked O. J. Simpson if being big, fast and elusive was an advantage for a halfback.

The boy looked at the bandage and then back at Cummings.

"Yeah. Bandage," Larry Wilkins said.

"Has your wrist been injured in some way, Larry?" Cummings asked.

"Who are you?" the boy said.

"Jerry Cummings, 'Just Up the Street' at the Getz home in Rochester, New York," Cummings said.

"What's all this stuff?" the boy asked.

"Our equipment. You're on television, Larry," Cummings said.

"Yeah?"

"Now tell us about your injury," Cummings said.

In another post-game locker room show, Cummings had asked Kareem Jabbar if he thought his future was still ahead of him.

"I sprained my thumb a little when I gouged Johnny Ryan's eye at school," the boy said. "But I'll be okay to pitch Saturday."

Into the headset Nathanson said, "Hey, shut Cummings up with the interview and let the boy go inside."

"What brings you to the Getz house, Larry?" Cummings asked.

"You ever get a look at Roxie?" the boy said.

In CBC Control, Nathanson said, "Dissolve inside . . . and . . . put it up."

Now America saw Ralph Getz as he sat quietly scowling on the couch in his living room. The black Lab slept at Ralph's bare feet. The table where Roxie had been doing her homework was now being set for dinner by Ann.

Suddenly Ralph spoke. But not to Ann.

Ralph spoke to the black Labrador.

"Tell you what, Daphne, if I'd known it was gonna involve all this just to get ourselves on television so Roxie can be famous, I believe I'd of told these TV boys the Getz family don't need it," Ralph said.

Daphne, the black Lab, sat up and looked at Ralph.

"We voted to revolt and kill our bosses, Daphne, did I tell you that?" Ralph said. "I tried to tell Ann but she said to wait until the show is over. When the show is over, they're gonna take those cables out of the beans and tomato plants, too, Daphne."

"Someone's at the door. Oh, it must be Larry for Roxie," Ann said.

Our mini-cam guy followed Ann Getz down the hall.

Nathanson put the mini-cam shot on the Preview Screen.

On the air, Ralph was saying, "Daphne, if I give you a dollar, would you go to the store for some ice cream?"

Nathanson cut the mini-cam shot onto the nation's TV screens just as Ann Getz opened the door at the end of the hall.

And anybody who was watching "Just Up the Street" on CBC at that moment saw the lovely, young, naked body of Roxie Getz.

You saw her from behind, but she was standing at a full-length mirror, so you also saw her from in front. She was brushing her long hair. She turned and smiled toward her mother.

Then Roxie seemed to notice the mini-cam for the first time, just as Roxie's mother saw in the mirror that the mini-cam was poking over her shoulder.

Roxie covered her pubes with the hairbrush and held an arm across her breasts.

Ann Getz grappled for the mini-cam and we got a shot of the ceiling before Jack cut the picture back to the living room.

Certain critics later accused Jack Nathanson of being too slow to cut away from the naked nymphet.

In fact, CBC had another minute of Roxie before Ann Getz shut the door in the mini-cam guy's face. But you had to be in the control room to see it on the monitor.

On the Air Screen, being fed to a hundred and eighty stations, Ralph Getz was telling Daphne that he was thinking seriously about giving up fishing.

"Ask if the dog can do tricks," I said to Nathanson.

Ralph Getz glanced offscreen as the question was relayed.

Ralph nodded and said, "Sing, Daphne."

The black Lab put back her head and we all agreed you could honestly hear "Tea for Two."

Ralph sang along.

In fact, I heard Stanley singing along in the VIP room.

"Hey, guys, we're getting some greenies back!" Stanley yelled.

"What happened to the kid who came to see Roxie?" I said.

Nathanson found the shot and put it up.

On the front porch of the Getz house, Jerry Cummings was still interviewing Larry Wilkins. But now there were at least a dozen more teenage boys on the porch.

And a guy in a raincoat was trying to reach the camera.

Hank Judson did the transition for a fast cut to Akron. Rod DeRoache, looking ill, explained the odd gathering in the yard. After the argument at the remote truck, DeRoache said, the Perrys' real TV set had been returned. The Perrys and neighbors had been on their way back inside the house to watch "Just Up the Street," when Sergeant Jackson arrived with a five-hundred-pound Roman candle.

"That's right, the boys are getting it down off the truck right now," Sergeant Jackson said, walking into the picture beside DeRoache.

Sergeant Jackson was about sixty and had grizzled white hair beneath his American Legion cap.

"Furthermore, we are going to shoot this five-hundred-pound Roman candle from a thirty-six-inch mortar. We got it loaded in there already," Sergeant Jaclson said. "When this booger goes off, the world is gonna know it."

Rod DeRoache smiled and flicked his eyes from side to side, checking what else might confront him.

"This Roman candle is gonna shoot a thousand feet

275

in the air," Sergeant Jackson said. "Then it's gonna open into a million twinkling stars in the shape of Mount Rushmore. I mean with all the faces on it, too, Clyde. It's a gift to the people of America from Legion Post 937."

"Four dollars it don't," said a man in a softball uniform.

"Save your money, brother, this thing gonna light up the sky from here to Schenectady," Sergeant Jackson said.

"I got four dollars say it do," Franklin Lincoln Perry said.

"You covered," said the man in the softball uniform.

"Brother, you ever see Mount Rushmore?" Sergeant Jackson said. "Well, in case you don't recall, Mount Rushmore is a big mountain where some cat carved four Presidents' faces on it. He put George Washington on there. Lincoln. Uh, Roosevelt, I believe. And one more dude. Ulysses S. Grant, I think it was."

"Don't make a shit, this ain't gonna light up no sky from here to Schenectady and it ain't gonna make no faces," said the softball player.

"Twenty say it do," somebody yelled, and four fat Legionnaires staggered past pulling the enormous, Roman-candle-loaded mortar on a sled.

On a monitor in the upper left corner I saw Tom Parsons, the Georgetown commentator, waving his arms and kicking the curb. I asked Nathanson what was going on.

"Parsons has run into a Senator he knows out front of the Skidmore house," Jack said. "Parsons wants to interview the guy. I reminded him no interviews if we can avoid it, and he said this is important because the Senator is going inside to visit the Skidmores."

"Let him do a bit with the Senator," I said.

Nathanson looked around at me and said, "I *am* directing this show. Right, Frank?"

I said, "Right, Jack."

Nathanson moved "Just Up the Street" to Georgetown, where Parsons introduced the distinguished Senator Frick.

Senator Frick said it was a surprise to run into Parsons. The Senator said he had been for a walk, mulling over committee matters, and he had noted he was nearly at the Skidmore house and he thought he would drop in and tell Bob Skidmore it was about time we all got to pulling together to solve the country's problems. Bob Skidmore, he said, was a brilliant fellow who represented a great company, but the Senator spoke for all America when he said it was a team game.

On the air a gray Mercedes 450 SL whined around the corner, stopped hard on the bricks, backed up and parked at a fireplug. A tall, bearded man hopped out of the driver's seat and tucked a pair of horn-rimmed glasses into the breast pocket of his navy-blue linen blazer. Out of the other side of the car stepped a very leggy blonde who looked like a taller and slightly older version of Dorothea Skidmore.

The Senator identified them to Parsons as Gladys and Phil de Menil from Easton, Maryland. Dorothea's sister and brother-in-law.

"Yes, in the car wash business," Parsons said.

"De Menil? In the car wash business?" the Senator said. "Yes, I suppose it's possible that he might somewhere own some car washes."

I put my mouth against Jack Nathanson's ear and said, "Jack, I ask you for one more thing. Go inside the house."

On a monitor we saw Bob and Dorothea Skidmore posing almost exactly as before, and on the earphones

277

we heard Dorothea talking about the need to improve the quality of after-dinner theater in America.

"Do it anyway," I said to Jack.

I glanced at D. Wayne Cooper, who was off in the corner of the control room with a headset on. He grinned sink-hole dimples at me.

Nathanson took us into the living room of the townhouse of the Skidmores, where Dorothea was saying:

"I think it's time we redid this room."

"Funny, I was thinking the same thing," Bob said.

"It's funny how often we think alike," Dorothea said.

The telephone rang.

"Probably Gladys and Phil calling from the club to say they'll be late," Bob Skidmore said.

Bob picked up the phone and said, "Hello."

Watching "Just Up the Street," you could not hear what Bob Skidmore was hearing on the phone, of course. But you could look at his face and tell it was not a pitch for lifetime light bulbs.

I knew what Bob Skidmore was hearing, because I knew who he was listening to.

D. Wayne Cooper was saying to Bob Skidmore, ". . . that little blonde is my wife, bubba, and she done told me the whole story. I know this here is Washington and you all think you're pretty smart. But I'm from Texas and I'm drunk and I say by god you don't go fucking another man's wife unless you're ready to get your goddam head blowed off."

"Who is it, Bob?" Dorothea asked.

Skidmore shrugged.

"Well, what do they want?" Dorothea said.

On the phone to Skidmore, Cooper said, "Man, that tight blond pussy better have been worth it, because in about two minutes I'm gonna be at your door."

Our viewers watched Bob Skidmore put down the phone and then heard him say to his wife:

"It's a terrorist threat. Get in gear, Dorothea! This is serious!"

Followed by the mini-cam, Bob and Dorothea ran into the bedroom where the six-year-old and the four-year-old were sleeping. The mini-cam guy switched on a light as the Skidmores picked up the kids.

"Bob, this is Georgetown!" Dorothea said. "What kind of terrorists would threaten us in Georgetown? We'll call the police. God, Bob, terrorists can't kill us on *television!*"

By now, Cooper's accent and threat had sunk in deep on Bob Skidmore.

He broke.

"You know Monday nights I play poker," he said. "I don't play poker . . . I go to this joint . . . I met a woman there . . . she's married to a Texas Congressman's aide."

Skidmore was blurting this with a sleepy, squirmy kid under each arm.

"She's not all that good-looking, but I nailed her anyhow!" Skidmore said.

Jack Nathanson switched your home TV picture to Hank Judson and then to Akron.

Looking at the monitors and wearing a headset, you could keep watching the Skidmores.

"I love our children, Bob, don't you?" Dorothea said.

"Damn it, Dorothea, can't you hurry?" Bob said. "There's two more kids to get!"

"But to think of you *screwing* with the wife of a Congressman's aide from *Texas,* makes me feel I must have a disease," Dorothea said.

"Stop the mouth, Dorothea! I've heard of that Texas guy. Grab the kids!" Bob shouted.

In Akron they were about to shoot the five-hundred-pound Roman candle that would light up the sky with the faces of Mount Rushmore.

So Jack called the Perry frontyard in Akron onto the network. The crowd was standing at a respectful distance from the five-hundred-pound Roman candle in the thirty-six-inch mortar. Except for Sergeant Jackson, who stood six feet from the Roman candle at the end of the fuse.

With his face on the left side of the Air Screen and the Roman candle on the right, Sergeant Jackson looked into the camera and pulled out of his pocket a brass belt buckle with a hole in it.

"I would of been shot to death in New Guinea if I had of not been laying behind a brother who got shot through the navel," Sergeant Jackson said.

He pulled an old cigarette lighter out of another pocket and said, "I don't need to tell any of you veterans what Zippo meant to us in the South Pacific. You know how hard it was to strike a match in the jungle when it was raining all the time and you was sweating and the little red stuff come off the match on your finger?"

"Get on with it, man," said the softball player.

"All right! Here come Mount Rushmore," Sergeant Jackson said.

Sergeant Jackson flicked his Zippo and lit the fuse to the five-hundred-pound Roman candle.

We watched the spark sizzle along the fuse and disappear into the base of the thirty-six-inch mortar.

All was quiet except for a gasp from the crowd as black smoke spurted out of the base of the mortar.

"Looks to me like they got the base plate of that sucker stuck in the ground at a funny angle," Cooper said.

The black smoke reduced to a dribble and then stopped.

For thirty seconds everyone in the Perrys' frontyard

and everyone watching "Just Up the Street" on CBC stared at the silent thirty-six-inch mortar.

"From here to Schenectady? That what you say, turkey?" laughed the softball player.

Sergeant Jackson said, "Well, now, when you got a whole Mount Rushmore packed in a tube, you got to expect . . ."

Then the five-hundred-pound Roman candle went off with a blast and a flash that reminded me of an ammo dump exploding.

A whirling comet of fire shot out of the mortar that had been mounted at a careless angle, as Cooper had noted.

The comet tore into our remote truck, and all the pictures from Akron went to black.

Jack Nathanson threw Hank Judson onto America's TV screens. Hank turned in his leather swivel chair to face the camera and said, "When critics of this country say we are losing our soul, I'll remind them of Sergeant Jackson, a dreamer and man of action, and his valiant attempt to put Mount Rushmore in the sky over . . . hold on a moment . . . we are receiving an audio report from Rod DeRoache on the scene in Akron. . . ."

On your home TV screen you saw Hank Judson but you heard the voice of Rod DeRoache.

"Frankly, it's a real mess 'Just Up the Street' in Akron, Ohio," said the voice of DeRoache. "Apparently nobody is seriously hurt. I saw Sergeant Jackson on the ground, but he was searching for his cap. No homes are burning, but our CBC remote unit is engulfed in orange. . . ."

There was a silence. Hank Judson explained to America that he had lost contact momentarily with Akron, and meanwhile "Just Up the Street" was returning to the Georgetown home of Bob and Dorothea Skidmore, where a controversy had developed.

Hank certainly hadn't overstated it.

281

In the control room we had been watching Georgetown on the monitors, and Nathanson had put Georgetown in the Preview Screen.

But Nathanson hesitated moving Georgetown onto the full CBC–TV network. Jack glanced around at me. I nodded, urging him to do it.

Nathanson shrugged, spoke to the technical director at his left and did his orchestra conductor gesture.

This is what our audience was treated to:

Bob and Dorothea Skidmore were screaming at each other in their foyer. Bob was trying to carry all four children. He kept dropping a little one in bunny-jamas. When he picked that one up he would drop one or two more.

"Dorothea, could you help me with this? They're your kids, too, you know!" Bob screamed.

"You're not only a cheat and a scum, you're a coward!" Dorothea screamed.

"You want me to stay here and shoot it out with that Texas lunatic?" Bob screamed.

"That's what a real man would do, yes!" Dorothea screamed.

The four children were crying.

If this hadn't been show business, I might have felt about half rotten for that phone call.

"Where did you take this tacky little person on Monday nights? To the Lucky Motel? Or did you parade her through the lobby of the Carlton so some of my friends could see her?" Dorothea screamed.

"It wasn't always Monday nights! Sometimes it was nooners during the week!" Bob screamed. "I nailed her on the grass in front of the Washington Monument one day! Now will you pick up one of these kids?"

Dorothea raised her chin, threw back her shoulders, turned her palms out at hip level and screamed, "Oh, Bob, you are low! low! low!"

"I'm going to be dead! dead! dead!" Bob screamed.

Several people in the control room, including Stanley, looked at Nathanson and me, wondering if we would really keep the Skidmores on the air.

"Okay, Frank, our ass is on the line," Nathanson said.

"Let's go out punching," I said.

A concealed camera was giving America a fine view of the Skidmores. But our mini-cam guy crept closer, trying for a tight shot of Dorothea's open mouth while she screamed.

Bob Skidmore thrust the tiny child in the bunny-jamas into our mini-cam guy's hands and yelled, "Here, fella, make yourself useful!"

The mini-cam guy later said he got letters from all over the country telling him he had held the child up-side down.

The sight of the mini-cam reminded Dorothea that she was on television. How much of this might have been seen at Easton, Maryland, or at the River Oaks Country Club in Houston, or even next door?

"I'm so ashamed of you!" Dorothea screamed.

"Shut the fuck up!" Bob screamed.

In the control room, Nathanson said, "Give me Three on Preview . . . okay, good . . . take Three."

Our outside camera in Georgetown picked up Bob Skidmore as he opened his front door carrying three kids and ran down the steps of the townhouse.

He ran straight into Gladys and Phil de Menil, Senator Frick and Parsons.

Into the headset Jack Nathanson said, "Tell Marty to give the kid to the mother and get the mini-cam going again. We need him on the street."

On the home TV screen was a shot of Bob Skidmore attempting to greet the arrivals while looking around wildly for a Texas assassin.

"Did we come on the wrong night, old spoke?" Phil de Menil said.

"Bob, I need to talk to you about teamwork," Senator Frick said.

"Why are the little lambs crying so?" Gladys de Menil said.

Bob Skidmore's eyes looked like fried eggs.

He cackled and screamed at the same time:

"Go on in! All of you! Go right on in! We're expecting company from Texas! Make him feel at home! Throw the football with him, Phil!"

Bob Skidmore rushed to his Lincoln parked at the curb and threw the three kids inside. He counted them and realized one was missing. You could tell that for an instant he considered going back for the fourth.

But he jumped behind the wheel of the Lincoln, started the motor, put the car in reverse and crashed into the de Menils' Mercedes.

"De Menil, you fucking pea-headed jackass! Move your car away from that fire hydrant so I can get out of here!" Bob screamed.

"See here, Bob, your sense of humor is a bit sick, isn't it? You have bashed in my grille," Phil de Menil said.

With that, Bob Skidmore leaped out of the Lincoln and ran off down the cobbled streets of Georgetown carrying two of the kids with him. The third looked out a window in the back seat.

With Akron still black, Hank Judson assured America that no one had been injured in Akron when the five-hundred-pound Roman candle missed the entire sky and hit our truck, but that the explosion was causing technical difficulties.

Hank then said "Just Up the Street" was moving back to the Tampa home of Angie Rocco, the plumber.

Lewis, the Tampa commentator, did a quick update on the Roccos. Mario had not yet come out of the bathroom. Carmen had invited Mr. Kaplan to have dinner with them.

284

Carmen had loaded Kaplan's plate with rigatoni, veal and garlic bread. On another plate for Kaplan were a dozen mushrooms stuffed with mozzarella. A thicket of salad grew from a nearby bowl. Carmen refilled the chianti glass Kaplan had just emptied.

"Mario, come out here and eat," Carmen Rocco said.

There was no answer from Mario.

Carmen leaned one hundred and thirty pounds of bosoms across Kaplan's head and poured the chianti glass up to the rim again the moment Kaplan took it away from his lips.

"You know, I could probably get you in trouble if I told your bosses you drink while you're working on a case," Carmen laughed.

"Aw, you wouldn't do that, Mrs. Rocco," Kaplan smiled.

"Carmen. Call me Carmen. We're friendly people here," Mrs. Rocco said.

"I'm Seymour," Kaplan said.

Carmen touched her chianti glass to her chin and lowered her eyelids and licked her lips.

"Seymour," she said.

"It's no good trying to stonewall it," Angie Rocco said with a sigh. "It'll come out sooner or later. You might as well hear it from me, Kaplan."

"Call me Seymour," Kaplan said.

"I ain't gonna call no Fed Seymour," Angie Rocco said.

"Who sent you here, Seymour?" Carmen Rocco said.

"We've been observing your family, Carmen," Kaplan said.

"Yeah, that's what I mean. What's the use of fighting the Feds? They listen to your phone and look in your window," Angie Rocco said. "I might as well tell you the story, Kaplan. It was just little things at first. One year I deducted some wrenches that hadn't really been stolen. I added a few thousand miles that I didn't really drive my truck. Little things like that. And it was easy. I never thought I'd get caught. I didn't know I was drifting into a life of crime. Sure, sure, the government needs money, Kaplan, but so do I."

Mario came out of the bathroom, sat down at the table and started scooping rigatoni into his mouth.

"Mario, go back and flush the toilet," Carmen Rocco said.

"What for? I didn't use it," Mario said.

"That trip where I went to Acapulco to bid on the job to keep the pipes open at the Hilton?" Angie Rocco said. "I didn't really have no chance at that job. They got their own guys that keep the pipes open. Mexican guys. They got a union. But I wrote the trip off as business. You might lock me up on that one, Kaplan. But what if I *had* of got the job? I got a right to hope, ain't I?"

Before Angie Rocco could plunge deeper into confession and probably reveal himself as a felon on the CBC–TV network to all of America, we replaced Angie on the screen with Hank Judson in his study.

Hank told the country everybody has a right to hope.

Then we moved "Just Up the Street" to Rochester, where several hundred people had gathered outside the home of Ralph and Ann Getz. Our commentator, Jerry Cummings, was still on the front porch doing interviews, but even on the earphones we could barely hear him in the noise of the crowd. So Jack left the outside of the house on just long enough to establish to you in your living room that you were now looking at Rochester.

Then Jack moved inside the Getz house.

Roxie wore a gold-spangled leotard and was twirling a baton. Ann Getz was playing Auto-Gammon. Ralph was talking to one of our technicians, who had wired an RF mike on Daphne, the singing Labrador.

"First I knew it was one day I was singing in the

shower, and I thought I heard my wife Ann singing harmony with me from the bedroom," Ralph said. "I thought that was real strange because Ann don't sing a note. So I wrapped a towel around me and went into the bedroom. Ann wasn't even in the room. It was Daphne throwing her head back and singing. That explained it. Hell, I knew it couldn't of been Ann."

Ralph scratched Daphne's ears and said, "Sweetheart, seeing as how you got a mike on now, just like me, let's do our all-time favorite."

Daphne cocked back her head, and Ralph lowered his head to the level of the black Lab's, and put his arm around Daphne.

If you saw it on your home TV, you would probably agree that it sounded like "Limehouse Blues."

The big clock in the CBC control room indicated that "Just Up the Street" had less than five minutes to go.

Nathanson called for the final whip-around from the commentators in Akron, Rochester, Georgetown and Tampa.

"This is the round-robin. Ready on the billboard," he said.

Akron was back on the air because our Akron affiliate had rushed its own remote truck to the Perry house. The other Akron radio and TV stations had sent news crews, making "Just Up the Street" a very well-publicized event in Akron. Three fire trucks had arrived to douse our remote unit. The Perrys, Sergeant Jackson and the others were being interviewed by the media.

Even our man Rod DeRoache was being queried by our competitors at the same time he was on the air for CBC–TV:

". . . well, you can see that the Perrys and their friends, after a tough day of making those steel-belted radials, like to loosen up and have a good laugh. This is Rod DeRoache, 'Just Up the Street,' in Akron, Ohio," he said into a multi-network battery of microphones and cameras.

Next, the show switched to Parsons and the Senator in front of the Skidmore townhouse in Georgetown.

"Yes, they're all back inside now—Dorothea Skidmore, two of her children, her sister Gladys and her brother-in-law Phil de Menil," Parsons said. "Bob Skidmore and the other two children have gone 'Just Up the Street' in Georgetown. . . ."

Jerry Cummings couldn't do the Rochester cleanup because the crowd on the porch of the Getz house had mashed him into a corner where he couldn't be seen or heard.

So with a lead-in by Hank Judson, we had Ralph and Daphne sing us off the air. They sang "After the Ball Is Over."

We faded out of that into Robert Lewis speaking from the driveway of the Rocco home in Tampa. Behind Lewis, Angie Rocco was showing his boat and trailer to Kaplan. If you wore a headset and could tune into the right monitor, you could hear Angie Rocco asking Kaplan what the boat might be worth in a settlement.

But on the home screens all that could be heard was Lewis signing off from Tampa.

Then a shot of Hank Judson in his study. Hank Judson was saying . . .

To tell the truth, I don't know what he said.

The fact that Hank Judson was on the screen winding up "Just Up the Street" was all I needed to know.

Chapter
Thirty-two

∽∽∽∽∽∽∽∽∽∽∽∽∽∽∽∽∽∽∽∽∽∽∽

Jack Nathanson said, "Okay, in twenty seconds let's round up the suspects." That meant stand by to roll the credits. Executive producer. Produced and directed by. Technical director. Air travel arrangements made by. This has been a live network presentation of. Nathanson was throwing it back to local, or, to take it out of TV language, our show was going off the air.

Nathanson said into his headset, "Hell of an effort out there, fellows. You can read the names of the dead and wounded in tomorrow's papers."

An A.D. said, "Nine . . . eight . . ."

Nathanson said, "Speed the credits . . . bring the music up full . . . and . . ."

We were off.

The way to know we were off for sure was to look up at the Air Screen and see that a commercial had replaced Hank Judson's face. A group of young ladies dressed in giant Spearmint gum packages and tricorn hats were playing fifes and drums on the deck of a tugboat circling the Statue of Liberty.

A few minutes earlier, the way to know we were

getting ready to go off was Stanley Coffman's party. He began making preparations for it at the top of the final hour.

At that point Stanley had rushed into the control room and said, "We must have the whole fucking country, guys. The board looks like Libby's green peas."

Long before the credits were crawling up the screen, then, I had three different glasses of champagne handed to me along with three different helpings of caviar, and at least four production girls—and maybe one guy—had already kissed me.

People who work in live TV production usually say something ritualistic to one another at the end of a show, a remark that might have some bearing on the lives we all lead. When I reached out to shake Jack Nathanson's hand and give him my thanks, he grinned and said:

"You get the luggage and I'll get the police escort."

Now Stanley Coffman was back in the control room. He had his own personal bottle of champagne, open and foaming. Behind him came a Frenchman in a tuxedo pushing a cart of iced-down magnums. And behind them came a half dozen waiters carrying trays of food and cocktails.

Staff people flooded in and out of the room, laughing, sloshing drinks and doing what they generally refer to as unwinding.

Stanley not only had his champagne. On his other arm he had the tall, long-haired production girl, Melissa.

"Jesus, in the second hour we kicked the private eye's ass four to one," Stanley said. "Know where the 'Movie of the Week' went? Right in the old shitter."

Stanley licked Melissa across the mouth. She did not seem to mind.

Stanley said, "Jesus, was that some show? A whole pile of niggers . . . The wops in there threshing around

. . . The guy in Georgetown eating a mile of shit . . . Hey, do I love that dog? . . . Do me a favor, Frank. Fuck Melissa. I'm taking the dog to Elaine's."

And Stanley roared.

I moved away to look for Cindy or Sally or Cooper.

As I was easing through the crowd I brushed against Hank Judson, who was having a grand-grand final.

"Good job, Hank," I said.

"Well, live television's where it is, Frank. We all know that, don't we?" Hank Judson said.

I said Hank handled all of the surprises we were confronted with in his usual professional manner.

"It's just experience, old bloke," he said.

We heard shouting and applause behind us.

I turned around to see Stanley had climbed up on the desk in front of the central panel.

Stanley asked for quiet from the crowd and said, "The little Wasp just wants to make a brief announcement."

With that, Stanley unzipped his pants and hollered:

"Right here, Nielsen! Here you go, guy! The old whanger!"

He then bent over and did a racing dive—a full Mark Spitz, he called it later—into Melissa and the party.

I lingered at the door to see if anyone was injured. I gathered not. When everyone peeled off, Melissa was swigging from the champagne bottle and Stanley's head was under her skirt.

There is no happier human, for a day or two anyhow, than a network president with a prime-time hit.

Cindy and Cooper were sitting down eating off their laps in a corner of the VIP room. Cindy was blending three desserts together: chocolate sundae, strawberry shortcake and lemon pie. Cooper was wrestling with a crab claw.

"If they don't get 'em some bologna and American

cheese in here, folks are liable to starve to death," Cooper said.

"Where's Sally?" I said.

Cooper said, "I think she went to rope one of them Frenchmen and get a cocktail."

My search for Sally included one more dip into a passing tureen of caviar, one more glass of champagne, and two invitations to a Cluster starting in a Village loft at midnight.

I spotted Sally as she came out of the powder room in a hall.

I didn't think she kissed me all that fiercely, as a matter of fact, considering my heroic stature of the moment.

"Kaplan, huh?" she said.

"Kaplan what?"

"Wonderful old unrehearsed and spontaneous 'Just Up the Street,' " she said.

Her tone was not explicitly what I had hoped for.

"You didn't enjoy the show?" I said.

"It isn't a question of whether I enjoyed it," Sally said. "Of course I enjoyed it."

"Then what's the problem?"

"It was a fake, Frank," she said. "If Kaplan was a fake, then maybe the rest of it was. Kaplan I know about for sure."

"Kaplan?"

"*Come on*," Sally said. "I was with you at Elaine's the night Watts and Travers came in. That insane stuff about a series? A series about an IRS agent? *Kaplan?* You took that idea and used it tonight to shake things up."

"If you're trying to say that we added a new dimension to the banality of TV comedy, just blurt it out," I said.

That was part of a line from one of Sally's old columns.

She lit a cigarette and said, "I speak as a critic now, and not as a person who might care for you."

"You called me a fake," I said.

"You are," Sally said. "I mean the *show* was."

"The situation wasn't fake," I said. "Does the plumber cheat on his income tax or doesn't he?"

I had skipped to what I considered to be the larger issue.

"He does. So what?" Sally said.

"So Kaplan comes in and whether Kaplan is a plant or not no longer matters. The plumber thought Kaplan was real and the plumber reacted. Because the plumber knows the real thing is, he cheats on his taxes," I said.

Sally said, "Kaplan *was* a plant. You can cut the bullshit. Thus, to me, the important point is that you provoked action with an outside influence, and that is not what the show was intended to be, or promoted to be or advertised to be, or what the hell ever."

She grabbed the champagne out of my hand and drank it.

"Is this the review?" I said. "Do I get to read about the opaque concept of the show itself, or how we did nothing more than present a potpourri of cartoon characters?"

Other lines of Sally's.

"You made up a reality, that's all," Sally said.

"Reality is what we had on that screen for three hours," I said.

She said, "I don't know why you didn't just use a script and Hollywood actors."

"You're wrong, you know that?" I said. "I could have put three hours up there tonight of nothing but supper time. And how many viewers would we have had? These were real people. Real things happened to them."

"*What* real things?" she said.

"Everything that happened was real. How about Georgetown? Let's say for the sake of discussion that the phone call to Skidmore was a joke. The fact is, Skidmore *does* jack around on his wife. And everything that happened after the phone call was plenty real, wouldn't you agree?"

"You probably did fake the phone call," Sally said. "That's absolutely something you would do. You had spies in Washington and you knew about Skidmore slipping around."

"That's absurd," I said. "But mainly it's unimportant."

She said, "A motivation, Frank, whether we're talking about human or fictionalized drama, has to be deeply felt, personal and honest."

"What's that? Inter-relation of the Arts?" I said.

"You resorted to tricks," Sally said. "I'm surprised you didn't have a bunch of bra-burners turn up in Rochester after Roxie got caught naked."

I said, "You're being stubborn. I'll say it again. Real things happened tonight to real people. And the real things represented a *substantial* truth in their lives."

Sally said, "Go get me a drink and I'll work on that for a minute. I don't want to break a date for the Prom with a cadet colonel for the wrong reason."

Not moving, I said, "Don't tell me you never made up a quote in a story."

"I write the truth, buddy," she said. "And I write about things that *I* didn't make happen."

"Good," I said. "Then I won't have to read in *New York* magazine that 'Just Up the Street' was so bland as to be unwatchable."

Sally said, "Stop quoting me, damn it."

In the next instant the elevator door in the hall opened and Watts and Travers leaped out. Thurlow Watts wearing a 1943 zoot suit with pegged pants and a broad-shouldered coat hanging to his knees. Larry Travers in a 1948 gabardine Eisenhower jacket, gym shorts, and a motorcycle helmet.

"Frank!" said Watts. "It's a series!"

Travers said, "Nitroglycerin!"

Watts said, "First episode. Key West and Birmingham. Turtle fisherman gambles it all on fan-tan! Steelworker's widow tries to raise a family of nine!"

Travers said, "Columbus and Oklahoma City. Ex-fullback selling encyclopedias breaks up with a debutante. Three cowgirls share a Winnebago with a German shepherd!"

Pushing the elevator button, Sally said, "Case closed."

"Where do you think you're going?" I said. "I've got a lot more to say about this."

Sally said, "I'm going to get a real cab to take me to my real apartment. In my life, cabs are real. Limos aren't. How come I forgot that for a while?"

And she was gone.

As calmly as possible then, I turned to Watts and Travers.

"Okay," I said. "Who thought up the goddam Roman candle?"

It took some time but Watts and Travers convinced me they had not planted Sergeant Jackson. He was real. So was Daphne. Watts and Travers did confess to sneaking the line into the bios about Gladys and Phil de Menil owning a chain of car washes.

D. Wayne Cooper came over. With his keen eyesight that could spot enemy targets radar couldn't pick up, he could naturally spot a girlfriend angrily getting on an elevator from across a room.

"Old Sally split, did she?" Cooper said. "Reckon show binness done blowed another one for you?"

Chapter
Thirty-three

~~~~~~

The Silver Goblet rolled into the driveway of the old family lodge in Pelham Manor around 1 A.M. The brass carriage lamps were burning. A light was on in the living room. A frail glow came from a window of the upstairs bedroom where Marcie had delivered many of her finest lectures.

"Mom's awake. Must be something good on TV," Cindy said.

"Swamp Fiend Women."

Lines like that hopped out on impulse when I got anywhere near Pelham. Cindy understood it.

When the doors of the limo slammed, they seemed to turn on more lights in the house.

Marcie was coming down the stairs as Cindy and I entered.

She had on a white velour caftan and her hair was not in curlers like the ladies browsing through the K-Mart. Her hair was longer and it had been streaked in pale gold. It looked good, as I was sure Marcie had been told by Dr. Ridley, Rex the Wonder Horse, Eddie Burns, and several suburban husbands on the prowl.

Marcie looked good all over, in fact. The white caftan barely clung to her shoulders and it contrasted nicely with her summer tan, which was doing nicely. By the end of a summer, Marcie could look like a blond Jamaican. She hadn't removed her earrings, and she was still wearing her eyes for the evening out; the kind of eyes some women needed more time to create than the Sistine Chapel required.

To be truthful, Marcie looked about as good as she had ever looked in the twenty-two years I had known her. Twenty-two years. Lord. She was thirty-eight, but all of a sudden a trim new racing sloop was cruising around Westchester County. Marcie was a book title: *Brett Ashley Goes to Pelham.*

"Oh, Frank, it's you," she said. "I thought it would just be Cooper. I missed the show. Did it go well?"

"It was *so* funny," Cindy said.

I asked Marcie if I should wake up Frankie and say hello. She said he was spending the night at a friend's. Some kid had got some new amplifiers for his birthday. Frankie didn't deserve to be allowed to go, Marcie said, but she had weakened.

Cindy said, "Mom, these people on Dad's show. They were so radical. There was this plumber, and these black people in Ohio. And there was this man in Washington who was cheating on his wi—"

Cindy faked a cough.

Good points on awareness, kid. The subtlety needed work.

"Anyhow, it was really fun," Cindy said.

"Why don't you run up to bed, angel," Marcie said. "You've had a big day, obviously."

Cindy squeezed me.

"Thanks, Dad, really. It was great. For sure."

297

"Don't forget to make up that list of movie stars you want to meet," I said.

I explained to Marcie that I might take Cindy to the Left Coast with me in a month or so, just for a few days. "We'll talk about it." Marcie smiled at Cindy. That always meant yes.

"Night, Mom," Cindy said, kissing her mother. She took the stairs two at a time. From the landing above, I heard:

"Love you two guys."

Marcie asked if I wanted a drink, as long as I was there. I said certainly. She became the bartendress in the room I called a den and she called a library. Marcie never drank Scotch, so she made a drink the way most stewardesses do. When Marcie poured a cocktail it was either all Scotch or all ice and water. This one was all Scotch and ice, and it wasn't even any of the gallons of J&B I'd left behind.

"Marcie, I can't drink Teachers," I said. "Maybe I'll just have some wine."

"Taste this," she said, handing me the glass of red wine she had chosen for herself.

"Let me have some of that," I said, having decided that some crafty devil had introduced Marcie to a damn good $3.99 California burgundy.

Marcie lit a cigarette without a trace of guilt as we sat down for a minute. "What did you say about the show again?" she asked, now remembering to remove her earrings.

I said it had gone okay, and the ratings would be surprisingly good. She said congratulations, then, on another triumph. Cindy, she said, had built it up around the house as something very important to my job. I said I didn't know how the critics would look at it. It might get rapped, here and there, I said.

"Would that be fair in your estimation?" she said, exhaling.

"Not very."

"Then I wouldn't be concerned about it, if I were you," she said. "You won the night, which was the most important thing." It crossed my mind that Marcie could debate the issue with Sally better than I could.

Marcie asked if any of the critics would trouble themselves to mention me personally.

"If they try to get their facts straight," I said, "I suppose they will have to say that I coordinated the luau."

I stood up to leave and Marcie began walking me to the door.

"Frank, I want to tell you something," she said. "I want you to know that *I* know we are doing the best thing for both of us, and the children. You said that from the beginning, and I've always really known it. I want you to try to forgive some of my outbursts these past two or three years. I don't enjoy being angry, whether you realize it or not. I don't hate you, Frank. I'm no longer in love with you—thank heavens—but I don't hate you. I'll always be marvelously fond of you. You are a very special person and you have a very special life. I've always told the children that."

She smiled with a sweetness I hadn't seen in a long time.

"I just never was very good at trying to ride a tidal wave," she said. "Let's let it go at that."

"Oh, you didn't do so badly, most of the time," I said, paying back the smile.

It was a perfect moment for me to say all that stuff about wishing there was a way for people to be able to forget the words that opened all the wounds which couldn't be healed. To say that a human being could only put those words out of mind for a day, maybe, sometimes two or three, and occasionally from a drunken bout of love-making. But they would always

299

come back. And if you didn't want to go on living the rest of your life with a cage of rabbits in your stomach, and arthritis of the heart, well, then you had a choice. Marcie and I were making that choice: divorce.

At the door I took one of her hands and kind of squeezed on it because it seemed all right with Marcie to do it.

Smiling again, I said, "It sure is amazing what people do to each other without intending to."

She gave me a look that combined her old, natural radiance with some sort of new agreement and understanding.

I took that look with me to the limo, never looking back.

In the Goblet I turned on all four TV sets, without the sound, to whatever programs were on, and I sank down in the seat to let the magic pictures compete with the dozens of images of Marcie, good and bad, and the dozens of images of Sally, mostly good, that were flashing through my head.

All four screens had a solemn news commentator staring at me. I turned up the volume on one of the sets and got my last jolt of the night.

The commentator was telling me that a great American, a pioneer in broadcasting, Harley O. Chambers, the Big Guy, was dead.

Chapter
Thirty-four

〰〰〰〰〰〰〰〰〰〰〰〰〰〰〰〰〰〰〰

It would have been easier for me to believe a Swiss Alp had died. Shriveled up unexpectedly and melted into a carton of low-fat milk right there in front of all the eyes on all the sundecks of Zermatt.

But a Big Guy couldn't die.

A Harley O. Chambers never died.

He could get old, senile, wheelchair-ridden, incoherent, blind, deaf, voiceless, motionless, and of no more use to anyone than the brain of a tuna.

And he could then have his breathing sustained only by each day's phenomenal scientific advances in tubes, valves, pumps and transplants.

And he might have to be observed in a plastic tent around the clock by the best medical minds, who would stand over him like the chefs of Lyon stand over an omelette.

For the next two billion years.

But a Big Guy never got poor, he never got powerless—and he certainly never died.

Herb Grant said he died gallantly.

Stanley and I were in Grant's office on the thirty-fourth floor.

"He liked the show very much, Mallory. He would want you to know that," Grant said. "He got excited right from the opening billboard. The old logo looked pretty damn good, I can tell you, on that forty-foot screen."

It was a good party, Grant said, until Harley was called Upstairs.

The forty-foot screen had made it easy for the Big Guy to arrange the seating for his guests in the den.

It was no problem for everyone to see around or between the life-sized stuffed animals. Giraffes, tigers and polar bears. Or any of the World War II treasures. In fact, Grant said he saw two people—Packey and Deeny from Hobe Sound—sit for a while in the model of a foxhole which had been re-created in a corner of the room.

Most of the male guests were on the Chambers board of directors. Packey, I remembered, was seventy-seven. Same age as the Big Guy. Deeny, his seventh wife, was twenty-two. She had flown for Delta.

Grant said the Big Guy sat by the controls of the forty-foot contraption between Batten Down Boynton and Shotsy Stovall. Mrs. Chambers, whose first name was known to very few people—Eula—wore a sailor suit and mainly occupied herself supervising the staff.

"In a way," said Grant, "I suppose he would still be here today if it hadn't been for that damn recording device on the Stroganschleiger."

It seems the Big Guy videotaped the show as he watched it, and thus he had it to run back again.

"He must have shown those segments with the plumber at least eight times," Grant said. "Each time, he got more worked up."

It was the last time that did it, according to Grant.

Nearly all of the guests had slumped into their chairs

302

and sofas asleep, including Bat and Shotsy. Grant said he had just returned from strolling down to the yacht basin to show Deeny the submarine and mine-sweeper.

Looking at the forty-foot screen, Grant said he suddenly realized there was a shadow on it—the shadow of a figure pointing a finger.

It was the Big Guy's shadow on the screen, which at the time was showing a closeup of the plumber. A moment when Angie Rocco was pleading with Kaplan about his income tax.

The sound volume was turned down low, so Grant could clearly hear the Big Guy's voice.

"Let's see your contemptuous gaze now!" the Big Guy screamed at the plumber.

Grant vividly remembered that much.

Stanley and I pressed Grant for every detail of the Big Guy's last actions and words.

It took a while to get most of the story. For one thing, the three of us needed to talk a good bit about something other than the Big Guy's actual departure. We were going on the air that evening with a two-hour memorial special—"Harley O. Chambers Tonight: A Tribute to a Great American."

Realizing he had been in on a part of history, Grant tried to tell us all that he saw and heard.

And I think by combining that information with only a little journalistic license, I can pretty well describe the Big Guy's final few minutes.

It went something like this.

"Come down here into our homes *now* with your contempt!" the Big Guy yelled at the plumber on the screen. "You can't fool with Uncle Sam! How does it feel to hear the rat-tat-tat-tat of the IRS on your padded repair bills?"

With that, the Big Guy picked up an empty buttermilk glass and spoke into it, not knowing it would be for the last time.

"Burrrroooom!" he said. "Ta-ta-ta-ta! . . . Deee-eeeyow! . . . Wooooo-up, woooo-up, woooo-up! . . .

"A bitter surface battle is raging around me while I stand here on the pitching deck of this carrier. I'm out here in the middle of the wild, heaving Pacific near a whacky chunk of coral that I won't try to spell or pronounce. . . . It wouldn't mean much to you, anyway. . . .

"This is Harley O. Chambers, and I'm counting angels. . . . Some of their wings are clipped, but they're fluttering back here to their nest . . . I've got a bunch of grease monkeys standing here with me—and they're counting, too. . . .

"They know, like I do, that we've got a lot of fresh-faced kids up there in that crazy, deformed, kamikaze sky. . . . Kids out of the corner drug stores of our home towns back in Duluth and Joplin . . .

"Yeah, they're kids. But today they're wearing the collars of their flight jackets turned up and their crushed caps in the jaunty angles of older men. . . . You know why, America? . . .

"Because they've just dropped a bundle of red, white and blue kisses on the filthy little slant-eyed yellow dwarfs who started this whole stinking mess. . . .

"*Achtung,* plumbers! . . . *I-cho, ki-ma, oh-so, Mai Tai, chocko* . . . Send us more Japs! . . . Now hear this, now hear this . . . The hard-fighting Russians pushed further into the Urals today. . . . *Ein deeter bine der klingin! Stroke das vine kutz!* . . .

"The rag-tag remnants of the British fighting forces today defied all the odds of mangled limbs and withering supplies and hurled themselves against the blazing, steel-girded might of Von Stilson's panzer faucets. . . .

"What, Mr. Rankin? . . . I went . . . The gutty little leatherneck knew he was out of ammo. . . . I saw the slimy yellow midget plumbers crawling toward him through the jungle rot. . . .

"Saddle up, Marines! . . . Ya had a good girl but she . . . she . . . lef . . . she right . . . she . . . she . . ."

The Big Guy staggered backward.

He gasped. It was the old ticker, all right.

He whirled in a half-circle. He stumbled and tried to clutch at all the teeth, ears, hair and toenails of the objects in the room.

He finally collapsed and died with a silly last whimper, like Cagney riddled with bullets on the cathedral steps.

Except the Big Guy was near a stuffed giraffe, stretched across the pride of his den—the seat on an authentic anti-aircraft gun from a World War II destroyer.

"Well, a great man has left us," said Herb Grant. "Sure. He was strange in many ways. But in his whole career he never made a bad business decision. He was even right about Juts."

"What?" said Stanley.

" 'Just Up the Street,' " I said. "It was a smasheroo, remember?"

Stanley looked out of the window in Herb Grant's office.

Then he said:

"Jesus, you know what the hell of it was? I mean, when you think about him playing the show back, over and over. The fucking guy spun out watching reruns."

305

Chapter
Thirty-five

〰〰〰〰〰〰〰〰〰〰〰〰〰〰

Our two-hour memorial special, "Harley
O. Chambers Tonight: A Tribute to a Great American," lit up its share of green bulbs. It could have
been the competition. NBC was in its eighty-fourth
week of serializing the Bible. CBS reran the sympo-
sium of city managers. ABC presented its own special: "Parole versus Capital Punishment." We might
also have concluded, where our broadcast was concerned, that the public's avid interest in nostalgia had
not flagged.

We had the Big Guy sitting on the verandas of resort hotels with presidents, kings, shahs and Mary
Pickfords. We had him at the track in Saratoga with
J. Edgar Hoover. On the promenade deck of the
Queen Mary with Sinclair Lewis, Marlene Dietrich and
Jerome Kern. Presenting a trophy to a polo player.
Snow-plowing down a beginner's slope in Sun Valley
with Norma Shearer and Lowell Thomas. In the cock-
pit of an airplane with Howard Hughes. In a songfest
around a piano with Knute Rockne, Ring Lardner
and Grantland Rice. Boarding a campaign train with

Wendell Willkie and Henry Luce. Teeing off for a round of golf with Bobby Jones, Adolphe Menjou and the Prince of Wales. And none of us could resist using a two-minute shot from Berlin, 1938: The Big Guy smiling proudly as Hermann Goering pinned a medal on Charles Lindbergh.

For a thirty-minute segment we were live. Hank Judson left his anchor position in the Big Guy's office on the thirty-fourth floor and went browsing through the display cases in the museum along with Herb Grant, Stanley Coffman, Chase Morgan and myself.

We all spoke of how much the Big Guy meant to broadcasting—and to each of us personally.

Herb Grant called the Big Guy "the Father of prime time."

Hank Judson said he was "the man who put the opera in the soap."

Chase Morgan admired him as "one of the geniuses of TV journalism—an electronics-stained wretch in the noblest sense of the phrase."

Stanley Coffman saw him as "the man who put the peep show in the Emerson."

I said I would miss, more than anything, his sense of humor.

On and off throughout the day I had phoned Sally Hawks and never got an answer. When I left the Chambers building after the special, around 9:30, Cooper took me to her apartment.

Sally wasn't home, but she had replaced the Rita Hayworth poster on her door with a typewritten note that was obviously intended for me.

All the note said was: *Loved her, hated him.*

Cooper and I went to Clarke's. I was only there long enough for two drinks, a cup of chili, and a conversational replay of Bob Skidmore's exit, when a waiter said I had a call.

I went to the private phone in the coat room behind the front bar.

"You got a stay of execution," Sally said. "I'll have to do an obit column on the Big Guy before I can get around to 'Just Up the Street.' Maybe by then I'll have thought more succinctly about the uncertain terrain you were trying to cover, if I may quote myself before you do."

"Where have you been?" I asked.

"At a screening," she said. "Strictly middle-period Truffaut."

"You weren't home all day," I said.

"I was out."

"Doing what?"

"I got stoned and went to Zabar's to look at cheese."

"I want to see you," I said.

"I don't want to see you."

I said that wasn't true.

"Yeah, you're right. I do want to see you. That's why I called. If we don't do something about the songs in the second act we're never going to get out of New Haven with this mess," she said.

I heard cocktail chatter behind Sally's voice.

"What bar are you in?" I said.

"The laughs are uneven. The structure is disjointed. We're in real trouble," she said.

"You haven't been to a screening," I said. "You're drunk."

She said, "The problem with television, as we know, is that by its very nature it must cling to the unsettling habit of shifting too abruptly from what it considers entertainment to the virtues of Di-Gel and Listerine."

"Sally," I said.

"It would still seem possible, however, for television to prevent art from evoking a discontinuity, and leaving us adrift in the electronic kaleidoscope," she said.

"Time out," I said.

"One does not actually ask, from the abysmal fragments the networks serve us, that one's body be energized . . . one's mind be occupied . . . one's heart be touched. . . ."

"Hey!" I said.

"One does not seek nor expect from television the faultlessly esthetic work. . . ."

I think I heard a hiccup.

Sally said, "But in the case of 'Just Up the Street,' a telecast with the seductive opportunity to give us three hours of unprepossessing reality, Frank Mallory succeeded only in driving us more swiftly toward the safest alternative to television itself, which is, I submit, mystical asceticism."

"Where the hell are you?" I said.

"At this moment," she said, "I am in the first-class departure lounge of Pan-Am. In about twenty minutes I shall be leaving JFK on a Twentieth-Century Fox junket to Geneva."

"You're on a movie junket?"

She said, "As I speak, I am reeling from the contrapuntal density of film talk."

That is exactly where Sally was, and precisely what she was doing.

The studio was taking a group of film writers to Switzerland for a week. As a promotion, Twentieth was going to let the writers observe the progress being made on a four-and-one-half-hour musical version of *The Magic Mountain* starring Glen Campbell as Hans Castorp.

I said, "I'll take you to Europe. I didn't know you had a valid passport."

The point of going away for a few days, Sally said, was not to see Europe. Which hadn't changed any. It was to avoid me.

"Why?" I said.

"I have to straighten out this reality business in my head," she said. "If I can't, then you and me won't ever be able to rob banks together or . . . uh . . . discuss . . . uh . . ."

"Mendelssohn?"

"Yeah," she said. "And O. E. Rolvaag . . . and pedigreed chicken parts . . . and everything."

I did not talk Sally out of going on the junket. I'm not sure anyone could have.

She said, "May your days during my absence be filled with the tawdry discomfort of 'Just Up the Street.'"

"Just do me one favor when you get back," I said.

"What's that?"

I said, "Don't trade me to the San Diego Chargers."

Chapter
Thirty-six

~~~~~~

For a couple of days Stanley Coffman delighted in circulating the rumor that there would be no funeral for the Big Guy.

"They can't shit me, he's in Frankfurt," Stanley said. "They've got him frozen in a vault. Soon as the fucking scientists work out the rough edges on the old Krupp-Opel life-restorer, he'll be back in the office."

The funeral in fact was held on the Big Guy's estate in Connecticut.

Since the Big Guy had left instructions that he be cremated, most of us guessed that Rear Admiral Cletus (Batten Down) Boynton and Lieutenant General Merle (Shotsy) Stovall would sprinkle the remains from a helicopter over that sector of the estate where the Arnhem bridge had been reproduced rather vividly.

We were wrong.

The Big Guy's ashes were poured into a simple urn and given to his widow, Eula. We then followed her as she marched up a hill, to the highest point on the property, and we watched as she carefully tossed handfuls of Harley O. Chambers into the sky, letting the winds take them where they might.

She explained that she was doing what the Big Guy wished—putting him up there with his air waves.

"Good luck and good show, Harley," she said. "I'm throwing you back to local."

Chapter
Thirty-seven

〜〜〜〜〜〜〜〜〜〜〜〜〜〜〜〜〜〜

The door of my office was open so I could easily hear Arleene when she yelled, "Herbert L. Motherfucking Grant!"

Arleene had just learned from an interoffice memo what I had heard only a moment earlier on the phone from Stanley: that Herb Grant had been elected Chairman of the Board of the Chambers Corporation.

Herb Grant, in effect, was the new Big Guy.

Arleene came to the doorway.

"It was unanimous," she said. "Not a single vote for Manson or Starkweather."

She then read aloud:

"Mr. Herbert Lynne Grant, Group President, Communications, was unanimously elected Chairman of the Board of the Chambers enterprises today.

"Mr. Grant, fifty-two, who resides in Locust Valley and Southampton, has served the company with distinction for the past twelve years, during which time he worked closely on all phases of operations with our great and departed leader, Harley O. Chambers.

"Mr. Grant joined the Chambers Corporation in the advertising department of our pet food division after a brilliant career with the agency of Doodle and Wimple. One year later Mr. Grant moved into communications where his creative ability quickly came to the front.

"While Mr. Grant had only a brief tenure as president of our television network, it was under Mr. Grant's leadership that many of CBC–TV's hit shows were developed during the 1960s. Most Americans still remember with fondness such programs developed by Mr. Grant as 'Albert the Talking Zebra,' 'Bootsy and the Harpsichord,' 'Sledgehammer Sam,' and 'Sing Along with Fridl.'

"Mr. Grant is married to the former Anabel Sprott Keeler-Gates.

"Mr. and Mrs. Grant have two children. Their son Dink, twenty-six, is currently touring with the well-known musical group, Speed. Their daughter Pamela, eighteen, is working with the Lambs of Light, a religious order in Greensboro, North Carolina.

"Mr. Grant has already assumed his duties as chairman. He plans to retain his present office until Mrs. Grant has had an opportunity to redecorate the thirty-fourth floor.

"The board is also pleased to announce that Mr. Irving K. Beckerman, our company comptroller, has agreed to fill the post of Group President, Communications, on an interim basis for the next six months until the board has completed its search for an able and experienced successor for the job Mr. Grant filled so capably.

"Although we will hardly be saying goodbye to Mr. Grant, who will only be moving down the hall, we hope you can join us for a little pouring at 5 P.M. today in the rotunda on the thirty-fourth floor to let Herb know how we feel about his contributions to

314

communications and send him along to his new responsibilities with our very best wishes."

The memo was signed by P.R. and R.V.K.—Packey Robertson and Rich Von Klammer—co-chairmen of the executive committee.

Arleene had scarcely had time to fold the memo into a paper airplane and sail it toward the wastebasket when my phone rang and I was ordered to the thirty-fourth floor to meet with the new chairman of the board.

"Don't take any crap," Arleene said. "We can always wait tables for Cooper."

Stanley was in Grant's office when I got there. If Stanley had been called at the same time I was, I did not see how he could have reached the thirty-fourth floor so quickly unless he had defied gravitation with some form of spiritual energy.

We were offered a drink and we accepted.

"Couple of tighteners for the troops, Blakey!" Grant called out with the joviality of a man whose annual income had just risen to $850,000.

Congratulations, we said.

Grant thanked us and then said he thought the word of his appointment would have a healthy effect on Wall Street, and might possibly even serve as an inspiration to other executives of other large corporations who might be restless and discontent.

Blakey brought the drinks.

"Guess you've seen all the reviews on Juts," Grant said.

"On what?" I said.

" 'Just Up the Street,' " said Stanley.

I had, of course.

Outside of New York, the show mostly got raves. In and around New York, I pointed out, it was called odious, bombastic, frenzied, sadomasochistic, ludicrous, jaded, dim, out of cadence, episodic, gyrating, obsessed with cruelty, diabolical, negligent, stylistically vulgar, revisionistic, despotic, contemptible, dissonant and artistically frazzled, but all in all a robust effort.

"That's the best fucking description I ever heard of a hit series," Stanley said.

Grant said, "Well, when you win the ratings you're playing in my ball park, and it doesn't make a damn what the critics say. I never knew a critic anyhow who wouldn't trade in the old typewriter for his own talk show."

I thought to myself that I knew one who wouldn't.

Grant said, "Glad you mentioned the series aspect, Stanley. I saw Styve Butler at The Numbers and he said he'd buy the whole thing for Alka-Seltzer if we'd make it a weekly comedy."

"I know a couple of writers who feel the same way," I said.

"Our people?" Grant said.

"They freelance," I said.

"Anybody I've ever heard of?" said Grant.

"Possibly," I said. "Loeb and Leopold?"

Herb Grant said, "What do you think of it as a series, Mallory?"

"Am I still employed?" I said.

Grant said, "I'll be direct, old man. I don't especially like you, but you may have a chance to become the best programmer in the business."

What Grant meant was, I could make him look good. That wasn't the most positively vague thing I ever thought about myself, but then of course I had a cocktail in my hand and that made it excusable, according to my friend J&B.

Grant's remark was also a signal that this was the time for the old power play, if there was ever going to be one. I detested power plays. But it was the only kind of game Herb Grant understood or even respected.

316

And being a lad from South Dallas, survival and competition were very much a part of my embodiment, as Marcie had so often said.

"I'll want some concessions," I said.

"That's an ears-up," Stanley said, nervously.

Stanley then asked if we could have another drink.

"Blakey!" Grant shouted. "Need some more water for the horses!"

Grant leaned back and said, "Fire away, old man."

I did not want, need or covet half of the things I babbled, and some of them did not even occur to me until that instant. But I said:

"Five-year contract starting with a fifty-thousand-dollar raise. Bonuses for every show I develop that makes the top ten. Four of my own specials a year with your money. Ten million on the table to put into forty new pilots right away. No conversations with Irv Beckerman. Stanley gets serious consideration for group president. If I win a season, we re-negotiate from this point upward."

Herb Grant laughed and said, "Tell you something, Mallory. I'll take that job and you can have this one."

Stanley and I traded our empty glasses for full ones with Blakey.

"What happens, old man, if I can't find that kind of money around here?" Grant said.

"I walk," I said.

I didn't quite know where, but I thought it sounded good. Maybe I was thinking about running Bobby Maitlow's studio. I also wondered if Bobby Maitlow, at that moment, lay dying somewhere."

"You'll have to give in a few areas," Grant said.

"I'll give on the raise," I said.

"The other networks don't see more than twenty-five pilots a year," he said.

"They're not fourth," I said.

Herb Grant focused on Stanley.

317

"I'll put your name in the hat for the group job," he said. "But I'm not sure you know what it entails. You'd spend most of your time in Washington with the FCC."

"Jesus, I haven't even thought about it, Herb," Stanley said. "But I guess you just run 'em all through the old suite in the Mayflower and lay a pile of sauce and nigger hooks on 'em, right?"

Coming back to me, Grant said, "All right, Mallory, you'll get most of it. Have it drawn up. If you get the results you seem to think you can get, you'll wind up being a bargain—and I'll be the big winner."

From somewhere in a college course in business I remembered hearing that a deal was only good if both parties benefitted. So I said as much as I got up to leave.

"Let's get started on Juts right away as a comedy," Grant said.

"On what?" said Stanley.

" 'Just Up the Street,' " I said. "It's my baby. I'll rock it."

"Jesus, is that gonna be some raffle?" Stanley said. "Styve Butler may have to go for sixty grand a thirty and a thermos of warm blood."

We were out in the hall when Stanley said:

"You forgot to ask Grant the most important question of all. From now on, do we call him Big Guy or Fuckhead?"

Chapter
Thirty-eight

~~~~~~

I skipped the cocktail party for Herb Grant in the Chambers building and had a little pouring of my own at Cooper's Country.

If you got to Cooper's early enough in the afternoons, before the truckers came in, you could select a bar stool near the front where you could look out the window on Park Avenue South and across the street to Union Square.

The sights through the window were not all that remarkable in the daytime. But there were trees in Union Square and occasionally people: pantomime fags and elderly insurrectionists. And you could be treated to the odd traffic snarl along the avenue—and the operetta that went with it.

The window was convenient, in other words, if you got tired of watching the mechanism inside Cooper's jukebox, or meditating on the hand-lettered sign which hung above the mirror behind the bar—a sign which said: TOO MUCH AIN'T ENOUGH.

That motto had been Cooper's favorite ever since

Billy Joe Shaver used the line in a song titled "Old Five and Dimers."

I had been drinking alone but enjoying it when Cooper finally leaned in beside me at the bar.

D. Wayne had been running around acting like an owner, talking to the four or five other customers in the place, whom he no doubt suspected to be undercover fire insurance inspectors and juvenile officers.

When I told Cooper about Herb Grant and my power play in the limo as we drove down to his joint, D. Wayne only grinned and said, "Too much ain't E-nough."

Now as he slouched at the bar he said he thought it was time for him to switch from beer to a South Dallas martini.

The bartender gave Cooper his drink and gave me another J&B.

"Well, here's to all them little blondes at poolside," Cooper said.

He put away most of his South Dallas martini in one gulp.

He said, "You know, one thing you're gonna be needing, Frank . . . which I been intending to bring up . . . except you've been busy . . . is what you might call your basic new driver for the Silver Goblet."

"Where are you going?" I said. "Back in the Marines to keep from getting married?"

"That's another thing," D. Wayne said. "Looks like I ain't gonna get married."

"Why not?"

"Same reason I can't drive for you no more," he said. "This joint we're sittin' in."

"If it's taking too much of your time, get somebody to run it for you," I said.

"Frank, that just shows how much you know about certain things," Cooper said. "You can't let nobody run a joint for you. If you let somebody run a joint for you,

320

the first thing you know, it'll be their joint, and you'll be phonin' up trying to get a reservation for dinner."

"You must know somebody who could handle it," I said.

"Yeah, I know all kinds of people who'd be real good in this binniss," Cooper said. "But there ain't none I'd let run my joint unless I had me some damned old lettuce I wanted to send somewhere by way of a rabbit."

D. Wayne asked the bartender to do it again.

He said, "Looks like this sucker's gonna be a gold mine, is what it looks like. It needs my full attention, Frank. I can't tend to that silver auto-mobile and this gold mine at the same time and do either one of 'em much good. I can't go flogging it out to the Left Coast and all that, either. I got to watch my joint, Frank, is what I'm tryin' to say."

"What happened with Katherine?" I said.

"That's a real fine woman, old Katherine," said Cooper.

"Katherine's a singer," I said.

"We were about as much in love as any two people could be who didn't exactly agree on everything," Cooper said.

"Did you have an argument?"

"Naw, there wasn't no argument or anything," Cooper said. "It wasn't no argument on my part at least."

I said, "It's not like Katherine all of a sudden to develop a dislike for gold mines."

Cooper said, "What happened was, she sat in here one night and started talking about how good it would be if I had a different kind of entertainment on Tuesdays. Or maybe on Tuesdays and Fridays both. She mentioned Cole Porter and some of them folks."

"I suppose she suggested that she could even appear on the bill now and then," I said.

321

"Now, Frank, I didn't want her to give up her singin'," Cooper said. "Katherine's singin' was too important to her. I never would have said that. Her singin' was one of the reasons me and her fell in love. All I said was, I wouldn't mind her singin' in my joint if she could do a whole lot more 'Honky-Tonk Angels' and a whole lot less 'Poor Fuckin' Butterfly.' "

"I don't see why that would upset her," I said.

"Aw, it didn't really," he said. "Katherine don't actually have a temper, as you know. She looks about half tame even when she's hot."

Cooper was right about that. Katherine had a cynical placidness to her that was part of her allure. But if you looked deep, you began to see all the years in the piano bars. If those years had ever given her that thing show business calls the bruised-by-life quality to her voice, she might have become a big star, and the years would have been worth it to her. But they hadn't. The years had only given her the loser's disease. It wasn't the worst disease in the world, and Katherine certainly had other virtues, but she had the disease, and it was one without a cure.

"I guess she said it was better for everybody if she just took it on to another cabin," I said.

"That's pretty near it," Cooper said. "There ain't no hard feelings or anything."

I motioned to the bartender for another backup.

"Life's a funny old raccoon," I said.

"Ain't she?" said Cooper.

I asked D. Wayne how he was going to like being wealthy, seeing as how Cooper's Country was a gold mine.

"Tell you what," he said. "I believe I can tolerate it. I don't think it'll be a shuck harder than bitin' down on a dandy old pair of titties and prayin' for lockjaw."

Chapter
Thirty-nine

Cooper pardoned himself for a while to go check the arithmetic of his bartenders and waitresses. And he said he also wanted to see if his chef had learned how to say chicken fried steak in Puerto Rican yet.

I was looking out of the window at the traffic just as a taxi double-parked in the street and a door opened. Sally Hawks got out and walked around the Silver Goblet to step onto the sidewalk and head for the entrance to Cooper's Country.

I twisted around to face the mirror.

Sally eased into a bar stool next to mine and took the cigarettes out of her shoulder bag. She lit a Winston and blew the smoke at an angle slightly away from me.

"Also," she said, "you knew the dog could sing."

I ordered Sally a drink.

"How was Switzerland?" I said.

"Very Swiss."

Where around Geneva, I asked, were they shooting the movie.

"Across the border in a French village," she said.

"They're shooting *The Magic Mountain* in France?" I said.

Sally said, "The director says the location looks more like Davos than Davos."

It occurred to me that Sally had returned home a day early. I asked if the junket had been cut short, or did she miss me?

"I got tired of hearing words like idiosyncratic," she said. "Listen, I want to talk about what you know I want to talk about, so let's talk about it."

"How'd you know where I was?"

"Arleene," she said.

"She tell you about Grant?"

"Yes."

"And me?"

"She said you outdrew him, but you only winged him," Sally said.

"When did your flight get in?"

She said, "We're not talking about what I want to talk about, are we?"

"What do you want me to say?"

"I want you to tell me that you're more than just a hired gun," she said.

"I intend to be," I said. "But I have to win first. That's my charter. Is this for journalism or for us?"

"I don't know yet," she said.

I took a swig of Scotch and said, "Kaplan was an actor."

"Gee, that's surprising," she said.

"D. Wayne made the phone call to Skidmore," I said.

I watched Sally as she seemed to dwell on that news for a moment, and I thought I detected an effort on her part to fight back a grin.

"I didn't think the Skidmores were bringing a lot to the dance," I said.

324

She said, "So you figured you'd give them a little massage?"

"Something like that," I said. "But I didn't know I'd get that much makeup on my hands."

Sally asked about the rest of it.

"Believe it or not, I didn't know about the Roman candle. And I didn't know the dog could sing," I said.

"Watts and Travers?" she said.

"They didn't know it, either," I said. "I had a couple of other things standing by, of course. But they wouldn't have been as real as what really turned out to be real."

Sally finished her drink. She put out her cigarette. She picked up her bag. Then she pulled me off the bar stool and started dragging me out the front door by the arm.

"What are you doing?" I said, in something of a giggle.

She pushed me into the rear seat of the limo and got in behind me.

She flicked on all four TV sets, which happened to be showing a soap opera, a game show, a movie and a panel discussion, and she raised the volume on each set to its peak.

"All right, tough guy," Sally said. "Of all the things you're surrounded by right now, tell me which one is real."

She removed her tinted glasses and did something to her hair that made it fall around her shoulders. Her hands worked their way over a path on my chest and up past my neck where they caressed my lips and one of my ears. Her body began to fit into mine and she gave me the longest, dampest, most vigorous kiss I ever got from a famous author.

"You'll have to tell me what's real," I said, coming out of it. "You're the executive producer on this one."

Looking back on how Sally then forced the two of

us lower into the seat, and thinking about all of the stunning late-afternoon theater that followed, I have wondered how I would shoot the scene for the ending of a movie.

The way that seems to appeal the most to Sally and me, us being romantics, is to open on the first kiss through the back window of the Silver Goblet, and then move gradually into an aerial view of Gotham with the limo sparkling like a diamond in all you can see below.

DAN JENKINS AND EDWIN SHRAKE are native Texans and lifelong friends. They attended the same high school and college in Fort Worth, have worked on the same Texas newspapers together, and presently they are both by-line writers for *Sports Illustrated* magazines. Mr. Jenkins, the author of five previous books including the bestseller, *Semi-Tough,* lives in Manhattan with his wife and three children. Mr. Shrake, himself the author of five previous novels including the critically acclaimed *Blessed Mcgill,* lives with his wife in Austin, Texas. *Limo* is their first collaboration —at least on a novel.

Keep Up With The BESTSELLERS!